MW01171150

DR. HARLEY

CITY OF SISTERLY LOVE BOOK 2

AK LANDOW

ISBN: 978-1-962575-00-3

Cover Design By: K.B. Designs

❀ Created with Vellum

DEDICATION

I would like to thank my husband and daughters for their loyalty and patience. To my friends and family who supported Knight, I appreciate each and every one of you. To those who helped me make Dr. Harley what it is, I can't thank you enough. To my readers, especially the Swan Squad ladies, I am constantly blown away by the encouragement. To the queen, TL Swan, you have helped to create a new generation of authors, giving countless women a new outlet of creativity and passion.

"Every woman's success should be an inspiration to another. We're strongest when we cheer each other on."
~Serena Williams

PROLOGUE

THE PAST ~ THREE YEARS AGO

HARLEY

"Reagan, you don't need to transfer here. Stay where you are. Skylar and I can handle things." I'm on the phone, walking down the sidewalk in high heels, trying not to bump into people.

"Harley, Mom is a disaster. Dad died a month ago, and the only time she has left the house has been for the funeral and her weekly visits to his grave. She barely leaves her bedroom. She won't even consider going into the family room of her own house." That's where she found Dad. He collapsed after having a heart attack. He was already gone by the time she found him.

"You don't need to do this. We've got it."

"Skylar is only just starting college. She's going to be busy making new friends, rushing, going to parties, and things like that.

You've got your second year of medical school about to begin. You guys won't have time."

"You're in college too, Reagan."

"I know, but I think the three of us can cover more territory. Between our three busy schedules, one of us should be available at most times to check on Mom. Aunt Cass is sleeping there, so she's got the nights and early mornings covered." She pauses for a moment. "Harley, I just need to be here in town for her right now. She needs all of us."

I sigh. "I guess I understand. I feel bad though. You love school so much."

The volume of the music increases as I get closer to the club.

"I'm fine with it. Really. I know a ton of people here. My plan is to open a business in Philly anyway. I can make some good contacts by going to school here. The transfer paperwork has already been filed. I start in a week." The music picks up. "Where the hell are you? It sounds like my freshman dorm on a Thursday night."

"I'm meeting Angelina and some of the girls at Club Liberty tonight."

"You're going out? Let me mark this date on my calendar."

"Very funny. Medical school starts back up on Monday. I'll be buried in books in no time. The past month has been nothing short of hell. I need one night to have a few drinks and have a little fun."

"Why the fuck wasn't I invited? I'm the most fun person you know." This is true. I wish I could let loose and have fun like Reagan. I've never been like that. I've always been focused on my studies.

"Sorry. It was last minute. The girls actually pushed me to go out. They said they know this will be my last night of fun for a year." Unfortunately, this is also true.

"Good. I'm glad. Do shots, dance up a storm, and find yourself a man. You could use a little action." She pauses for a moment. "Actually, I could use some too."

I smile and shake my head. I wish I could. "Not really my style, but I'll definitely have a few drinks and dance."

"I'm telling Aunt Cass on you."

I laugh. "No, no. I don't need her meddling. I'll compromise and dance with a few guys. I promise."

"Do more than dance with them."

I shake my head. "Good-bye. I'll see you at Mom's tomorrow."

"See you then."

I spot Angelina, Olivia, and Sophie waiting for me out front. "Sorry I'm late."

Angelina looks at her watch. "You're literally exactly on time." That's late for me. "You look hot. Nicely done. Let's go have some fun."

I'm wearing a short tight royal blue dress that more than shows off my figure. It's low cut and my boobs are practically spilling out. Reagan bought it for me for Christmas last year. It's not something I would normally wear. This is the first time I've ever worn it.

The bouncer lets us butt in front of the line. It's the one perk of being fairly attractive. No lines. We head straight to the bar and order eight lemon drop shots and four margaritas.

The bartender brings us our drinks. Olivia holds a shot glass up in the air. "To Harley actually being out." We all clink glasses and down the shot.

Sophie holds the second shot glass up in the air. "To Harley letting loose." The three of them hold their shot glasses up. I stare at them. "Come on Harley. Just one night. Forget the past month. Forget studying. Live in the moment. Do something just because it feels good."

I reluctantly hold my shot glass up with theirs. They all smile. "That's my girl!" We down the second round of shots, followed quickly thereafter by our margaritas.

Angelina grabs my hand. "Let's dance."

We dance for over two hours, taking breaks here and there for drinks. We're having a great time. There are a lot of men surrounding our group trying jump in, but we pay them no attention. We're doing our own thing tonight.

I offer to go buy the next round. I head to the bar and order four more margaritas.

The bartender brings me the drinks and I go to hand her my credit card. A big hand grabs mine from behind and I hear him say, "I've got it." He attempts to hand the bartender his card instead.

I shake my head. "No thanks, *I've* got it." I give her my card and she leaves to run it through.

The man chuckles. I turn around and look up and up until I'm met with big blue eyes. I see him smiling. "Wow, you and your friends are really putting out the *fuck off* vibe tonight."

I laugh. "Yea, we're just here letting off some steam. Not looking for extra company." He smiles again. He's really attractive. He's very tall, with wavy blonde hair, and a square chin with a dimple.

"I don't think those guys got the memo." He points his thumb to my friends. There's a circle of at least ten guys around them. "You and your friends haven't let them in for one dance, and yet they just stand there waiting like puppy dogs."

I laugh. "That's life in the big city."

"More like the life of beautiful women in the big city. One in particular."

We're uncomfortably silent for a moment. "Like I said, we're just here to have a bit of fun together. We've all got some things going on and we're looking to have a rare good time with close friends."

His face gets serious for a moment. "What do you have going on that you can't have a good time? You should always make time for a little fun."

"Nothing I'm interested in discussing. Nice to meet you. I'm going to head back to my friends." I go to grab the drinks sitting on the bar, but he stops me.

"We didn't really meet. I don't know your name. You don't know mine." We stare at each other for a few moments. He's really cute. If I actually had time in my life to date, I'd be into this guy, but I don't. "I'm Brody by the way."

I grab the drinks and wave with an open finger. "Bye Brody." I walk away and head back to my friends to give them their margaritas.

We're back dancing in our own world when I feel big hands on my shoulders and hot breath on my ear. "You forgot something." I turn around and Brody is holding up my credit card. Whoops. I must have left it at the bar. I go to grab it, but he pulls it away. "One dance. I'll give it back to you if you dance with me for one song."

I roll my eyes. "Fine. One song." One dance with a hot guy won't kill me. I promised that to Reagan anyway.

A slow sensual song starts playing. Figures. I go to put my hands on his shoulders but he grabs my shoulders and turns me around. He wraps his arms around me and pulls my back to his chest. My hips to his. My backside to his front.

He starts moving us in rhythm together, swaying to the slow beat of the music. We stay like that for a while. He starts moving his hands up and down my hips, and runs his lips along my neck. I close my eyes. God this feels good. He feels good.

Before I know it, three songs have gone by and we haven't

moved from this position. He whispers in my ear. "Come home with me."

That breaks my momentary trance. I turn around and put my hands on my hips. "You've got the wrong girl, buddy." I hold out my hand for the card. He gives it to me.

I turn to leave, but he puts his hand on the small of my back and pulls me close to him, locking his eyes with mine. He's silent for a moment, doing nothing but staring at me.

He takes his other hand and gently runs his thumb across my bottom lip. "You're so incredibly beautiful." He bends down and takes my bottom lip into his mouth and slowly sucks it. I close my eyes and moan at the sensation. I can feel it in my whole body. I have a strong ache forming between my legs.

I have no idea what comes over me. Maybe it's the alcohol. Maybe it's the emotions of the past month. Maybe it's the fact that I know I'll be buried in my studies in a few days. Maybe it's the insanely hot guy sucking on my lip. Maybe it's my pledge to do something that just feels good tonight. Whatever it is, I grab his hand and lead him into the stairwell.

We walk up two flights of stairs in silence to the roof. There are several large, wide columns up on the roof affording some privacy from the outside world.

I push him against the wall of one of the columns, grab his face, and crash my lips to his. Our mouths immediately open. Our tongues relentlessly exploring one another. The kiss is passionate and warm, yet his lips are soft and tender.

He grabs my waist and pulls me close. I run my fingers up through his hair, grabbing it by the handful. He turns us so that my back is now to the wall, and pushes himself against me. I can feel his massive erection on my stomach.

He slowly moves his hands up my body and grabs my breasts. Even though he has big hands, they're still not big enough to fit around my breasts. He yanks my dress and bra down so that my breasts pop out.

He pulls away from my lips and looks down, slowly running his fingertips around my chest, and brushing his thumbs across my nipples. They harden immediately. "You have the most perfect body I've ever seen."

He bends his head down and takes one of my nipples into his warm mouth. He sucks it hard. I lay my head back on the wall and moan in pleasure. He moves along to the other nipple, and gives it the same heavenly treatment. It feels so good.

He gets down on his knees as he kisses his way down my body. He slowly pulls the bottom of my dress up to my waist. He runs his fingers up my legs until he reaches my white lace thong. He pulls it down my legs and off my body. He rolls it up and puts it in his pocket.

He open mouth kisses his way up from my knees to the apex of my thighs. He throws one of my legs over his shoulder and moves the other leg out wide. He spreads my lips and takes a long lick.

"Oh god," I moan. He smiles up at me for a brief moment, and then brings his mouth back to me again. He's moving his tongue up and down, licking me everywhere. He starts sucking on my clit. I'm on stimulation overload. I don't know the last time I came, but it's definitely going to happen for me now.

He takes one of his thumbs and slides it through me until it's at my entrance. He slowly pushes it in.

The dual sensation feels too good. I don't think I can stand on my one leg anymore. He must sense it because he throws that leg over his shoulder too. He's completely supporting me on his shoulders, using the wall to support my back. I don't know how he's doing it. I don't care.

He continues alternating licking and sucking my clit while

pumping me with his thumb. I can feel myself starting to slip over the edge. I feel my walls trembling.

A few more licks and pumps, and I explode on his tongue and thumb with a very loud moan. I think I nearly blackout from the pleasure.

He lets me ride out my orgasm as he continues to lick up my juices.

He gradually sets my shaky legs down. I'm not sure I can fully stand, but I use the wall to lean back and support most of my weight. I'm panting, and I didn't even do anything. I can't see straight yet.

I hear his belt buckle and zipper, and then the tearing open of a condom wrapper. He kisses my mouth again and whispers into it. "Are you with me? I'm not done with you." I nod at a loss for words. I'm not done yet either. I need him inside of me.

I feel him grab the underside of my ass with two hands, spread my legs, and pick me up. My senses are starting to come back to me. I wrap my legs around him. His tip is at my entrance as he slowly enters me. He keeps going and going and going. Oh shit. He must be huge. I didn't see him before he entered me, but I've never felt anything so big inside of me. It's all-encompassing.

Once he's all the way in, he stops. I'm looking down hoping this sucker is actually all the way in. I don't think I can take any more, but it's stretching me in the best way possible.

I feel the pleasure slowly spreading throughout my body. He removes one hand from my ass and he tilts my chin up so that I'm looking at him. "Are you okay?"

I wrap my arms around his neck, kissing my way up to his ear. I whisper, "God yes. I'm good. Please keep going."

He starts pumping into me. In and out. I'm so full of him. It feels amazing.

I grab his cheeks and bite his bottom lip. I move down to his neck. He tastes good. He smells good too. I'm sucking on his neck. He moans out in pleasure. "You feel incredible. You're so tight and wet. You're squeezing me so hard."

I throw my head back. This is too much. I'm going to come again. I've never come this quickly from penetrative sex.

With my head back, he moves onto my neck and kisses his way down to my breasts again. He circles my nipple with his tongue. He takes my nipple into his mouth. Once he sucks on it, that's my tipping point. "Ah, Brody. I'm coming."

I hold onto his shirt for dear life and squeeze my eyes shut. I feel myself pulse and then explode. The sensation is indescribable. He continues to moan loudly, until he grunts into his own release.

We're still for a few moments, as we both pant and regain an awareness of our surroundings. As my senses return, I realize that I just had sex with a complete stranger. I can't believe I did that. I've never done anything like this before in my life. He slowly pulls out, and sets my legs on the ground. I fix my dress as he pulls off the condom and zips up his pants.

He gives me a soft kiss on my lips. As he moves away, he tilts his head to the side and pulls his eyebrows together. "What's your name?"

Oh. My. God. I never gave him my name, and just had mind-blowing sex with him on the roof of a club. Who am I right now?

I take a breath and then a big gulp. "Let's not go there. We both know exactly what this was. Let's not spoil it."

He looks a little sad and shrugs his shoulders. "If that's what you want."

"It is." I fidget for a moment and then look up at him with my hand out. "Can I have my underwear back?"

He smiles. "No, beautiful. I need to hold onto something from tonight."

It's not worth arguing with him. I just want to get away from him as quickly as possible.

He leads me back into the stairwell. We reach the dance floor. I see my friends and turn to him. "Bye Brody. Have a good life." I head back to my friends to finish out the evening and head home.

———

It's Sunday night and I'm heading to Mom's for dinner. Aunt Cass said she was just ordering Chinese food since there's no way Mom is up for cooking, and Aunt Cass doesn't know what to do in a kitchen. I have no clue what I'm walking into. Hopefully, Mom is in a better mood and is out of bed.

I open the door and walk into the house. Aunt Cass, Skylar, and Reagan are all sitting at the kitchen table. No Mom. Damn. When will she snap out of this?

Reagan looks me up and down and squints her eyes. "You had sex."

My eyes widen. "What? No, I didn't."

Aunt Cass turns her head to me and also looks me up and down. "Yes, you totally did." Skylar nods in agreement.

I stare at them all. "Are you three witches?"

Reagan turns to Aunt Cass "That sounds like a yes to me."

Aunt Cass nods. "Sure does. Good for you, kiddo."

I sit down and sigh. "How the hell do you guys know? Am I wearing a sign?"

Aunt Cass grabs my hand. "Harley, I love you like you're my own, but you are the most uptight woman on the face of the planet. There's something bizarrely relaxed about you right now. Something that only a good time in the sheets could possibly achieve. Frankly, it's unsettling to see you like this." She smirks at me.

I roll my eyes. "I'm not that uptight."

Skylar and Reagan respond in unison. "Yes, you are."

Reagan couldn't possibly be more excited. "So, did you bring in a bench player or someone new?" She thinks she's making a joke.

"I met a guy at the club last night."

Reagan looks shocked. "What was his name?"

"Brody."

"Brody what?"

I look down, preferring not to answer that. She's staring at me, clearly not letting me get away with avoiding the question.

I mumble, "I didn't get his last name."

She has a huge grin on her face. "I'm sorry, who are you and what have you done with my sister?"

Skylar interrupts. "Seriously Harley. That's so unlike you." She smiles at Reagan and Aunt Cass. "I'm so excited."

"You guys make me sound like a prude."

Reagan rolls her eyes. "We didn't say that you're a prude. You've just never had sex with someone you weren't in a relationship with. You're a serial monogamist."

Aunt Cass shivers. "Ugh, monogamy. Don't use that word in my presence."

"Fine, I agree. It wasn't like me. But I did it, so deal with it."

"How was it?" Reagan just wants details.

I blow out a long breath. "Really fucking good. Like best sex of my life good."

She smiles. "Are you going to see him again?"

"No."

"He didn't want your number? I find that hard to believe. Look at you."

"I didn't give him the chance. I wouldn't even give him my

name." I pause for a moment, not making eye contact with any of them. "And it was against the wall on the roof of the club."

Reagan, Skylar, and Aunt Cass look at each other with their mouths wide open in shock. Reagan turns back. "I'm not even joking. Who are you? Where's Harley?"

"Shut up." I put my head in my hands. "I don't know what came over me."

"Sounds like he came over you, or was it under you?" Skylar is clearly amusing herself.

I give her a nasty look. "The last month has been hell. I lost my father. I have a shell of a mother. I'm about to start a hellish year of studying with no chance at dating. A gorgeous guy wanted me, and I went with it. For the first time in my life, I went with it. It was great. It was more than great. But it's over now. School starts tomorrow. Back to the grind."

Reagan rubs my back. "Good. For. You, sis. I'm thrilled for you."

Aunt Cass grabs all of our hands, looking sad. "I know your mother is a shell of herself right now. She's only forty-five and she lost the love of her life. Just give her some time. She'll be back to her old awesome self in no time. I promise."

I hope she's right.

It's Monday morning. My first day of the second year of medical school. I see my friend Megan when I walk in. "Hey Meg. What class do you have this morning?"

"Hey babe. I have neuro."

"Me too. Who do you have?"

"I have Dr. Waters." She scrunches up her nose. "I had him last year too, for anatomy. He's old as dirt and boring as fuck."

He's actually only in his forties, but he's definitely a boring teacher. He's a little creepy too. He used to stare at me and unnecessarily touch my arm whenever he was near me.

"True, he is a bit dull. I must be in a different section this year. I have the new professor, Dr. Cooper. He's supposed to be the best spinal surgeon in the country. I heard he's young, so maybe he'll be more interesting."

"I hope so. I'll see you for lunch?"

I nod. "Yep, see you then."

I make my way into the classroom. The professor hasn't arrived yet. I sit front and center, as always. Students are filing in. Though there are plenty of empty seats, two guys sit on either side of me and smile at me. I roll my eyes.

The classroom eventually fills and it's 8:00, our start time. There's a faculty only door at the front of the classroom. It opens and a tall man walks through with his head down. He eventually looks up at no one in particular and smiles. "Good morning class. I'm Dr. Cooper."

Oh my fucking God. It's Brody. He sets his stuff down and then looks up, right at me. His smile instantly fades and his eyes just about pop out of his head in realization.

I can't believe this. I had sex with my neuro professor. This is bad. Really bad.

CHAPTER ONE

THE PAST

BRODY

I'm completely freaking out. This cannot be happening. It's the green-eyed, brunette bombshell with the killer body. The goddess that I haven't been able to get out of my mind since Saturday. The first woman in my thirty-two years that left me wanting for more. She's sitting right here in my class as my student. What are the chances?

I can't manage to put words together right now. I'm in shock. Judging by the look on her face, she's in shock too. Everyone is staring at me, but I can't seem to get a sentence out of my mouth. Get it together, Brody.

I try to gather myself. "Um, hello. Like I said, I'm Dr. Cooper. I'll be your neurology professor this term. We'll learn how to diagnose and treat conditions and diseases involving the central and peripheral nervous systems."

I look around. No one seems to notice that I'm off-kilter. "A little about me. I am a neurosurgeon myself. Kind of like Dr. McDreamy on Grey's Anatomy." I pause and get a few laughs.

"I work across the street at Pennsylvania Hospital, specializing in complex spinal cord injuries. I grew up in Southern California, where I went to school and worked up until two weeks ago when I moved here. As part of my job at Pennsylvania Hospital, they asked that I teach one class here with the purpose being to impart my experience and wisdom to the next generation of doctors. So, here I am with you beautiful people." One beautiful person in particular.

"This is the first class I've ever taught, so please bear with me. I may not be very good at it." I get a few more laughs.

"I'm a big believer in learning beyond the pages of your textbooks. We'll spend a good amount of time discussing real cases, and you all will spend time in the lab learning surgical techniques."

I look down at the class roster. She could be any one of the women on here. I at least need her name. It's been driving me nuts all weekend that I never got her name. I feel like I've been given a second chance. I intend to take advantage of it.

I could just take attendance, but I suppose I could also take this opportunity to learn a little bit more about her. "I was thinking that for today we could go around the classroom and introduce ourselves. Please stand when I call your name.

Tell us what type of medicine you're considering and why, your favorite food, and since I'm new in town and don't know much about Philadelphia, why don't you tell me one of your favorite spots." Everyone seems to nod in acknowledgement.

"We'll go in alphabetical order. I'll also pass around the class roster. Please give me your cell phone numbers so that I can create a group text for class information. Being almost as young as you all, I know that emails are passe. It's all about the texting." It's actually all about needing to get in touch with this woman.

"I'm leaving my cell number on the board for all of you, in case you have any questions or concerns. Please don't hesitate to reach out." I write my number on the board. They all seem to note my number, including my gorgeous mystery woman.

I start running through the class roster. There are definitely a lot of cheesesteak lovers in this class. There also seems to be a great amount of disagreement over where to get the best cheesesteak. There are sadly many students who want to go into *whatever type of medicine makes the most money*. That's a shame.

I'm halfway through the list and I haven't gotten to my real target yet. "Next up, Harley Lawrence."

She stands up. Finally. What a great name. It suits her perfectly. I can't help but smile.

I look at her. She's even more beautiful than I remember. She's totally natural today, and she takes my breath away. She looks a bit nervous, but once she starts speaking, she has complete composure.

"Hello. I'm Harley Lawrence. I want to be a surgeon. I have since I was a little girl. I came here thinking that I'd like to go into neurosurgery, enjoying the challenges and complexities of it, but I've since changed my mind."

"Well, Ms. Lawrence, I'm going to spend this year trying to change it back." A few students snicker. "What made you change your mind?"

"My father passed away this summer from a heart attack at only fifty-three years old. We have a strong family history of losing people too young to heart disease. I think I'd like to switch to cardiothoracic and see if I can't make a difference in that regard." I nod with sympathy. That hits pretty close to home for me.

"My favorite food is sushi, but I'm very particular as to where I get my sushi. There are only a few special restaurants that truly satisfy me." I gulp at that word choice.

"As for my favorite spot, it's a little different than the rest. It's not exactly in Philadelphia, but it's less than an hour away, and considered part of the Philadelphia spirit. I really love the Jersey shore. I love the beach and the ocean and the peace it brings."

I smile. "Well, Ms. Lawrence, I can certainly understand that, being from Southern California. I'm a bit of a beach bum myself." She simply nods her head in acknowledgment as she sits back down in her seat.

We finish the class introductions and I dismiss the students for the day. I'm not sure what to do about Harley. I'm clearly extremely attracted to her, but she's my student and there are obviously significant issues with that.

There's definitely a part of me that can't shake the feeling that I've been gifted a second chance with the woman who rocked my world. I'm confused as to the best course of action.

I head to lunch. I see the only faculty member that I knew before I arrived, Dr. Elizabeth Powers. Liz is around my age. She's fairly attractive, with long auburn hair and blue eyes. We worked together briefly at the hospital in California as surgical residents. She ended up specializing in cardiothoracic surgery. We always got along quite well. "Hey Liz. Do you mind if I sit with you?"

She motions to an empty chair at her table. "Please, Brody. Have a seat. How's your first day going?"

"It's been fine. Just some general class introductions today. Nothing too heavy just yet."

"Did anyone stand out?"

"Well, I was simply getting to know them a bit, but I'd say a student by the name of Harley Lawrence stood out."

Liz smiles knowingly. "Of course, she did."

Oh shit. Did I give something away? "I'm sorry. I'm not following."

"She's the most brilliant student in this school. I taught her last year. In all my years of teaching, I've never had a student stimulate and challenge me the way she did. Her mind is a unique gift. I can't wait to see what she does with it. It's a shame so many people don't see past her exterior."

I pinch my eyebrows in surprise. "What do you mean?"

She gives me a knowing look. "What do I mean? I assume you have eyes. She looks like a Sports Illustrated swimsuit model." I inwardly laugh. She has no idea just how model-like that body is.

Liz continues, "She spends half of her time fighting off unwanted advances from fellow students, and the other half trying to get those students, and certain professors, to take her seriously. It's not right. She deserves more respect than that. She's truly gifted."

I put my head down in guilt for a moment. The other night I asked her to come home with me after three minutes of talking to her, and I told her that she's beautiful and has a perfect body. All I've thought about since is seeing that body again. I'm ashamed of myself.

"There's something special about that girl, Brody. She's going to make a wonderful doctor one day."

"Well, thanks for the heads up. I'll certainly be sure to take her seriously and see to it that her classmates do the same." I mean that. I'm not going to contact her as I considered either. I think I need to do nothing but treat her as a student, and respect her accordingly. I should probably avoid too much interaction with her outside of class, given my obvious attraction to her.

"Good. She deserves that. This school needs to nurture and support minds like hers. That's our job. It's our responsibility." I nod in determination.

Just then, I hear my phone beep with a text notification.

> Unknown: Dr. Cooper, this is Harley Lawrence from your neurology class. May I get a moment of your time?

So much for avoiding contact.

> Me: No problem. Why don't you meet me in my office in 5 minutes.

> Unknown: Thank you. I'll see you then.

I say my goodbyes to Liz and make my way up to my office. A few minutes later, Harley arrives at the door. I tell her to close it. She hesitates for a moment, but eventually does close the door.

She sits in one of the chairs in front of my desk. "Dr. Cooper, there's an obvious elephant in the room. I'd really like to deal with it head-on. I want to talk to you about the other night."

Wow. She's very mature. I imagine most women her age would play the avoidance game. I expected her to.

I smile at her. "In light of everything, I feel like you should call me Brody."

"I'd rather not."

What was I thinking? I shake my head. "You're right. I'm sorry. Dr. Cooper it is."

"Look, I did something completely out of my comfort zone the other night, and now I'm clearly being punished for it. Please know that it was very uncharacteristic of me. I'm mortified. I hope you understand that I had no clue who you were or that you were going to be my professor."

"Of course, you didn't. Just as I didn't know that you were going to be my student."

She nods her head. "Yes. I'm glad we understand each other. I'm going to ask for a transfer to Dr. Waters' neuro class. In light of the circumstances, I think that makes the most sense. I would never want to be accused of anything inappropriate. I imagine you feel the same?"

I think for a moment about what Liz said. About the brilliant mind sitting in front of me and our responsibility to nurture someone like her. "Look Har...Ms. Lawrence. I understand why you feel like a class transfer is appropriate. In all honesty, it probably is the best course of action. However, not to sound like a pompous ass, but you do know that I'm considered one of the leading spinal surgeons in this country?"

She nods.

"I've come to learn that you have a very unique mind for medicine, Ms. Lawrence. I would hate for what happened the other night to deprive you of the opportunity to learn from me, and me of the opportunity to help impart my expertise to a special student like yourself." I can see her deep in thought. "Besides, I've heard that Dr. Waters is a snooze fest, and I'm still hoping you'll consider switching back to neurosurgery."

She smiles at that. God that smile is a thing of pure beauty. Stop it.

She considers my words for a few moments. "Well, Dr. Cooper, do you think we can maintain an appropriate student-teacher relationship, and put this past weekend behind us?"

I nod. "I can if you can."

"Are you're comfortable keeping the events of this past weekend just between the two of us?"

I nod again. "I am if you are."

"Okay then. I'll stay in your class as your student, and *only* your student. Thank you for your time. I really appreciate it."

She puts out her hand for me to shake it. When I do, there's something electric that runs through me the moment we touch. I feel it in my whole body. I can tell in her face that she feels it too. I quickly pull my hand away, breaking our touch.

I mumble out, "See you in class tomorrow, Ms. Lawrence."

"I'll see you then Dr. Cooper." There's some part of me that knows that I may have just committed the biggest mistake of my life, but I simply couldn't help myself.

HARLEY

"Hey Meg. Sorry I'm late for lunch. I was meeting with a professor."

She stares at me with her mouth wide open. "Already? You're such a nerd, Harley. It's the first day of classes. What could you possibly have to discuss?"

I laugh. "Just some curriculum-based questions."

She shakes her head. "So, how was Dr. Cooper? The gossip is spreading like crazy." Oh my god. Everyone knows already? How did this happen?

I croak out, "What gossip?"

"That he's hot as hell. Did you not notice?" Phew.

"I guess he's attractive. Frankly, I didn't think about it," I lie. It's all I thought about the entire class. He's insanely attractive. Even more so than I thought the other night. And when he touched me in his office, I felt it in every part of my body. I'm pretty sure he felt it too.

"Of course, you didn't. Anyway, Shelly Summers said she saw a big hickey on his neck. He took his tie off after class and she saw it just under his shirt collar."

I choke on my drink. "A hickey?"

"Yep, she said it looked fresh. Sounds like Dr. Cooper had himself some fun this weekend." She giggles.

I'm all of a sudden having a flashback of me sucking on his neck, while my legs are wrapped around him, and he's pounding into me. My whole body is now warm and flushed.

"Are you feeling okay, Harley? You look all red."

I start to fan myself with my hand. "It's just really hot in here."

It's time to steer this conversation in a new direction. "How was class with Dr. Waters?"

"It was boring. He's so full of himself. That class is going to be brutal. I need to find a way to transfer into the hot professor's class. He's all anyone is talking about."

It's going to be a long year.

CHAPTER TWO

THE PRESENT

HARLEY

Aunt Cass holds up a glass of champagne. "To Harley on her medical school graduation."

Aunt Cass, my sisters, and even Mom, hold up their glasses. "To Harley." We all sip our champagne.

"Thanks, everyone. I still have to study for and pass my Boards, but finishing medical school is certainly a big step." I grab Mom's hand. "Thank you, Mom, for coming to the graduation and coming out to dinner. I know it's not easy for you."

She looks embarrassed. I didn't mean to make her feel that way. I meant to let her know how happy I am that she's here. She so rarely leaves the house. We had to drag her out last year for Reagan's college graduation. She's been a little bit better about going out this past year though. It's not too often, but it's certainly more than the first two years after Dad died. The only time she consistently leaves the house is every Friday morning when she visits his grave to talk to him. She also leaves to watch football with my father's group of high school friends.

She rubs my back. "Of course, Harley. I wouldn't miss this for anything in the world. I'm so incredibly proud of you. I know Dad would be proud too." Tears start to well in her eyes, but she keeps them at bay. That's certainly progress. Normally she can't talk about him without crying. "I have your letter for you at the house whenever you want to come by."

"I'll come by this weekend and grab it."

Even though Dad died suddenly of a heart attack, because of his extensive family history of heart disease, he always assumed he would die relatively young. Mom would never talk about it, but he knew the likelihood, and planned accordingly. He left a series of letters for all of us when we reach certain life milestones. Mom won't tell us which ones, only when she has one for us. I did assume my medical school graduation would be one of those milestones. It's incredible to be able to hear from him. I can't wait to read my letter this weekend.

Mom doesn't know it, but I have one letter saved for her that he entrusted to my sisters and me. We're supposed to give it to her when she falls in love again and is having a crisis of conscience over it. I can't imagine her dating, let alone falling in love, but I'm hopeful that one day she will move on from my father.

She's only forty-eight years old and is absolutely stunning. It's weird for me to think that because she and I really do look so much alike, everyone says so, but no one could possibly deny that my mother is a beautiful woman. She's incredibly funny, loving, and smart too. At least she *was* before he passed.

It would be amazing for her to find someone new to share her life with. Reagan, Skylar, and I want that so much for her. But right now, she barely leaves the house, so I don't think love is coming her way anytime soon. Aunt Cass tries desperately to get her to go out, but she's only been successful a small handful of times.

Reagan always attempts to lighten the mood when things get too heavy. "Aunt Cass, any good dating stories for us?" Aunt Cass often indulges us with her latest and greatest crazy stories. Especially her crazy dating stories. Her nickname among Mom and their friends is actually Crazy Cassandra.

"Hmmm. Nothing too out of the ordinary lately. As I get older, the men get more mature and more boring. Frankly, I prefer someone who makes me laugh before they make my toes curl."

She's deep in thought for a moment. "Oh, I've got one. I was on a date with a new guy last week. He was super flirty the whole time, which I don't mind at all. In fact, I prefer that as long as I'm into him, and I was definitely into him. He was really good-looking. At some point during the meal, he slipped me something across the table. At first, I thought it was money, and that maybe he thought I was a prostitute. But it wasn't money. It was a condom. It wasn't your regular run-of-the-mill condom though. It was a personalized condom with his face on it." We're now all hysterically laughing, as we usually are with her absurd stories.

"He then tells me that it's the only head he gives, and that's why he has them. Well, a man who doesn't give head is as useful to me as a condom machine at the Vatican. So, I pulled out my phone and quickly texted Dennis." We've all heard of Dennis. He's a police officer who is Aunt Cass's fuck buddy when she doesn't have anyone else. He's probably the only steady man in her life, but he seems to understand her concrete walls, and they're able to keep it completely casual.

I've never been able to engage in casual sex. Well, except that once, and it sort of blew up in my face. I still haven't gotten him out of my mind, but it's been years since I've seen or heard from him. It's for the better. Nothing could ever happen between us anyway.

"I told Dennis it was a Code 69 and gave him the address." I don't know what a *Code 69* is, and I'm afraid to ask. "Dennis shows up fifteen minutes later in his uniform, and places me under arrest for prostitution. Right there at the table, he bent me over and cuffed me. You should have seen my date's face. It was priceless. Anyway, I took Dennis home with me instead. We definitely made use of those cuffs and that guy's printed condom."

She tells us these stories completely nonchalantly, as if she's telling us about a mundane trip to the supermarket. We're all giggling and shaking our heads. Aunt Cass never fails with her stories. Reagan loves them the most. Probably because she's as close to carefree like Aunt Cass as any of us. "Aunt Cass, you're my idol."

Aunt Cass smiles. "Reagan, it takes a special woman to be like me. I think you have what it takes though." They laugh together.

She turns to me. "Harley, are we still on for tomorrow?"

I narrow my eyes at her. "I suppose. Are you going to tell me what we're doing?"

She just gives me a trademark Aunt Cass smile. "No, I'm not. You'll have to trust me." Fat chance. "Meet me at 21st and Walnut at noon."

I sigh. "Fine. I'll see you then."

THE NEXT DAY I head down to 21st and Walnut to meet Aunt Cass. When I arrive, I see that Reagan and Skylar are with her. I shake my head. "I can only imagine what we're doing here."

They all grin, and they're definitely conspiratorial grins. What have I gotten myself into? We turn into a shop called "The Pleasure Chest". I've never heard of it. As we take a few steps inside, I realize exactly what it is. It's sex toy shop. I turn to leave, but Aunt Cass grabs me. "Oh no you don't. You're coming in, and we're loading you up."

"No. I don't need any of this. I definitely won't use it."

"Sweetheart, you most definitely need it. When was the last time you got laid?" I'm silent. I would be embarrassed to tell them how long it's been. "Exactly. When is the last time you came?"

"Ummm...I don't know. It's been a while. We don't need to discuss this. I'm not sure it's really any of your business."

"Of course, it's my business, and exactly. It's been a long while. That's why you're so uptight. You're going to be studying all summer for your Boards. You need some stress relief. Reagan, Skylar, don't you agree with me?"

They both immediately say, "Yes," and nod enthusiastically.

I look at them. "How often is it normal to come? When was the last time each of you came?"

I don't know why I bothered to ask. Aunt Cass and Reagan happily announce that it was last night for each of them. For Skylar, it was this morning. They all laugh, seemingly at my expense.

I sigh. "Fine, we can look around. I get final approval of all purchases though."

Aunt Cass shakes her head. "No, you can pick one thing, but I'll be picking the rest. I know the kinds of things you need."

I cross my arms in disgust. "Whatever. Let's just get this over with."

We walk all the way into the store. As soon as we do, the salesclerk comes up to us. "Hey Cassandra. Back so soon?" I can't believe the salesclerk knows her by name.

"Hey Frankie. Yes. My friend Harley here is a bit uptight. She needs some of your magic. Load her up with all of the standards. Vibrator, handcuffs, lube, butt plugs…"

"Butt plugs? I'm not using that!"

Cassandra brushes me off with her hand. "All of that stuff please, Frankie. What are some special things that a really uptight person might need?"

Frankie looks around. "Hmmm. What about a remote-control bullet?"

"Yes, we'll take that. What else?

"Excuse me. This is my body. What's a remote-control bullet?"

Reagan rolls her eyes as if my naivety is a nuisance. "It's a relatively small device you insert inside yourself. There's a remote that controls the vibrations. You can use it, a partner can use it, or even I can use it." She smiles at me.

I shake my head. "That's a *no* for me."

Aunt Cass nods her head. "That's a *yes* for her, Frankie. What's the latest and greatest gadget?"

"Remote-control, vibrating nipple clamps?"

"We'll take one of those, along with regular nipple clamps. What else? Wow me with something I haven't heard of." What the fuck? Remote control, vibrating nipple clamps? What else could there possibly be?

Frankie looks like she's deep in thought. "Well, have you heard of the Smart Bead?"

Aunt Cass's eyes light up. "No. Tell me about it."

"It's sized and inserted much the same way as the bullet, but there's no remote control. You activate it with an app, but it's your body that controls when it goes on and off. It basically learns your body and senses when you need an orgasm. It measures your orgasm potential. It's like a pleasure and stress trainer. The more stressed and uptight you are, the more it vibrates. When you relax, it stops. Its goal is to train your body to relax through orgasms."

Aunt Cass, Reagan, and Skylar stare at me with their mouths wide open. I look back at them. "What?"

"It's as if a device was specifically created with you in mind. It's perfect."

Aunt Cass turns back to Frankie. "She'll take two of those, just in case one breaks from overuse." I roll my eyes at her. "Reagan, Skylar, you'll see to it that she uses it?"

"Of course, Aunt Cass." Skylar smiles at me.

"Definitely. We're *on* it, and we'll make sure it's *in* her." Reagan cracks herself up.

I frown. "You three are completely ridiculous."

We spend another half an hour in there. Aunt Cass keeps adding things to our cart. Yes, we now have so much stuff that it necessitates a cart. She spends over a thousand dollars on me.

She holds out her arms when we're done. "Happy graduation, Harley. I love you."

I scowl at her. "I hate you."

She laughs. "No, you don't. You'll love me for this stuff. I promise."

Reagan and Skylar leave after our trip to the "Pleasure Chest", but Aunt Cass and I head to lunch. It's a beautiful day, so we eat outside on Rittenhouse Square. We sit down at our table, and I put my three large, unmarked, black, opaque bags on the ground next to me. At least they're discreet.

We order two glasses of white wine before Aunt Cass takes my hand. "Harley, talk to me. What's going on with you?"

I pinch my eyebrows. "I don't understand. What do you mean?"

"What do I mean? Harley, this should be a happy time in your life, yet you're sad. You've achieved all of your goals in life, yet you are completely stressed out. You're young and stunningly beautiful, yet you never date. Need I go on?"

"No. It's not necessary." I put my head in my hands. "I don't know what's wrong with me. Maybe it's Mom. I'm always worried about her."

"I know it's been a rough couple of years with your mom, but I see signs of life in her. She's going to break out of this funk very soon. She's been my best friend for thirty years, Harley. No one knows her better than I do. I'm telling you that she's close to getting back on track. You just leave that to me. I'll take care of her."

She takes a deep breath. "Look Harley, I know your mother's depression weighs heavily on you, but I think it's something more than that. Did anything else happen at school, beyond what I know?"

"No, you know everything." Tears start to well in my eyes. She squeezes my hand. The simple fact is that Aunt Cass has been our surrogate mother since Dad died. Mom hasn't been mentally present at all. We feel like we walk on eggshells around her. She teeters on the edge of tears at all times. If I'm going to talk to anyone about this, it would be Aunt Cass.

She studies my face. "Are you dating at all?"

Now the tears spill over. I look up at her. "I don't know how to explain it without sounding like I'm crazy."

"Harley, I'm the queen of crazy. It's literally my nickname. If anyone will understand, it's me."

I sigh. "I've been on a few dates." I'm nervously playing with my napkin. I put my head down, not able to look at her in the eyes. "When things start to get intimate, my body just won't react like it's supposed to." I look up, hoping she knows what I mean. "It's like I'm dead inside. Nothing, and no one, turns me on. I make up an excuse to end it and leave. It's gotten so embarrassing, that now I've honestly stopped trying." My face is a wet mess of tears.

"Oh, sweetie come here." She pulls her chair next to mine and hugs me. "Why do you think that is? When was the last time it felt good? When did it last feel right?"

I close my eyes. "You know when."

"Oh. When did you last see him?"

"I haven't seen him in years."

She's next to me holding my hand. "Not to sound insensitive, but you need to get over him."

"I am. In my head, I'm over him. Apparently, my body has a different idea." My heart too.

"I see. Well, I think your new toys might be helpful in that regard." I give her a look. "I'm not kidding. You need to break out of this slump. Just give it a try. I'm telling you it will help."

"Let me get through studying for my Boards. Then I'll think about it." She's not thrilled with that reply, but at least I've given her some hope. Even if I have none.

It's Saturday afternoon. I'm about to arrive at Mom's house. I never know what I'm going to get when I go there. Sometimes she's a mess, and sometimes she's okay. She's never really more than just okay though. Reagan, Skylar, and I usually rotate coming to check on her at least twice a week. I know Aunt Cass comes by a few days a week as well. We also have a group dinner, along with Aunt Cass, every Sunday night. That's become a bit of a fun tradition.

When I arrive, I see her outside doing gardening work. I don't think I've ever seen her do that before in my entire life. I pull up and she turns. She has a big smile. What? Wow, that's great to see.

She waves at me as I get out of my car. "Hey, doll. I forgot that you were coming." She hugs me. "So good to see you." She looks down and notices that she got a little bit of dirt on me. "Shit. I'm sorry. You're all dirty now."

I honestly have tears welling in my eyes. This is the most *normal* I've seen her in a long time. "It's fine, Mom. I didn't know you were a gardener."

She laughs. "I'm definitely not. Look at this mess. I've heard that it's therapeutic, so I'm giving it a go."

I smile at her new hobby. "It suits you. Soon you'll be living off of the land like a farmer."

She laughs again. Wow. It's nice to see that big smile and hear her laugh. "I'm sure. Let's go inside."

She pours us two glasses of iced tea as we sit on the stools at her kitchen island. "How's studying going?"

"It's good. I've only just begun."

"Don't make yourself crazy. We both know you'll breeze past your Boards."

"I didn't come this far to half-ass my way through the finish line."

"I suppose. Just don't work too hard. You'll be fine."

"I know. What have you been up to?"

"I spent some time in the office this week." I'm shocked. She runs her own law firm, but she's barely gone in since Dad passed. She wasn't in full-time before he died, but she has left the office mostly in the hands of her associates since his death.

She must see the shock on my face. "What? I *do* own a business. I *am* a professional."

"Oh, I know. I just didn't think you were going in very much. That's great. I'm so thrilled to hear it."

"Yep. Just keeping myself busy. Cassandra is trying to get me to go out more with her, Gennifer, and Alexandra. I did have drinks with them one night a few weeks ago." What? I didn't know this.

"That's great, Mom. You should definitely go out and have fun with your friends."

She scrunches her nose. "You think?"

I nod. "Absolutely."

"I don't mind hanging out with my friends. It's really fun, but Cassandra tries to get me to talk to men. A few men have approached me, but I sent them away. I don't think I'm quite ready for that." She bites her lip.

"I think it's great that you're going out. Maybe take baby steps on talking to men. Work your way up to it." I smile at her. "Just so you know, Reagan, Skylar, and I are totally okay if you want to start dating. We want you to be happy."

"Thanks, baby. I'm not there quite yet. Maybe I will be soon." She refills our glasses. "How about you? Are you dating?"

I shake my head. "I don't have any time for that right now. I went on a few dates this year. No one really did anything for me. I'm kind of sick of all the guys from medical school. Maybe I'll have more interest in the fall once studying is behind me. I'm sure I'll meet new people when my residency begins."

She nods. "That makes sense. Just make sure you enjoy yourself, Harley. Trust me, life goes by very fast."

She's drifting. "Mom, can I grab my letter."

"Yep, let me get it from the safe." She comes back a few minutes later and hands it to me. I head into the guestroom so that I can read it alone. I sit on the bed and look at the front of the envelope. *To Harley Madison Lawrence Upon Your Medical School Graduation.* I open it and start to read.

Harley:

Congratulations, baby girl! I'm so proud of you. Twenty-six years of studying your ass off has finally come to a successful close. There was never a doubt in my mind that this day would come.

When you pass your Boards, and officially become a doctor, I'll have a lot more to say about what you've accomplished. Today, your dear old Dad wants to talk to you about life. Of course, you've been an adult since you turned eighteen years old (and have acted like one since you were about three), but you've been in school until now, so your actual adult life really begins today.

Baby doll, stop and take a breath. Smell the roses. Enjoy your life. For so many years, you've been entirely focused on the goal of becoming a doctor, that I think you've missed out on life a bit. I don't want that for you. Spend time with your mother and sisters. Enjoy one another. Go to the shore more. I know you love that. Smell the ocean. Take long walks in the sand. Go out with friends. Drink too much. Laugh too much. Go out on dates. I won't elaborate on what you should do on those dates, but I imagine you catch my drift at this point.

I'm thrilled that you are about to achieve your lifetime goal of becoming a doctor, and I'm incredibly proud of you, but there's more to life than that. Do you think my successful business career would have meant anything at all to me if I didn't have you girls and your mother? Find someone special to share your life *with you. My wish for you is to find the kind of love your mother and I had, and to create a family together. You're a 21st-century woman. You can have it all.*

I know you're going to spend the next several weeks studying for your Boards. That's what you have to do. Once that's behind you, live it up. Find happiness.

I'll talk to you again in a few months once those pesky Boards are behind you.

I love you always,
Dad

I'm crying. I cry at all his letters. He's not wrong. I know it in my heart. Maybe that's why I've been so down. I thought that finally achieving my lifetime goal would make me happy, and make me feel fulfilled, but that's not how I feel at all. I feel like something's missing.

I'm hesitant to show Mom my letter. She's having such a good day. I hate to make her cry, and she'll most definitely cry from this letter. I wipe my tears, so she doesn't see them. I put a smile on my face, and walk back into the kitchen, where she's anxiously waiting.

"Hey, Mom. It wasn't really what I thought it was going to be. It wasn't as much about congratulating me on my graduation. It was him giving me some good life advice. I think I needed to hear it. Would you like to read it?"

She looks at me with trepidation. "You don't mind?"

"Of course not." I hand it to her. I watch her read it. She has tears in her eyes as she finishes it, but she's not hysterical.

She grabs my hand. "He's right. You do need to start having

things in your life that are more than just school and medicine. You need to find happiness, Harley."

"I know he's right." I look at her. "I think it applies to you too, Mom. You're too young and too beautiful to sit here alone all the time. You need to find happiness too."

She wipes her tears and stands up straight. She gives me a big smile and holds out her other hand. I take it. "How about you and I both pledge to push ourselves out of our comfort zones over the next year?"

I remove my hands from hers and hug her. When I pull back, I squeeze her hand and shake on it. She shakes mine back. "Mom, we have ourselves a deal."

CHAPTER THREE

THE PAST

BRODY

"Good morning, class. Today I want to tell you the story of a man we'll call Phillip. Phillip was a high school football player who was injured in a helmet-to-helmet collision. The C-3 and C-4 vertebrae in his neck were fractured. In fact, the vertebrae literally exploded, as he crushed the front of his spinal cord." Harley raises her hand and I nod toward her.

"Professor Cooper, that sounds a lot like the same injury as the actor Christopher Reeve." She's so damn smart. I've had her in my class for nearly three months now. Liz was right. She's got a brilliant mind. She works harder than any of the students in the class. She sees things that others just don't see. She's always at least one step ahead of everyone else, me included.

I've also had to bear witness to every man, and even a few women, in this class hitting on her. She does absolutely nothing to encourage it, yet it's a daily occurrence for her.

Though she shouldn't have to, she goes so far as to wear baggy clothes to hide her sensational body. It's in such contrast to what I saw her wearing the night we met. If possible, she's sexier like this. I haven't seen her wear a speck of make-up since that night, and her face is simply flawless. She's the epitome of effortless beauty.

Despite my feelings, I've done nothing other than sneak a few longing glances now and then. I have been completely professional around her. I've only spoken to her in class. We haven't remotely acknowledged what happened between us since the first day of class in my office.

"Yes, very good Ms. Lawrence. It's the exact same injury that he suffered when he fell from his horse. Do you know what happened to him, Ms. Lawrence?"

"As I understand it, he was left a quadriplegic and died about ten years later due to the toll of the injuries on his body."

I nod. "That's correct. Excellent. As for Phillip, his EMTs were very smart, and very quick-acting. They cooled and provided oxygen directly to the injured area, and they administered steroids to relieve the swelling and inflammation on the way to the hospital."

"Phillip arrived at my hospital within twenty minutes of the injury and was in my O.R. fifteen minutes later. We worked extremely quickly to fuse the vertebrae and relieve the pressure around the spinal cord. Today, Phillip is walking. Though his football career is over, he's able to otherwise live a very normal life."

I continue, "It's my belief that it was the combination of the competent EMTs and our quick-moving surgical team." I show them all a recent photo of Phillip, as humanizing these cases is especially important for medical students.

"I have two assignments for all of you. First, I am handing out the file of a woman who had a surfing accident. I've removed her name for her privacy but make no mistake that this is the real file, of a real patient. I'd like you to review it and let me know if the doctors did all they could to prevent her paralysis. I want a short write-up in explanation sent to me one week from today."

They all seem to understand the assignment. "Second, I want you all to spend the next week in the lab working on both your spinal fusion technique, *and* the efficiency of that technique. You can use class time. We learned in the case of Phillip that the speed at which we fused the vertebrae was the difference in Phillip walking or spending his life in a wheelchair unable to move anything from his neck down. But please understand that I would never want you to value speed over quality of care. I suggest you work on the technique first, without concern for speed, and then work your way up to completing the procedure more and more efficiently."

The students look excited to get into the lab.

"At the end of the week, we will all gather, and the person with the most precise *and* efficient performance will receive some sort of reward."

Of course, the class starts buzzing about extra credit. I roll my eyes. "Don't hesitate to reach out with questions. I look forward to seeing you all in the lab. Class is dismissed."

Harley comes up to my desk after class. "Professor Cooper, would it be possible to get ahold of Phillip's surgical notes to compare to your surfer?" That makes a lot of sense.

"Of course, Ms. Lawrence. I will email them to you this evening."

"Thank you." She smiles and leaves. I can't help but watch her walk up the stairs and out of the class. There's just something about her that I can't let go of.

A clearing throat brings me out of my Harley trance. I see Greg Waters standing there. "Can't keep your eyes off of her, can you?"

I give him a confused face. "I'm sorry?"

"Harley Lawrence. You were just looking at her ass the whole way up those stairs." I wasn't staring at her ass. It's all of her that intoxicates me.

"I don't know what you're talking about. Ms. Lawrence simply asked for the surgical notes on a case file that we discussed in class today."

He gives me an arrogant smile. "Don't worry, Brody. I get it. Believe me, I get it. She's one hot piece of ass." He wiggles his eyebrows up and down. "The things I could do to that ass." He smiles suggestively. I want to punch him in the face.

I don't give him the satisfaction of a returning smile. "Greg, she's the smartest person in the class. She's going to be an incredible doctor. That's what I see when I look at her."

He scoffs at me. "I call bullshit. You're a human man after all. We're both smart enough to know what's lying underneath those baggy clothes she wears." He looks around to make sure no one else is around. "You know, she's totally obsessed with her grades. You could probably get her to do just about anything for an A in your class."

"Greg, there's no need to disrespect her. I think she's more than earned our respect. In my experience to date, she's not obsessed with grades so much as wanting to learn. She's a sponge, hungry for information. I would never attempt to put her in a compromising position. In part because she appears to be an honorable woman, and in part, because I'm not a harassing asshole. Additionally, she doesn't need help in the grades department. She earns straight A's based on actual merit."

"I think there's an opportunity there. You may be missing out." He shrugs his shoulders. "Want to grab lunch?"

"No."

THREE DAYS LATER, I'm in my office at the school finishing some paperwork. It's nighttime and I don't think there are any students still around. I walk by the lab door and notice that the light is on. That's odd.

I peek in and see Harley hard at work, concentrating, oblivious to the outside world. She doesn't see me yet, focused on the task at hand. I can't take my eyes off of her. It's not just her distinct beauty. It's watching her work. The obvious passion she has for what she's doing. She stirs something in me that no one else ever has.

I know I shouldn't, but I walk inside the lab. I find myself wanting to interact with her, even if just professionally. "Ms. Lawrence, how's it going?"

She looks up in surprise that anyone else is in the

building. "Oh, hey Dr. Cooper. Everything's fine. I'm just problem solving here."

"Is there anything I can help with?"

She thinks for a moment. She puts her pen in her mouth. It's distracting. "Well, I'm struggling a bit with not clipping any major veins or arteries during the fusion." She points to a specific spot. "You see, when the tool enters here, I don't see how it's possible to slide it all the way in without bumping anything."

"Ah. I see. Have you tried coming at it from a different angle?"

She pinches her eyebrows together. "What do you mean?"

I walk behind her and place my hand near hers. "May I?" She nods. I place my hand over hers. She's so soft. I place my other hand on her hip and switch her positioning in front of the spine.

I close my eyes for a second. This is the first physical contact we've had in months. It feels so nice. Both of our breaths have noticeably deepened.

"If you stand over here, and move your fingers this way, you'll be safe." I manipulate her body and her fingers. I'm bent over, and my face is so close to her neck. I inhale her scent. She smells amazing. It's like vanilla and strawberries. Everything about her being in my arms feels right. I close my eyes for one more second and take it in.

She whispers, "Dr. Cooper."

My mouth is right next to her ear. I whisper back, "Harley." I rub my nose up and down her neck. I just can't help myself.

She swallows hard. "We can't do this." But she makes no attempt to move.

As if I have no control over my body, I slowly remove my hand from hers, rub it down her cheek and allow it to trickle down onto her neck. She lets out a soft moan as she leans back into me. I'm hard as a rock. She no doubt can feel it, as I'm now pressed against her backside. I have such a strong urge to bend her over this table.

I can feel her let out the breath she was undoubtedly holding, as she again whispers to me. "Dr. Cooper. We can't do this. I can't do this." She still makes no attempt to move. "You know what would happen to my reputation if this came out."

That's the bucket of ice water that I needed. I immediately back away. I rub my hand over my face. "You're right. I'm so sorry, Ms. Lawrence. It won't happen again." I walk toward the door. "I hope that position shift helps. Good night, Ms. Lawrence."

"Good night. Thank you for the tip, Dr. Cooper." I simply nod with my back to her as I exit the door. I need to get out of here, and away from her, immediately.

HARLEY

It's the night before the contest. I've been working crazy hours this week in the lab to perfect the surgical technique. I see Dr. Cooper at the door. I enthusiastically wave him in and smile. "Look, I think I've got it right, and my speed gets better each time. Your tip was a game-changer for me. Thank you." I'm so excited.

He walks over scanning my work. He bends down to get a closer look, ensuring my tools aren't touching any veins or arteries. He's in my face again. He's so gorgeous. That freaking chin dimple. I stare at it all the time. He's so close that I could touch it if I wanted to.

He lifts his head just a bit as he smiles up at me. "You've mastered it, Ms. Lawrence. I'm pretty sure that you've got this competition in the bag. I don't think anyone else ever stood a chance against you. The prize is all but yours."

I laugh. "What will a win, a Hershey Kiss?" Why did I say kiss? Why? Because I wish it could be a real one. I'm staring at his lips while licking mine. His face turns serious when he notices, and now he's staring at me. The tension is palpable. I can't help myself. I reach my hand out, and run my fingertips down his bottom lip into his chin dimple. The dimple that has a starring role in all of my dreams. Every night I replay when he was on his knees between my legs looking up at me. His dimple covered in my juices.

I'm so drawn to him. I feel myself physically aching for him. I'm throbbing between my legs. I move my hand over to cup his cheek. I don't care anymore. I need to kiss him. I need to taste him again. I move my lips towards his. He's not moving away. Our lips are almost touching when a noise outside the door breaks our collective daze.

We both jerk backward. "I...I...I'm so sorry. I don't know what came over me."

He holds up his hands. "No, no. It's completely my fault. I'll leave you to it, Ms. Lawrence. Good luck tomorrow." He leaves the lab.

I blow out a breath. This is a lot harder than I thought it would be. He almost kissed me the other night. I almost kissed him tonight. I think we're both struggling with this arrangement. This is a recipe for disaster. I can't see him every day. I think for the second semester I'm going to have to request a transfer into Dr. Waters' class. I don't want to, but I just don't see any other way around it.

THE DAY of the contest arrives. Half of the students don't have the proper technique. Of those with proper technique, most of them take way too much time. There are only a small handful that do it quickly. I know that I can do it faster. None of them are standing in the position that Dr. Cooper taught me.

It's my turn. I get into my spot as I wait for him to start the clock. I get it done exactly correctly. I know that much. I look up at him. "What was my time?" I'm pretty sure I was the fastest, but I was in the zone and wasn't totally aware of the time ticking by.

Dr. Cooper looks up from his timer with a huge smile. "Well Ms. Lawrence, your technique and quality of care were perfect, and your time was better than mine when I worked on Phillip. You too would have saved him from a terrible fate. Perhaps he'd be back on the football field if you were his surgeon. Congratulations. You're the winner." His smile widens even more. The whole class claps for me. It feels amazing. I love doing this. I can't wait until I'm a real surgeon and save real people.

"Ms. Lawrence, we'll think up an appropriate reward for you. Great job, class. If your technique was flawed today, I suggest you spend some more time in this lab in the next few weeks. You'll have to do this perfectly as part of your final exam. If you haven't done so already, please also make sure to get me your analysis paragraph on the paralyzed surfer. That's due today. Class is dismissed."

I stay in the lab after he dismisses us. "Dr. Cooper, can I have a word with you in your office?"

"Of course, Ms. Lawrence. Follow me." I follow him up to his office and close the door. I sit in one of the chairs at the front of his desk. He looks at me. "If this is about the reward, I'm sure we can find something appropriate."

"Dr. Cooper, do you honestly think I care about some silly reward? Knowing that I performed the procedure in a way that would possibly save someone's life is reward enough for me." He nods and smiles.

"I'm here because I want to give you the courtesy of letting you know that at the end of this semester, I'm going to request a transfer into Dr. Waters' class."

He goes to speak but I put up my hand. "No. It's time. I need to face the truth. I need to be honest with myself. The fact is that I'm extremely attracted to you. I thought I could bury my feelings, but clearly, I can't. I'm pretty sure you're attracted to me as well." He nods his head in agreement. "I think this is for the best. I've worked too hard to get where I am to let this attraction knock me off course. I think I need some distance from you."

He gives me a defeated smile. "I understand. Please know that I absolutely hate to lose you as a student, but I understand. Also, know that you are genuinely the brightest student in my class, and you're going to make a fantastic surgeon one day."

"Thank you."

He smiles. "Does this mean that you'll start calling me Brody?"

"No. I still can't have what happened getting out. You're my professor this semester, and you're a professor at this school."

"Harley, one day I won't be the professor and you won't be the student." He doesn't get that it can never happen between us.

"But you will have always been my professor, and I'll never be willing to have my abilities or credibility as a student put into question." He looks disappointed.

I need to change the topic. "The other reason I wanted to talk to you is about your surfer file." I hesitate a moment. "It was your mother, wasn't it?"

His eyes open wide. "How...how did you know that?"

"Well, it happened on Huntington Beach. I know you're from Huntington Beach. I saw the year it happened and the age of the victim. I figured there was some relation so I googled the accident. The last name is Cooper. It mentioned that her son was with her, and his age matches up."

He looks up at the ceiling for a moment and closes his eyes. He brings his head back down and looks at me. "Yes, it was my mother."

I nod. "Will you tell me what happened?" He doesn't respond right away. "I've already turned in my assignment, so there's no issue there."

He looks like he's in a different world right now. "We were surfing like we did every Saturday morning together. I remember that the waves were amazing that day. We were having such a great time. We alternated waves. The next wave was her turn. I don't even know exactly what happened, other than I saw her get up, and then I saw her crash down."

He pauses for a moment, clearly emotional. "She apparently went headfirst into the ocean floor at the worst angle possible. I knew something was wrong right away. I saw her board first. It was split down the middle. Then I saw her behind it. She was floating face down. I swam to her as fast as I could and lifted her onto my board. I was screaming for help as I tried to swim ashore. A few people on the beach swam out to us and helped me bring her in. I remember her looking and feeling so lifeless. Someone called 911 while someone else gave her CPR. I was in shock."

He has tears in his eyes now, as do I. I can't help myself. I grab his hand. He lets me hold it. "The EMTs were slow to arrive, but the surgeon was slower. Her injury was the exact same as Phillip's. They didn't get her into the O.R. for well over an hour. The surgeon performed the procedure slower than the slowest student in our class today." He slumps his head down, completely overcome with emotion.

I gently rub my thumb on his hand. "You were what, fifteen years old?"

He nods. "Yes."

"What happened to her?"

"She was rendered a quadriplegic. We didn't quite have the resources that Christopher Reeve had. She died less than two years later." Tears are freely flowing down both of our cheeks.

I squeeze his hand. "I'm so sorry, Brody." We sit in silence with me holding his hand for a few more minutes. I eventually look up at him. "Is this why you became a neurosurgeon?" He nods. "You understand more than anyone why I need my surgical specialty to be cardio? It feels like a calling. A way to right a past wrong."

He nods again. "Of course, I understand."

"How did your father handle things?"

"He was a mess for a long time. He took care of her for two years before she passed. I was still a teenager, so he had to take care of me too. It wasn't easy. When she passed, he was in a pretty bad place, but eventually got better. It took some time, but he moved on with his life. He had to. He dates now and then. It's never anything serious, but he lives his life."

He looks at me and recognizes a similar pain. "How's your mother managing?"

A big lump forms in my throat. "Honestly, she's an absolute disaster right now. We can't even get her out of bed. She still cries all day long. It's been nearly six months, but it's still very fresh for her. I suppose time heals all wounds though. At least the type she's suffering. I can only hope that one day she returns to the wonderful, vibrant woman that she once was."

"I'm sorry to hear that. It's hard. Just know that in time, she'll get it together. Just be patient with her. Let her mourn however she needs to and be there for her in whatever way she needs you."

"We are. My sisters and I constantly check in on her. My mother's best friend has practically moved in. She stays with her every night."

"How many sisters do you have?"

"I have two. I'm the oldest. They're both in college right now. One was local and one wasn't, but the one who was away transferred back here this year. She felt like she needed to be closer to home."

"You're lucky to have a support system. I don't have siblings, so it was just me and my father. I think that's why I ended up staying in Southern California for so long. Moving here is the first time I've ever lived away from my hometown. He was the one who encouraged me to try something new."

We're still holding hands, a little lost in the moment, when Dr. Waters barges through the door. He takes quick notice of our merged hands. We immediately break them apart. "Am I interrupting something?"

Brody stands. "Not at all Greg. I was just congratulating Ms. Lawrence on winning the surgical contest in our class. It was quite impressive."

"I bet it was." He says that with a tone I don't recognize.

I quickly wipe my eyes as I get up to leave. "Thank you, Dr. Cooper. I learned a lot from the fusion exercise. I look forward to the next competition."

Dr. Waters stops me before I can exit. "Actually, Ms. Lawrence, can you come with me to my office? I have a few opportunities to discuss with you."

Brody looks bothered. "I'm sure you can talk to her here, Greg. I don't mind at all."

"No, that's not necessary. My office is best." I have no clue what opportunities he's talking about, but I guess I have to follow him.

We walk down the hallway and enter his office. He closes and locks the door. Instead of sitting behind his desk, he sits down right next to me.

Something bad is about to happen. I know it. Before I can say anything, he speaks. "So, Ms. Lawrence. How's neuro going for you this year? I was sad when I learned that you weren't going to be in my class again."

"It's going really well. I'm learning so much. I like the practical approach. Having a top spinal surgeon in the country makes it particularly exciting."

He smirks at me. "Is that the only reason it's exciting?"

"I don't know what you mean."

"Sure you do. I saw you and Dr. Cooper embracing. Perhaps you've found another way to earn those good grades."

"Excuse me Dr. Waters, but that's insulting. My grades at this school are perfect because I study hard. I have no need for any of that behavior, nor would I ever engage in it."

He reaches over and grabs my inner thigh hard. I try to pull away but he's too strong. "You know I can help you get any residency you want." I don't bother to respond.

He uses his other hand to grab my chin. He roughly tilts it to him, as he moves his eyes up and down my body. "You're the hottest woman I've ever seen."

He rubs my bottom lip with his thumb. Unlike Brody's touch, his makes my stomach turn. "Your lips are so full. You know they could really help you secure that residency." I have tears welling in my eyes again, but this time for a different reason.

I manage to croak out, "No thank you." He's about to speak again when there's a loud banging at the door.

I hear Brody. "Greg, it's time for the faculty meeting. Let's get going." He loosens his grip enough for me to get free and run to the door. I unlock and open it. Brody's eyes widen when he sees the tears in my eyes. I run down the hall to get away from them both. I go into the bathroom, slide down the wall and start to sob.

I'm crying for a few minutes when I receive a text.

Brody: Are you okay? What did he do?

Me: He did what all men do to me. Think that I'm easy. Think that I'll do anything to get ahead.

Brody: I'm so sorry he did that. I never should've let you go with him. I didn't know how to get you out of it without sounding suspicious.

Me: Do you now understand why I can't ever date you? Everyone will assume you've given me good grades or special treatment because I'm giving you what Dr. Waters wanted from me.

Brody: I get it. Do you want me to report him?

Me: No, because then I'll always be 'that girl'. No one will see anything else I've ever done.

Brody: I'm sorry Harley. I really am.

Me: I know you are. Silver lining. I think I'll be staying in your class next semester. I'd rather take my chances there.

Brody: I won't lie. I'm doing a happy dance. Not just because of my feelings. Harley, you're the most intelligent person at this school. It's truly exciting to teach someone with your potential. I mean that. Know that I'm not the only professor here who feels that way. I'm not the only professor who respects your mind.

Me: Thanks for saying that (or I guess writing that).

Brody: It's true.

I put my phone down and get myself together.

THE NEXT WEEK is the annual faculty versus students flag football game. I think it's in part to get us medical students out of the library and moving around, and in part to humanize the faculty.

I'm one of the only women on the team. My mother was a college athlete. She would freak out if I didn't participate in stuff like this. I can hold my own though. I'm a pretty good athlete.

I see Brody making his way to the field. I've never seen him in athletic attire. He's in shorts and a t-shirt. He has long, thick, muscular, sexy legs. I know firsthand that it's not the only thick thing on his body. The t-shirt is tight across his broad chest. His arms are huge. He's quite muscular. I don't think I noticed that before in his buttoned-down shirts.

I honestly didn't need more material for my wet dreams, but here it is right before me. I think every female student and faculty member is drooling. I'm pretty sure getting to see him like this is the only reason they're here.

I never realized it before, mostly because I try to avoid seeing him outside of class, but he's extremely popular among the rest of the faculty. They're in a circle around him. He's got them all laughing about something.

I wish I wasn't, but I'm so attracted to him. In looking around at all the female faces right now, I'm clearly not the only one.

A whistle blows, breaking me out of my blatant ogling. We begin the game, and it quickly becomes clear that the medical students are not comprised of many athletes.

The game ends up being a lot of fun. Brody throws three touchdown passes for his team, while I catch two for mine.

Our team is down by one on the final play of the game. I catch the ball and am running down the sideline. Brody goes to grab my flag, but our feet tangle, causing us both to fall. Naturally, we fall with my back to the ground and him between my legs. We're both hysterically laughing until we notice the position we're in, and the fact that every single person is looking at us.

He should get up now, but he doesn't. I'm not sure I really want him to. Truth be told, he was the last person between my legs, and I'm not too upset having him back. His face turns serious as he stares at me. I look around at all the faces staring at us. "Dr. Cooper, you should get up. People are watching us."

"Harley, I'd really like to, but if I do, everyone here will know just how attracted I am to you." I look down and see what he's talking about. My eyes widen. It shouldn't, but it turns me on to see the effect I have on him.

I look at him. "Why don't we at least shift from this position. We can stay on the ground as long as you need to though. I'll fake an injury."

He gives me a small smile. "Thanks."

We untangle ourselves, but he stays laying on the ground as he pretends to examine my foot. A few of the other faculty members come over. "Everything okay, Ms. Lawrence?"

"Yes, I just twisted my ankle. Dr. Cooper is looking at it. Thank you." They fawn all over me, getting me ice and bandages. He mouths, "Thank you," and eventually stands.

Megan comes over to help me off the field. I fake limp my way to a seat. She looks at me. "Was having Dr. Cooper between your legs as hot as I would imagine?"

"He wasn't between my legs. We both fell."

"Between your legs."

"Whatever. It was an accident."

She laughs. "It made me want to play football." It made me want to do some other things.

CHAPTER FOUR

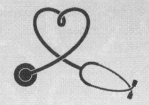

THE PRESENT

HARLEY

"Harley! Congrats on passing your Boards! I'm so proud of you, Dr. Lawrence. My big sister, the doctor."

"Thanks, Reagan. I just heard from Skylar too. It's exciting. I'm about to start my first residency shift."

"You're amazing, sis. I'm so proud of you. Have you read your letter from Dad yet?

"Not yet. I'll head to Mom's this weekend to grab it. My residency is keeping me busy all week. I can't get out there before then."

"Don't work too hard. Have a little fun. Do you want to go out sometime soon to celebrate?"

"I'm absolutely committed to going out more in the coming

months. I just need to get up and running in my residency. I need to get used to the schedule."

"Fine, but we're going out soon."

She screams. "Oh my god, I almost forgot to tell you. Guess what? I've got big news. Huge." She sounds so excited.

I have no clue what this could be. "What's the big news?"

"Mom met a guy at a bar. He asked her out and she's thinking about going out with him this weekend."

I'm truly shocked. "Shut the hell up. Are you serious?"

"Yep."

"That's amazing. This could be so great for her. She needs something like this."

"Agree. Frankly, Mom needs to get laid. Her dry spell is even longer than yours." Just barely.

"Thanks for that."

"Sorry, but you need to think about getting some action too."

"I know. You're right. Like I said, I promise to start going out more. I just need a little more time. This is great news about Mom though. You made my day. Do we know anything about him?"

"I couldn't get any more details out of Mom. I'll text Aunt Cass to see what I can find out."

"Okay. Let me know. I'll talk to you soon."

Exactly twenty seconds later, my cell phone pings with a text notification. I take my phone back out. I see it's my group chat with my sisters and Aunt Cass.

> Reagan: AC- Mom told me she met a guy at a bar and may go out with him this weekend. What's the deal?

> Aunt Cass: YES!!! She slow danced with him at Cover Me. They drank and talked at the bar all night. She was even flirting. He's hot AF.

> **Skylar:** WHAT??!! That's so awesome. She go home with him? Please say yes.

> **Aunt Cass:** No. He asked her out for this coming weekend. She initially said no because she was nervous, but he charmed her into agreeing to talk on the phone every night this week before she makes a decision about the date. She's going to go if I have to drag her ass out.

> **Me:** That's fantastic. Do we know anything about him other than he's "hot AF"?

> **Aunt Cass:** I did some research. I wouldn't let my BFF go out with a freaking serial killer. He's a very respected and successful businessman. Did I mention that he's hot AF?

> **Reagan:** This is awesome!! Good work Aunt Cass!! Got to get back to the shop. See you bitches at dinner on Sunday night.

I put my phone back in my purse and walk into the hospital. I have a huge smile on my face for Mom. I would be thrilled if she started dating.

I'm about thirty minutes early, but they get me started on my paperwork and my IDs. There's a pretty, young-looking woman, with long brown hair, sitting next to me filling out paperwork as well. She looks really nervous. Once we both finish, I'm handed a white coat, but she's not. I decide to introduce myself. "Hi, I'm Harley Lawrence. Is this your first day too?

"Yes, my first day as a surgical nurse. I'm really nervous. Does it show?"

"Everyone's nervous on their first day. What's your name?"

"Oh. Duh. I'm Jessica Shaw. It's nice to meet you." We shake hands. "Thanks for introducing yourself. It'll be nice to have a friendly face among the doctor staff." She nods her head towards my white coat.

"Yep, it's the first day of my surgical residency. I feel like I've been waiting for this day my whole life."

Just then my friend Megan walks in. I wave her over. "Jessica, this is my friend Megan. She's starting today as a doctor too, though she'll be down in pediatrics." They say their hellos, but Megan then takes off for the pediatrics floor.

Over the next twenty minutes, the room fills out a bit more. I meet the other people in my surgical residency group. A goofy guy named John Peters, a petite, attractive curly-haired blonde named Michele Black, and a standoffish tall guy name Marc La Porta.

The doctor seemingly in charge of our group comes in. He's an older man with salt and pepper hair. I've seen him around during the past few years, but I've never met him.

"Hello, ladies and gentlemen. Welcome to the first day of the best surgical residency in the country. Congratulations to all of you for making the cut. Everyone want-to-be surgeon applies to this residency, and you four were selected. My name is Dr. Phillip McCrevis. I'm the chief of surgery at this hospital. I'll be running your residency program."

Johns starts laughing. We all look at him, though he tries to play it off by clearing his throat like he was coughing. He whispers to me. "His name is Phil McCrevis. That was my fake ID name when I was a teenager. Do you think that's his real name?"

I look at him like he's crazy. I whisper back. "Uh, yes. He's not giving us a fake name."

Dr. McCrevis continues. "You all will spend the next four months in the ER." We look at each other in shock. None of us signed up for that.

"I know it's unconventional, but the ER is a wonderful place to get your feet wet. You see everything, and you'll see it happening at a rapid pace. You'll learn how to think quickly on your feet. We're making life and death decisions on a daily basis. It's my belief that the ER will get you the foundation that you need. It's not to say you won't be able to observe surgeries, you will. There will be plenty of emergency surgery situations that come through the ER."

The new surgical nurses will join you so that you can get comfortable working with one another. After your time in the ER, which will be about four months, you'll transition here to the surgical floor. That will be just after the new year. You'll be a part of surgeries in neuro, cardio, ortho, obstetrics, and several others. At some point, each of you will gravitate towards one over the others. There's no need to make the decision now. It may change once you spend time in trenches."

Just then, someone catches the attention of Dr. McCrevis. "Dr. Waters, can you come in here." Ugh. I had almost forgotten that I would run into him. Fortunately, he's not in charge of the residency program in neuro.

Dr. Waters comes in and gives me a slimy smile. "Dr. Waters, please meet our new surgical residents. Group, this is Dr. Gregory Waters, a brilliant neurosurgeon. He'll be co-running the neuro part of the residency program." What? That is not who is supposed to be in charge. I can't believe this.

"Hello all. Welcome to Pennsylvania Hospital. Dr. Lawrence, it's so good to see one of my former students accepted into our surgical residency program." He looks me up and down in a way that makes my skin crawl.

I give my best fake smile. "Good to see you too, Dr. Waters." I probably should say that I look forward to working with him, but I can't muster a second lie.

Fortunately, Dr. McCrevis begins speaking again. "Oh right, Dr. Lawrence went to medical school right here. I don't spend any time with medical students, but I thought you looked familiar. How lovely to have one of our own here with us." He gives me a genuine smile, and I give him one in return. "Well gang, let's head down to the ER. Thanks for stopping by Dr. Waters."

He looks me up and down again. "The pleasure was all mine. I can't wait to get my hands on you guys." I shiver.

As we're walking down the hallway to the ER, Michele whispers in my ear. "Was it me or did Dr. Waters give you one creepy eye fuck?"

"It wasn't you. He's extremely creepy. Don't let yourself end up in a room alone with him. He's a sleaze. What happened to Dr. Mancini? I thought he was in charge of the neurosurgical residents."

"You must not have heard. The hospital kept it under wraps. He got fired. Apparently, it was ugly. I heard he was caught in a supply closet with a resident. He was immediately asked to resign. That's hearsay though. I don't know anything firsthand. It was definitely something scandalous though. His exit was very sudden."

"Oh shit. I had no clue. Well, if it's against the rules for attendings to fraternize with residents, then perhaps Dr. Waters will keep his distance from us."

"Yea, that guy didn't really look like he's planning on distancing himself from you." She's not wrong. Damn it. I can never get away from this crap. It follows me everywhere.

I have lunch with my fellow residents that day. John and

Michele are very funny. I feel like they're flirting with each other. Marc is quiet and doesn't offer much to the conversation.

John tells us that when he was in college, he used to make money as a mascot for a professional sports team. I can see him having the personality for that. He tells us how many attractive women wanted to sleep with a mascot. He said he would have sex with random women after every single game.

We're laughing at how ridiculous this is. I can't help but ask the obvious question. "Did you wear your mascot uniform when you had sex with them?"

"Yes, they always wanted me to keep the mascot head on."

We're hysterically laughing now. Michele looks at all of us. "Is that a fetish now? Mascot sex?"

I shrug my shoulders. I have no clue. But John says, "Yes." Michele's eating up every word out of his mouth. There's something brewing with these two. I'm just happy to sit and laugh though.

CHAPTER FIVE

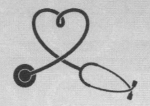

THE PAST

BRODY

As the months have gone by, it's only gotten harder to be around her. Harley Lawrence is official the most perfect woman on the planet. I watch her every single day. I'm convinced more and more that she's everything I could ever want in a woman. It's as if she was made for me.

She's probably the smartest person I've ever been around. I love the way her mind works.

She's one hundred percent authentic. There's not a fake bone in her body. There's not a bad bone in her body. And that body. I just keep playing our night together, all those months ago, over and over in my mind. I imagine those tits and that ass. I can still feel both in my hands. I know I appreciated them at the time, but I wish I appreciated them even more.

Sitting on top of that perfect body is the face of an angel. I long to touch it and kiss it. I'm officially going out of my mind. I can't even look at other women. They do nothing for me. I may set the world record for jerking off.

"Brody. Earth to Brody." My Harley spell is momentarily broken as I turn my head.

"Oh. Hey Liz. Sorry, I was in another world."

"You really were. I called your name like seven times. I was trying to ask if you want to grab a drink tonight. I realize I was likely the only person you knew when you moved here, and I never really took you out. I'd be more than happy to rectify that." She smiles up at me. I know that look. It's a *let's go out as more than friends* look.

"To be honest, I haven't gone out much, Liz. I'm swamped at the hospital and, frankly, I'm a little hung up on someone I was seeing." That's a bit of a stretch of the truth, but I am certainly hung up on someone.

I shrug. "I've kind of just been focusing on work, and not much else." I see the disappointment in her face, but Liz is a good person, I don't want to give her false hope or lead her on in any way.

"She really must have done a number on you. The Brody I knew in California went out nearly every night."

"You're right. I guess she did do a number on me."

"Well, if you change your mind, or even if you just want someone to talk to, you know where to find me."

"Thanks, Liz."

She's not wrong. I used to be the good-time guy who went out all the time. All I've done since I arrived in Philly eight months ago is pine for this woman who I can't have.

Maybe I just need to get out and meet new people. I need to meet new women.

I decide to text Nathan, a young, single architect who lives in my building. He's always asking me to hang out. I'm pretty sure he just needs a wingman. I think I can probably handle that.

> Me: Hey bud. I need to blow off some steam. What are you up to tomorrow night?

> Nathan: I'm meeting my little brother and his new girlfriend at Tonic and Tango. You're welcome to come with us. I think he mentioned that she may be bringing her sisters. He said they're all gorgeous.

> Me: Great. I'm in. What time?

> Nathan: 9:00.

> Me: See you there.

I ARRIVE at the club at 8:30. I need a few drinks in my system before this evening starts. I know that on some level I *need* to be here, but I also know that I don't actually *want* to be here.

I take three tequila shots before I remotely begin to loosen up.

I'm sitting at the bar, not paying attention to anything in particular when Nathan taps my shoulder. "Hey, buddy. I was looking for you. We have a table. Come join us."

"Great. I didn't see you come in. Let me settle up and I'll

meet you. I'll grab a round of shots too. How many are we and where's the table?"

"Back left corner booth. With you, there are six of us. By the way, my brother was right. The sisters are all hot as hell. Like model hot."

"Great. I'll be there in a few minutes." I order six tequila shots, and then make my way to the back left corner. I'm barely paying attention as I weave through all the people to the table. The club is dark, loud, and extremely crowded.

Nathan stands as I get there. He has to scream because it's so loud in here. "Hey, Brody. This is my little brother David." I shake his hand. "This is his girlfriend, Reagan." I smile and nod hello. "Her younger sister, Skylar." I smile and nod again. "And her older sister, Harley."

All of the air escapes my lungs. I may even gasp. My eyes meet the big green eyes that I've seen shaded with lust as an orgasm overtakes her body. The woman that I can't get out of my mind. The woman whose naked body has left a permanent mark on my soul. The perfect woman with the perfect brain.

I think my heart actually skips a beat. She's in a tight V-neck green dress. It's so different from what she normally wears to school. Unlike her appearance at school, her hair is styled, and her make-up is done. I love how she looks both ways, but tonight, she's just plain exquisite.

Her eyes widen just enough that I know she too is shocked to see me here. After a bit of an awkward pause, she subtly shakes her head. She doesn't want anyone to know that we know each other.

I give my best fake smile. "Nice to meet you ladies." I have to shout. "I brought tequila shots for everyone." They all yell out their thanks.

I look around the table. Wow, her sisters are beautiful too. Both of their hair colors are lighter than Harley's, and Reagan has blue eyes, but they undoubtedly resemble one another, and they're most definitely an extremely attractive family.

David's girlfriend Reagan hands out the shots, along with the salt and limes. We all silently cheers our shot glasses because we can't hear anything, and down our shots.

I move into the booth at the end next to Harley. The music is so loud that you can only hear the person right next to you. She leans into my ear. "Please don't say anything. I don't want my sisters to know."

"Okay." My eyes make a slow path down her body. I can't help myself. Her body calls to me. I adjust my jeans, as I can feel them getting tight. I can't believe the effect she has on me.

She looks down and knows exactly what's happening to me. I see her chest rise and fall a little faster and deeper, as her cheeks redden. She rubs her legs together. She's feeling the same thing. I can see it.

I know that I lack control in close proximity to her. It doesn't help matters that we're in an environment that affords us some anonymity, despite the crowd size.

I find myself needing to touch her. I put my hand on her upper thigh under the table where no one else can see. She doesn't stop me. Instead, she closes her eyes, and even with the insane noise level, I hear her let out a small moan.

She places her hand over mine, rubbing it with her thumb. We stay like that for a few songs. She even moves my hand a little bit higher on her thigh.

It's nice to just be able to touch each other. Neither of us wants it to end. I need more though. I need to touch more of her body.

At some point, I whisper in her ear. "Let's go get a drink." She looks me in the eyes and nods. Though I can't hear her, she clearly tells her sisters that we're headed over to the bar.

We make our way around the dance floor, which must have a thousand people out there by now. Once we're out of sight, I take her hand in mine, interlacing our fingers. She doesn't stop me.

I know she's struggling with control, just as I am. The attraction we share is like nothing I've ever experienced. It's palpable.

We approach the bar, and I order eight more tequila shots, two for Harley and me to drink now, and six for all of us at the table. I hand her one, nodding my head indicating that she should take it now. She looks at me while she seductively licks the salt off her hand, just ahead of taking the shot.

Watching it slide down her throat is so damn hot. Watching her lick her lips afterward is even hotter. I'm pretty sure that I visibly gulp, and she notices. I lick my lips. She notices that too. Her mouth is open, and her face is flushed.

I assume she's going to hand me the lime and salt when she's done, but she doesn't. She looks me dead in the eye, licks the lime, and subtly spreads it across the top of the exposed part of her breasts. She then sprinkles the salt across it. It sticks to her breasts in invitation.

I grab her hips and pull her close to me. I bend my head down and slowly lick across the top of her. I think we both moan. I know that I do. I'm desperate to pull her dress down to lick lower. I'm desperate to do anything to keep my mouth and hands on her.

I down the shot of tequila. She puts the lime into my mouth. She doesn't pull back though. She slowly trails her fingers down my lips, down my chin, and then across my neck to the top of my chest. I see her struggling, wanting to touch more of me. She keeps her hand on my chest as she runs her gaze down and then back up my body.

I pull the lime out and move my mouth to her ear. "I'm going to drop the shots at the table. I'll tell them you went to the bathroom. Meet me on the side of the dance floor closest to the back exit. It's out of their line of vision." She nods her head.

I make my way back to the table and drop the shots down. Skylar looks behind me. "Where's Harley?"

"I think she said she was going to the bathroom. I saw a friend of mine. I'm heading to the dance floor. I'll see you guys in a few." They nod in some form of acknowledgment, but I'm not sure they can hear me, or care to hear me.

I make my way toward the dance floor area near the back. I don't see her. I try to look through the crowd, but I still can't find her. There are so many people here.

All of a sudden, I feel arms snake around my waist from behind, and work their way down to my thighs.

I can smell Harley. I've come to love that smell of vanilla and strawberries. It permeates every space she inhabits. It fills the lab when she's working in there. It fills my classroom. It fills my office. I have a visceral reaction to that delicious smell.

We're swaying our hips to the beat as she works her way up and across my chest. I grab her hands, quickly turning us so that my front is now to her back. I wrap one arm around her waist, and pull her tight to my body, as we continue to sway to the beat. With the other arm, I take my hand and move her hair out of the way. She tilts her head to the side. I move my lips and tongue across her neck. She tastes so good.

We're dancing just as we did the night we met, with me wrapped around her, my hands on her body, and my lips on her neck. She grinds her ass against me, as she lifts one of her hands and grabs onto the back of my hair, pulling me closer. Her other hand runs up and down my thigh.

We stay like this for a while, enjoying the close proximity we've both clearly craved. I eventually kiss my way towards the front of her neck. As I do, she slowly turns around in my arms.

She runs all her fingers through my hair and grips it, pulling my face toward hers. Our lips come together. I immediately slip my tongue into her mouth. Oh god she tastes so good. I nearly forgot how great she tastes.

We have a substantial height difference, so I'm bent all the way down. I wrap my arms around her and lift her off the floor so that her face is at the same level as mine, even with me standing.

She tightens her arms around my neck. If possible, our kiss deepens further. We're both completely lost in one another. She's grabbing everywhere she can reach on my body. This feels exactly how I remember it feeling. Even better.

I've wanted this for so long. Now that it's here, I want to appreciate it. I have her in my arms again, and I'm not letting go this time.

I notice the back door toward the alley. Still holding her, I move us in that direction, and maneuver through the door to the outside. The door slams shut.

Without breaking our kiss, I look both ways. I see no one else in the alley. I move to press her back to the brick wall next to the door and push my body hard against hers.

She wraps her legs around me as she grinds onto me. I'm as hard as iron. I feel like I could explode. I have been since the second I saw her at the table. This girl is lighting me on fire in a way I've never experienced.

I kiss my way down her neck. I pull one side of her dress down freeing her breast. It's even bigger and more perfect than I remember. I grab it, taking her nipple into my mouth and sucking.

She arches her back. "Oh god, Brody. I need you inside of me. I need it more than I need to breathe. I've never wanted anything as much as I want you right now. Please." I know the feeling. I can't wait to be inside her again.

I move to her ear and whisper. "I'm going fuck you so hard tonight, Harley. You won't be walking straight for a week." She moans so loudly that they might have heard her over the music inside.

This is the moment I've been waiting for all these months. I move my hand to the hem of her dress, brushing my fingers across her thighs as I do. I feel her quiver at my touch. It drives me wild.

I'm about to pull up the bottom of her dress when I hear a police siren. We break our kiss, as we both look up the alley. We see a police car with its lights shining directly at us.

I panic. I pull up the top of her dress back over her breast, throw her over my shoulder, and I run the other way. The police yell for us to stop, but I don't.

I run like the wind for three blocks, cutting through alleyways, making sure they can't find us. I see an empty cab parked on a corner, place her inside and jump in. I yell as I hit the seat. "Go. Go."

He speeds off. I look behind us. The coast is clear.

She bursts out laughing. "Oh my god. That's the first time in my life that I've ever had to run from the cops."

"Technically, you didn't run. I did all the running." We're both laughing now.

"True." She takes out her phone. "I better text my sisters. I'm going to tell them that I wasn't feeling well and need to study. They'd believe that more than me leaving with a hot guy."

"That doesn't happen often?"

She shakes her head. "That doesn't happen ever, Dr. Cooper."

My smile fades. "Oh no. You're back to calling me Dr. Cooper."

She takes a deep breath and looks at me. "Yes, I suppose I am."

She finishes the text. She's silent for a bit as she lays her head against the back seat looking up. She eventually turns to me. "What is it about us and clubs?"

I look at her unable to answer. I shrug my shoulders. The cab driver turns his head back. "Anyone going to tell me where I'm going or am I just driving around all night spending your money?"

We briefly laugh again. I turn to Harley. It's her call. I'm hoping it's either her place or mine, not both.

She gives me an apologetic smile. "There will be two stops."

HARLEY

I almost had sex with Brody again this weekend. I can't believe how out of control I get around him. I've never been this way about anyone or anything in my entire life. The feeling takes on a life of its own. I can't manage my emotions or my body around him.

I actually spread lime and salt across my breasts and encouraged him to lick it off. I have no clue where I came up with that.

Sleeping with Brody again would have been a huge mistake. What was I thinking? I wasn't.

Thank god for the police interruption. If they didn't come, we would have had sex right there in the alley. I don't recognize myself around him.

It's Monday at 1:00 in the afternoon. Mercifully, my last class of the day was canceled, so I'm finished unusually early.

I'm in an irritable, terrible mood because of my momentary slip in judgment over the weekend. It's also possible that I'm in a terrible mood because I was more aroused on Saturday night than I've even been in my entire life, and it never came to fruition.

Thankfully, I didn't have neuro today. I don't think that I'm ready to face him just yet.

I walk out of the building, and down the front steps of the medical school. I see Aunt Cass in her car waiting for me. She motions for me to come over. I walk over. "What's up?"

"Get in."

"Why?"

"Because we're going for a drink."

"It's 1:00 on a Monday."

"And?"

I roll my eyes, make my way around to the passenger side, and get in. "Normally I have another class on Mondays. Were you just loitering or stalking me? Waiting out front on the off chance I came out two hours earlier than normal?"

She doesn't bat an eyelash. "I have my ways."

We get to an upscale bar. She orders us two vodka martinis. The bartender brings our drinks in less than thirty seconds. She winks at him. "Thanks, Ralph."

He winks back. "Anything for you, Cassandra." Of course, she knows the bartender. She's probably slept with him. Why can't I just sleep with random bartenders? My life would be so much less complicated.

I turn to her. "So, are you going to tell me why the fuck I'm drinking vodka at 1:00 on a Monday?"

"Quite a mouth on you today. Are you going to tell me why the fuck you looked like you were going to rip everyone to shreds at our dinner last night?"

"I was hungover." That's a lie.

"Bull. Fucking. Shit. Reagan and Skylar said you only had like two drinks, and then bailed early to study. Something has got you all twisted up. We're not leaving until you talk to me about it. It's more than your normal *never getting any action* uptight demeanor."

She's really pissing me off. It's not like I was in a great mood to begin with. "Fuck you! I don't need your shit right now! You're not my mother!"

She gives me a sympathetic look. "I'm temporarily the closest thing you have to it, so spill it."

I feel tears in my eyes. "What if it's not temporary?"

"It is. She just needs more time. It won't happen tomorrow, but she'll recover. I'll gladly pinch-hit in the meantime." She takes a sip of her drink. "Harley, give her a minute. She's completely broken-hearted."

I don't realize it, but I mumble, "She's not the only one." Oh crap. Why did I say that?

She looks surprised. "Who broke your heart?"

"Me. I broke my heart."

"I don't understand." I'm silent. She eventually raises her voice. "For crying out loud. Talk to me, Harley."

I down the whole martini at once, and motion to Ralph the fuck buddy that I need another.

I turn to her and look at her in the eyes with the defiance that I feel. "I *fucked* my professor. I want to keep *fucking* my professor. But I can't *fuck* him because he's my *fucking* professor. There. Now you've heard it. Are you happy?"

"Why would your unhappiness make me happy?"

I put my head down in defeat. "I'm not unhappy. I'm messed up in the head."

"Give me the story."

I sigh. "Remember the random guy I had sex with on the roof of the club right before school started?"

"Best sex of your life guy?"

"That's the one."

"Yes, but I thought you didn't know each other or exchange any information."

"We didn't. Imagine my surprise, when two days later I walked into my neurology class, and the stranger that I let bang me on the roof of Club Liberty turns out to be the best spinal surgeon in the country, and my neurology professor for the year."

"Oh shit."

"Oh shit is right."

She looks confused. "And you've been banging him since? You really haven't seemed like you've been getting laid on the regular. Certainly not with *Mr. Best Sex of My Life*."

I put my head in my hands. "No, I haven't had sex with him

since that night on the roof. We met after class that first day and mutually decided to keep things professional. We were both in a bit of shock over the circumstances but agreed to keep it quiet and keep it in the past."

"Good. That's what you should be doing. So, what's the problem?"

"The problem is that we're insanely attracted to each other. The attraction takes on a life of its own. We're both powerless against it. We've had so many near misses. There were a few times in the fall semester that we found ourselves alone in the lab and almost kissed."

"And then this past Saturday night he was at the club we went to." I blow out a breath and close my eyes. "My nipple was in his mouth, and he was about thirty seconds away from penetrating me in the alleyway when the police showed up and we had to run away."

I turn back to her. She looks shocked. "Aunt Cass, I can't fucking control myself around him. I've never been like that with anyone. I've never felt this way. I'm pretty sure he feels the same. I think that if I gave him the green light, we'd be together. I don't think he cares about the propriety of it anymore. The attraction is that powerful."

"Shit Harley."

"Yea. *Shit Harley* is right."

She's silent in contemplation for a moment before she looks at me. "You know I'm all for free love, and be with whoever you want, but women like you can't bang their professors."

"What's that supposed to mean?"

"You know exactly what it means. It means women that look like you, and have a body like yours, need to be twice as smart, because everyone just assumes you're using your good looks and banging your way to the top. Lucky for you, you actually are twice as smart, but you can't also bang the professors."

I put my head down on the bar. "I know. I've told him this. I'm not sure he totally gets it, but he at least tries to respect it. He really does. Sometimes we just lose control. It's like our bodies need the other. We have no control over it."

"How much longer is he your professor?"

"Just a few weeks. The school year is almost over. I won't have him for anything next year."

"You still can't be with him next year. You get that, right? Your grades will always be questioned if you are. Your integrity will be questioned."

"I know. I've also tried explaining that to him."

"Try harder. You need to tell him it's never happening."

"I'm trying. I really am."

"You've worked too hard to have it all flipped on you. You'd become the two-dollar whore that most people probably think you are."

"Thanks for that."

"I'm sorry, but it's the truth."

"I know. It's just so unfair."

"It's incredibly unfair. It's complete bullshit. But that's just the way it is."

I slowly nod my head. "It's not like I don't know the right answer. I'm not happy about it, but I know what to do."

"Then woman up and take care of it."

THE NEXT DAY I send Brody a text to meet me after class in his office. He texts back that he's available.

As soon as I close the door to his office, he's on me. He pushes me up against the door and kisses me. I love the way he kisses me. It's so passionate.

I go to push him away, but instead, I find myself grabbing his shirt pulling him to me. I lift my leg and grind against him. It's like he has a giant rod in his pants. Everything about his body on mine feels so right.

No. What am I doing? I pull my head away and push his chest. I'm out of breath from his kiss. "Stop. I didn't come here for this."

He looks disappointed. We both take a moment to catch our breath. "Sorry, I just assumed. Why did you want to see me then?"

"Why? Because we almost made another catastrophic mistake on Saturday. It can't ever happen again."

"In three weeks, I won't be your professor anymore. Then we can be together."

I sigh. "No, we can't. You'll have always been my professor. My grades can never be questioned. The integrity of what I'm doing here means everything to me. There's no *thing* and no *one* that's worth compromising that. I can't risk it. I won't risk it."

He moves back and falls into his chair in frustration. He looks like he's been shot. "Well, what if I resign my position as a professor? It would be easy enough to make excuses about it interfering with my surgical practice."

"That makes no difference, Brody."

He tilts his head to the side as he looks at me in the eyes. "Harley, I've completely fallen for you. I can't control this feeling. It's like I physically need you. I know you feel it too."

I close my eyes and lean my head back against the door. Tears are streaming down my cheeks. "Brody, I understand. Believe me, I understand. I've fallen for you too, but it changes nothing. It can never happen between us. I'm sorry."

CHAPTER SIX

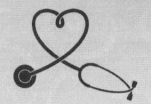

THE PRESENT

HARLEY

It's early in the morning on the day before Thanksgiving. Mom and her boyfriend Jackson are in some kind of fight. She's been back in bed crying for the past two weeks. I can't go through this nightmare again. We've had the most blissful few months since they started dating, but now we're almost back to where we started.

My sisters and I have a text group chat with his three sons, Payton, Hayden, and Trevor. Payton is thirty years old and married. Hayden is a twenty-three-year-old medical student. His crazy twin Trevor is in business school.

It sounds like Jackson is in the same shape as Mom. I don't know what happened between them, but I can't watch her slip back into a depression again.

I have a little over an hour before my shift at the hospital begins. I stop at Jackson's house and ring the doorbell. He answers the door. He looks like hell. He's in boxers and a T-shirt, with his hair sticking up all over the place. He clearly hasn't shaved in the two weeks they've been apart.

I look him up and down while shaking my head. "Jackson, throw on some clothes. We're going for a ride." He doesn't speak. He just turns and does as he's told.

We get in the car and pull out of his driveway. "What happened?"

He looks down. "I fucked up."

"Did you cheat on her?"

He looks up at me. "No. Why does everyone assume that when people have a fight it's always about that?"

"Because it usually is. If you cheated on her, I'll take you right back up your driveway to your house."

He shakes his head. "Well, it's not that. I love her. Not only would I never cheat on her, but I genuinely have no interest in other women. She's all I see. Harley, I miss her." He's practically in tears.

I like that answer. I know he really does love her. I've seen him with her. I'm pretty sure she loves him too. "Well then, what the hell happened between you two?"

"It would be disrespectful to your mother for me to tell you the details. She'll have to be the one to tell you." He looks down again. "Where are we going?"

"You're going to fix this. I won't watch her suffer through another broken heart." I see the corner of his mouth rise. He's happy that I'm taking him to see her. I grab his hand. "Jackson, don't screw this up. Make it right."

He nods. "I'll try. She's a stubborn woman." Don't I know it.

We arrive at her house. I walk in the front door and yell for her. I go into her bedroom. Of course, she's still curled up in bed. It's clear that she's been crying.

I'm not sure either of them has showered in days. I lock them in her room and tell them to fix it and shower.

I'm pulling into my parking spot in the hospital garage when I hear my text tone for Reagan.

> Reagan: You're coming out tonight.

> Me: Can't. I don't get off until 7:30.

> Reagan: We're not 80. We don't go out for the early bird specials.

> Me: You're such a pain.

> Reagan: You promised. You've been working for 3 months. It's time. Trevor and Hayden may come too. We're going to make a plan to get Mom and Jackson back together.

> Me: Taken care of. I just locked him in her room and told them that they can't come out until they kiss and make up.

> Reagan: You're a genius, sis!

> Me: Duh. Of course I am. ;)

> Reagan: I'll be at your place at 8:30 to help you get ready. Wash your hair before I come, and I'll blow it dry for you. I'll do your make-up too.

> Me: I don't know that I agreed to go out.

> Reagan: Funny, I remember it differently. See you at 8:30. Love you.

Me: Love you too, brat.

It's a normal morning in the ER. A few broken bones, several head injuries, a ton of people with colds who think it's an emergency when it's not, and one mild heart attack.

At some point I see Trevor walk in with a woman holding her eye. She's extremely attractive, but she seems older than him. Maybe in her early or mid-thirties. I walk over to him. "Trevor?"

He looks up. He seems a little embarrassed to see me. I'm not sure I've ever seen him as anything other than confident and playful. "Hey, Harley. I wasn't sure if you were going to be here today." He looks down. "Frankly, I was hoping that you weren't."

What? Why?

"I don't have to be the doctor that sees you. Just know that if I bring you back now as my patient, I can save you about five hours of time. If you sit in the regular waiting area, you're looking at a long day."

He motions to the woman, and she nods, clearly in pain. He looks back at me. "Okay. Thank you. This is Debbie by the way."

"Hey, Debbie. I'm Dr. Lawrence. I'll be helping you today. Why don't you head through those doors to room six. I'll be right with you in a few minutes. I just need to grab a nurse so we can take care of the paperwork."

She smiles. "Thanks Dr. Lawrence."

Debbie starts to walk through the doors. Trevor hangs back for a moment and whispers to me. "Hey, I don't know her last name, so don't ask me that in front of her."

I roll my eyes. "The nurse will be in to get her license and insurance information. Pay attention then."

He smiles. "Good idea."

I grab Jess and we walk into room six. "Debbie, this is nurse

Jessica. Jess, this is Trevor. Trevor is the son of my mother's boyfriend."

Trevor smiles at Jess. "Don't let her downplay it, Jess. We're practically siblings."

"Jess, I am most definitely not related to this guy. He's trouble with a capital *T*." Trevor laughs.

I turn back to Debbie. "Debbie, can you give Jess your ID and insurance cards?" Debbie hands her cards to Jess, and Jess starts to type away on the computer. "It looks like you're holding your right eye. Why don't you tell me exactly what happened to it."

Debbie looks down and then elbows Trevor. He looks at me with a sheepish grin. "Well, Debbie woke me up this morning in the manner in which all men would like to be awakened."

He pauses for a moment until I catch up. Okay, so she was giving him a blow job. I nod in understanding.

"I was trying to save her during the finale." I don't think I followed that. Clearly, he can tell. "I was pulling out." Ah. Got it. I nod again.

"Debbie, being the amazing woman she is, was going to finish the job how all men prefer the job to be finished." By swallowing. "We got our signals crossed, and I potentially finished right into her eye."

Jess and I both need to cover our smiles with our hands. We attempt to stifle our laughs. We fail miserably. It doesn't help that Trevor has a huge grin on his face. Poor Debbie.

After taking a few moments to compose myself, I get back into doctor mode. "Debbie, did his penis contact your eye, or just the ejaculation?"

Debbie is silent for a moment, so Trevor answers. "I'm pretty big, doc, but not quite that big. Just the massive ejaculation." He grins again.

"Okay, Debbie. We're going to wash your eye out with a

cleaning solution. Once it's clean, I'll take a look for any damage. Being that his micro penis wasn't big enough to hit your eye, I don't see any reason why you should have any real damage. It may just be irritated and red for a day or two." I give Trevor a big grin right back.

My dig doesn't remotely bother Trevor. "Thanks, sis. You're the best."

Jess leaves to get the solution and Trevor turns back to me. "By the way, we need to make sure Mom and Dad kiss and make up. Dad has been a grumpy bear for two weeks."

"*My* mom has been a mess too. I picked him up this morning. I dropped him at her house on my way to work. I locked them in a room and told them to work out their shit. They'll be fine. I don't think either of them is happy without the other."

"That was a good idea."

"I know." I nod towards Debbie. "Unlike you, I'm full of good ideas." He laughs.

Just then, my text tone rings. I pull out my phone. It's from Mom. It's a selfie of her and Jackson with huge smiles. Their hair is wet and they're in towels, clearly just having gotten out of the shower. Ugh. Gross. Couldn't they wait until they were dressed to take a photo? There's an accompanying text that reads, *thank you for knowing what we needed – we're back on track.*

I show it to Trevor. "See. I told you I'd fix it."

"Thank God. Thanksgiving dinner would have been depressing if they were still in a fight."

My text tone pings again. I read it and lift my head to Trevor. "Looks like we're having Thanksgiving together." We both smile. "My sister mentioned going out tonight too. Are you coming?"

"Yes, Reagan texted Hayden and me. I'm trying to get Payton to join us, but he rarely goes out."

"I rarely go out myself, but she's talked me into it. Maybe more like forced me into it."

"We'll have fun. I promise."

Jess returns and I take care of Debbie's eye. As I suspected, there was no major damage, so I send them on their way.

After they leave, Jess looks at me. "Wow, your brother is hot."

"He's not my brother, but yes, he's very good-looking. He looks exactly like his father, my mother's boyfriend, who is also very good-looking. But Trevor is a bit of a nut. I'd stay away from that one. I mean, he just came into the eye of a girl whose last name he doesn't even know." We both laugh. "His twin is really sweet though."

Her eyes pop open. "He has a twin? There are two of them? Sign me up for that."

I giggle. "They're not identical, but he's very attractive too. He's a medical school student right here. I'm sure he'll be in the hospital at some point. I'll introduce you to him."

She smiles. "Thank you."

I head to the supply closet to grab a few things, but when I open it, I'm surprised to see John standing between Michele's naked legs. She yells, "Pound the zone, Johnny."

I must gasp because they both stop and look at me. I manage to mumble, "Oh shit. I'm so sorry." I quickly walk out and close the door behind me.

A few minutes later, Michele finds me on the floor. "Sorry about that Harley."

"There's no need to apologize. I feel bad that I interrupted you guys."

She looks angry. "The idiot didn't lock the door."

"I didn't realize that you two are together."

"We're not. We're just fooling around. You won't tell anyone, will you?"

"Of course not. It's not anyone's business. Enjoy yourself." It feels like everyone is getting action except me. Maybe it's time for that to change. I know it is.

REAGAN ARRIVES at my place at precisely 8:30, with bottles of vodka and cranberry juice. She hands them to me when she walks in. "Here. Mix us a few drinks."

I salute her. "Yes ma'am. Should I make one for Skylar too?"

"No, she and Jason are meeting us at the bar." We both roll our eyes. We don't love Jason. We think he's cheating on her. He randomly disappears a night or two each week and doesn't respond to her texts for hours. She won't listen to reason. She won't confront him on it.

Reagan does a nice job on my hair and make-up. She's significantly better at both than I am.

She searches through my drawers and cabinets for my lipsticks and comes across three long-forgotten opaque black bags. She looks inside them and gives me an evil look. "What the fuck? You haven't opened any of this stuff. It's been like six months."

"I told you guys then that I wasn't going to use any of it."

"That is bullshit. It's going to change. Tonight." She takes one item out and smiles. I look at the package. It's the Smart Bead. She opens it and reads the instructions.

She seemingly downloads the app to her phone and creates an account. She hands me the bead. "Go put it in."

"Are you fucking insane? I'm not putting that inside of me. I'm not going out with something inside of me."

"Yes, you are."

"No, I'm not."

"If you don't, I'm going to call Aunt Cass and tell her that you haven't used any of the items she bought. How do you think she's going to take it? She will either come here and force you to use all of them in front of her, or she will publicly humiliate you until you use them. So, like I said, go put it in."

I grab it out of her hands and head to the toilet area. "I hate you." I close the door and slip it in me. I come out and wash my hands. "What now?"

"When I decide to activate it, I will. I imagine you'll figure it out pretty quickly."

"You're insane. I really think this is crossing a sister boundary line."

"When was your last orgasm?"

I roll my eyes and grab my purse. "Let's just go."

"Exactly."

TREVOR

Hayden and I are at the bar. Payton said he'd come for one drink, but that Kylie wasn't feeling great and was staying home. They're like an eighty-year-old couple.

Hayden and I are drinking our beers when Reagan and Harley walk in. They are truly gorgeous women. Every man in this place stops what he's doing and looks their way.

Reagan notices what's going on, but Harley seems totally oblivious to it. That or she just doesn't care.

They see us and make their way over. Every guy here is probably jealous of us. Little do they know. I kiss them both on the cheek hello. "Hey, pretty ladies. What can I get you to drink?"

Reagan grabs for her credit card. "Being that you have

zero chance of getting lucky with us tonight, we can get our own drinks."

I laugh. "Get your mind out of the gutter, Lawrence. I wasn't thinking that. We can rotate buying rounds like normal friends."

She looks at me skeptically for a moment. "Fine. Two shots of tequila and two margaritas. We'll get the next round."

"Coming right up." I blow her a kiss as I head to the bar to order their drinks, along with two extra tequila shots for Hayden and me.

While I'm gone, I count five guys who try to hit on Reagan and Harley. The girls just shoo them away as if they're fruit flies.

I see Skylar walk in holding hands with a guy who looks about her age. They head over to Harley, Reagan, and Hayden. I add two more shots and another margarita to my order, figuring they'll need drinks too.

By the time I return, they've found a table. I'm introduced to Skylar's boyfriend, Jason. He seems nice enough, but Harley and Reagan are a bit cold to him. I'm not sure why.

We all toast to our happy, reunited parents.

We're an hour and a few rounds into the evening. Anytime one of the girls gets up, they get hit on. It's amazing to watch. Reagan flirts with some of them, but Harley doesn't. She seems uncomfortable with it.

Skylar hasn't left Jason's side all night though. They're all over each other.

We haven't seen a waitress in a while, so at some point, Harley goes to the bar to buy us all another round. Reagan immediately takes out her phone and shows something on it to Skylar. They start cracking up.

I look at them. "What's going on? What am I missing? You two are about to cause some trouble, and I want in." Hayden smacks the back of my head.

Reagan checks over her shoulder for Harley one more time, seemingly making sure she's not on her way back yet. "Have you guys ever heard of the Smart Bead?"

Hayden and I look at each other in bewilderment. I shrug. "No. What is it?"

"It's sort of like a smart vibrator." What? "You stick the device up yourself. There's an app associated with it, and you can use the app to activate the device. It learns your body. When it senses that you're stressed and uptight, it vibrates. When you relax, it stops. It basically senses when you need an orgasm to relax."

I cross my arms. "I've never heard of it. Is that a real thing? It seems pretty far-fetched."

Reagan just smiles. She turns her phone to show me the app. She looks back again at Harley while she's at the bar. She then presses the green activation button on the app right in front of my face. "It's real, it's inside Harley right now, and I just activated it." She and Skylar high-five each other.

Harley is sitting alone at the bar. I see a guy very clearly making his way over to her. He taps her shoulder. As soon as she sees him, her eyes almost pop out of her head. She grabs the side of the bar. You can tell on her face that the device is definitely vibrating inside of her because she's freaking out, turning red, and biting her lip. I think the guy believes she's having a seizure and leaves.

Shortly after he goes, Harley seems to calm down. She turns around and mouths to Reagan, "fuck you."

Our whole table bursts out laughing. This is amazing. "Oh my god, Reagan, you're a genius. This is the greatest thing I've ever witnessed."

"Actually, Aunt Cass got it for her. You'll meet her tomorrow night. I just made Harley put it in before we left and downloaded the app to my phone. I'm so glad I did. This is going to be so much fun."

Another guy comes over to Harley, and the same thing happens. Harley is gripping the side of the bar with both hands like she's going to break it. Her eyes roll to the back of her head. We're dying with laughter at our table.

At some point, the guy leaves. She then visibly relaxes. She comes back with our drinks. "Reagan, I'm going to kill you."

Reagan just smirks at her. "Better not get too stressed, sis. Oh look, like ten guys seem as though they want to come talk to you. They're checking out your hot bod. They're all coming over here right now."

Harley almost drops the drinks. She quickly puts them on the table, sits down, crosses her legs, leans over, and buries her face in Skylar's arm. I can hear her cursing under her breath. She grabs Skylar's arm hard. Skylar moves so we can see some of Harley's face.

We're all laughing, which only makes Harley *more* stressed, which means the vibrations continue and intensify.

She squeezes her eyes shut and whispers, "Oh my god." Her mouth is wide open. I'm pretty sure I'm watching her orgasm face right now. After a few more moments, she's breathing heavily, but otherwise seems to have calmed down. I guess now that she had an orgasm, she's not as stressed.

She slowly lets go of her death grip on Skylar and looks up for the first time. I smile at her. "Feeling relaxed now, Harley?"

"I seriously hate all of you. Reagan and Skylar, in the bathroom now. I need to get this damn thing out of me."

I stand up. "I volunteer to help with that." Hayden hits me.

Harley sticks her finger in my face. "You sit your ass down, Knight, or I'm going to tell everyone here why you were in the ER today."

Hayden looks at me with concern. "You were in the ER today? Are you okay? Why didn't you call me?"

I look at Hayden. "I'm fine." I turn back to Harley. "You can't say anything. Doctor-patient confidentiality."

She smiles at me. "You weren't my patient." She's got me there. I sit back down, and the girls disappear.

When they're gone, Payton comes in. He grabs a beer from the bar, finds us, and comes to sit down.

"Hey, guys. Where are all the girls?"

"They went to the bathroom." I point to Jason. "This is Jason, Skylar's friend. Jason, this is our eighty-year-old brother, Payton." Payton and Jason shake hands. Payton gives me a dirty look.

The girls come back excited to see Payton. We have several more rounds.

Everyone except Payton is drunk. We're laughing and having a great time. The girls are really funny, especially when they're all together. We all get along so well.

At some point, I see Larry Clarrett walk into the bar. I

point him out to my brothers. "Look who just walked in. I can't stand that guy. He's such an asshole."

Reagan turns to look. "Who is?"

I show her Larry. "That guy. He and his father have it out for our father and his business. They threaten him all the time. They're snakes."

Payton interrupts. "I'm not going to tell you exactly what happened, because it's not my business to share, but Larry and his father are responsible for your mom and our dad's fight for the past two weeks. They did some terrible shit to Dad and Darian."

What? I didn't know this. "What was it? Is everything okay? I will beat his ass if I have to."

"It's not necessary, and I won't say. Just know that everything is fine now. Darian went all crazy lawyer on the guy. She demoralized him. It's all good, but those guys are bad news, and they definitely have it out for Dad. They basically tried to use Darian to get to him. Obviously, they put the two of them through the ringer for the past two weeks."

Reagan looks at all of us with a devious face. "Nobody fucks with my mother. Watch and learn boys."

All she has to do is make eye contact with Larry, and it's like he's under her spell. He walks right over to our table and grabs Reagan's hand.

"Hey, gorgeous girl. What are you doing over here with these pathetic losers? These guys don't deserve to be at the same table with a woman as beautiful as you." Reagan giggles. It's so fake, but Larry eats it up. "What's your name, gorgeous?"

Reagan answers, "I'm Penelope. What's yours, handsome?" Handsome? Not even close.

"I'm Larry. My friends call me hot dog."

Reagan doesn't miss a beat. "Is that because you have a footlong?"

"Why don't you come and find out?"

Reagan stands up and licks her lips seductively. "I think I will." He grabs her hand and moves to pull her away. She whispers back to the table, "Settle the tab and meet me at the front door in five minutes." They make their way back through the crowd, and toward the bathroom area.

We do as she says, and settle the tab. We're at the front door within a few minutes. All of a sudden, we hear a man scream, "Bitch." Reagan comes running out of the bathroom area, holding all of Larry's clothes in her hands. She yells, "Go, go, go." We all run out the door, and down the block out of view.

We sidestep into a small alley and stop. We're all panting and laughing. I look at Reagan. "Did you take all of his clothes?"

She smirks. "Every last item. Even his underwear, socks, and shoes. FYI, he definitely doesn't have a footlong. Not even half a footlong."

She holds out all of his clothes and drops them right into a big puddle. "Whoops."

We all burst out laughing. I pat her back. "Reagan, that was epic. Maybe you really are my twin."

Payton looks at his watch. "I need to get home to Kylie. Reagan, you made my night. I'm so glad I came and witnessed that." They high-five. "I'll see you all tomorrow night." He leaves.

Shortly thereafter, Jason leaves to go to his family's house for Thanksgiving. We have to stand there and suffer through him and Skylar kissing goodbye as though he's going off to war.

The five of us are left. I look around. "You guys want to hit Dad's hot tub?"

Harley gives me a look. "We don't have bathing suits."

"I'm not bothered by your nudity, Harley. In fact, I encourage it." I pause and let them get pissed.

"Just kidding. Your Mom has a ton of clothes at his house, including bathing suits." I look at their massive boobs. "You're all about the same size."

Hayden smacks the back of my head again. "You're an asshole. He'll behave, I promise. Come on. I ordered us an Uber."

We're all still pretty drunk and laughing as the Uber drops us at Dad's at 1:30 in the morning. Hayden puts his finger to his lips. "Shhhhhh. They're probably sleeping. We need to be quiet." We all nod.

I enter the code. We quietly tiptoe in, but as soon as we enter the house, we hear moans coming from the bedroom. "Oh god, Jackson. Yes, yes, yes!"

I start shaking with silent laughter. Harley, Reagan, and Skylar cover their ears. Harley motions for us to move. We quickly head out back. The screaming gets louder, until we're safely back outside by the hot tub, and the door is closed.

Harley shivers. "Ugh. I'm having flashbacks to my childhood."

Hayden looks at her in question. "What does that mean?"

"I mean our mother is a screamer, and we had to deal with extremely sexually active parents our whole lives. This isn't the first time we've heard her shouting in ecstasy."

Hayden and I look at each other. "Yea, that never once happened in our entire childhood. I'm not sure our parents ever had sex. In fact, I don't think they physically slept in the same bed for the last few years of their marriage."

Skylar crosses her arms. "Consider yourselves very lucky, at least as it pertains to that. We're *deeply* scarred from it. We used to hear Mom and Dad going at it all the time. And I mean *all* the time." Reagan and Harley nod in agreement.

We all head into the pool house, find bathing suits, and change. I uncover the hot tub and grab five beers from the outdoor kitchen refrigerator.

We get in and quietly relax for a few minutes without speaking. The hot water feels amazing in contrast to the colder November weather.

Reagan eventually breaks the silence. "Why don't we all reveal one major truth bomb slash fear." Everyone nods in agreement. "I'll go first. My biggest fear is that my business will fail and that I'll disappoint my mother." Wow, we're really digging into this.

Harley and Skylar immediately go to embrace Reagan. Harley lays her head on Reagan's shoulder. "Reagan, your business is crazy successful already. It's only getting bigger. Mom is so proud of you. Dad would be too."

Reagan has tears in her eyes. "Thanks for saying that. It's just very scary to own a business. I'm always stressed about it." I nod. I understand that. "It's such a trend-based business concept. I'm a little fearful of when the trend ends."

I look at her. "Then you just hit the next trend. Your business concept can be staying on top of the latest trends. It's smart."

"Thanks, Trevor. I appreciate it. Why don't you go next."

"Hmmm. I know this sounds weird, but I prefer older women. Women my age don't do it for me. I like them more mature. There's so much less drama with an older woman. They're significantly more secure, and honestly, they're better in bed."

Harley nods her head. "That explains today. I thought Debbie looked at least ten years older than you."

"Twelve, actually."

Hayden splashes me. "Are you going to tell us what happened today?"

I look at Harley. She puts her hands up. "You know I won't tell. It's up to you."

I sigh. "Fine. My friend Debbie was giving me a blow job this morning, and I blew my load into her eye." Everyone bursts out in laughter.

"Screw all of you. It really hurt her eye. I feel terrible about it."

Hayden pats my back. "Don't worry. We're not laughing at Debbie. We're laughing at you." They keep laughing. I guess it is pretty funny. "Do you like her?"

"Not particularly. It's probably over. We're not really dating anyway. We just hook up now and then. I hate to shoot and run, but..." They all laugh again.

I let them laugh for another minute or two. "Alright. Enough making fun of me. Skylar, you're up."

"Mine is probably obvious. I'm scared that Jason is cheating on me. I really like him, and I don't think he's cheating, but perhaps I'm just being naïve."

I'm surprised to hear that. They were all over each other tonight.

Reagan turns to Skylar. "You know I think he's cheating on you. He's a sketchy guy."

I look at Reagan. "Why?"

"Because he disappears a night or two a week and ghosts her. He doesn't respond to texts during those hours that he's gone. It's weird. It's even more weird that she doesn't confront him on it. I don't want her being taken advantage of."

"Hmmm. I saw him with her tonight. And I know guys. I don't think he's cheating on you, Skylar. His disappearing act is strange, I agree with that, but I don't think he's cheating on you. He just doesn't seem the type."

Skylar smiles at me. "Thank you, Trevor. I've been trying to tell them that."

"Also, if I had a girlfriend as hot as you, I would never cheat. Who the hell would cheat on you? You'd have to be a fucking idiot."

"I'm going to pretend that wasn't creepy and just say thank you. I know I'm not old enough for you anyway." She smirks at me and then turns to Hayden. "You're up."

"I know you guys probably think I will say something about medical school and being afraid of not making it through. That's obviously a fear of mine, but, if I'm being totally honest, my biggest fear is that I'm afraid I won't find someone to love, or more so, someone that loves me."

He looks sad. "My parents didn't love each other. I hated their marriage. I would never want that for myself. My father is forty-nine, and I think this is the first time in his life that he's ever been in love. I'm so happy for him. He's such a great guy and deserves it. But I don't want to wait until I'm forty-nine to fall in love. I know I don't have Trevor's fun, outgoing personality. I get that he's much more likable than me. What if no one ever loves me?"

I had no idea that my brother felt this way. It makes me sad. I refrain from any wise cracks.

All three girls go over to him and hug him. Harley grabs his cheeks and looks at him in the eyes. "Hayden, you're sweet, smart, and incredibly handsome. Any girl would be lucky to have you. I promise that you're lovable. I mean that." She kisses his cheek. Reagan and Skylar do the same.

Reagan squeezes his hand. "You know, if we didn't have this pseudo brother/sister thing going on, I'd be all over you, Hayden Knight." Hayden smiles. These are good girls. We're lucky to have them in our lives. I hope they stay.

Skylar motions her head toward the inside of the house. "Do you guys think they're in love?"

Hayden and I immediately say, "Yes," at the same time. "I can't totally speak for Darian, but Dad is definitely in love with her. As far as he's concerned, the sun rises and sets with her." I pause for a moment. "Do you guys think she loves him?"

All three of them tear up, but they all nod. Harley speaks first. "She definitely loves him. You guys know it took her forever to mourn the loss of our father, so there may be some bumps in the road, but she loves him. We know what to do when they hit a big bump." She nods at her sisters. They both seem to understand. Hayden and I don't intrude by asking.

Reagan looks at Harley. "You're up, sis."

"I think I already went." She smiles.

"Nice try. You should be extremely relaxed after your big public *O*. Just let out your truth bomb." Harley gives Reagan the finger, and Reagan giggles.

She leans her head back relaxing into the hot tub. She closes her eyes for an extended moment before she looks at us again. "I appreciate that you all were vulnerable tonight, so I'm going to try to give you the same courtesy." Tears well in her eyes as she takes a big breath. "I'm afraid that I may have pushed away *the one*." Reagan gasps.

"I'm afraid I'll never feel anywhere near the way I felt for a man that I sent away." This is clearly news to Reagan and Skylar. They are in complete shock. "I pushed him so far, that he doesn't even live in this country anymore, and it's 100% my fault."

CHAPTER SEVEN

THE PAST

BRODY

The past three weeks have been miserable. Harley shutting the door on anything ever happening between us has done something to me. I'm not okay. I need to make a change in my life. If I can't have her, I can't be around her anymore.

My cell phone rings, and I see that it's my father.

"Hey, Dad. Is everything okay?"

I hear him laugh. "I can't just call my son to say hello?"

I smile. "Of course, you can. How are you?"

"Actually, that's why I'm calling." Oh no. I hope he's not sick. "Brody, I met someone."

What a relief. "That's great, Dad." He's on and off dated

since Mom died. I've met a few of them. There's never been anyone too serious though.

"We're getting married in a few weeks. Do you think you can come out here for the wedding?" What? "It wouldn't be the same without you."

I think I need to sit down. "Wow, Dad. This is kind of shocking. Give me a second here to digest."

He laughs. "Take your time. I understand."

"I'm certainly happy for you. This just kind of came out of nowhere. I've never heard about her."

"Her name is Melanie. She's amazing. I don't know how to explain it to someone who's never been in love. When the right person comes into your life, you just know it. You can't think of anyone but them. They consume your every thought. You can't even see other women anymore." I get it more than he knows.

"That's great, Dad. You're a lucky man. Why don't you text me all the details. Of course, I'll be there. I wouldn't miss it."

"Fantastic. I wasn't sure you could get the time off. You haven't even been at that hospital for a year yet."

"I'm considering a highly specialized fellowship overseas. I may not be here much longer. I'm not sure that Philly is the right place for me."

"Oh, I didn't know you were struggling."

"I'm not struggling." That's a lie. "I might just need some different scenery. Frankly, this is a hard opportunity to pass up."

"Okay. We can discuss it more when you visit. I'll text you all the details. I can't wait to see you, and I can't wait for you to meet Melanie."

"If you love her, I'm sure I will too."

We say our goodbyes and he texts me the information. It's in three weeks. I think I know what I need to do.

IT's the last day of classes for the school year. I texted Harley before class and asked her to meet me in my office at the end of the day.

At precisely 3:00, she walks in the door to my office. My heart genuinely skips a beat when I see her. I can feel it. Her delicious scent immediately takes over the room. Every ounce of me is drawn to her. I won't ever be okay unless I'm far away from her.

She closes the door without having to be asked. She sits down in the chair in front of my desk. "Hey, Dr. Cooper. You wanted to see me?"

"Harley, I'm not your professor anymore. Please call me Brody."

She shakes her head. "You're still a professor at this school."

"That's what I want to talk to you about." I take a deep breath. "I want to confirm one final time, that if I were to resign from the medical school, you still wouldn't consider dating me?"

She looks pained. Nearly as pained as I do.

"Brody, I need you to understand me. I need you to *really* hear me because I'm being one-hundred percent honest with you. I want to be with you. I'm insanely attracted to you. Obviously to the point of losing control at times. It's a struggle every damn day not to be with you."

She pauses as she swallows hard. "But I've spent every day of my twenty-four years working toward the goal of becoming a surgeon. If I become the whore that slept with her professor, it will have all been for nothing. I can't do that to my family. I can't do it to myself."

She looks at me with tears brewing in her big, beautiful eyes. "I wish things were different, but they're not."

I nod. I genuinely think I would feel better if she said she wasn't attracted to me. That would make this easier. The fact that I want her, and she wants me, yet we can't be together, is enough to make my head explode.

"Okay. I understand and respect your decision. I don't agree with it, but I'll respect your wishes."

She pinches her eyebrows together. "You will?"

I give her a resigned smile. "I will. But please understand that I need to make some big life decisions based on this."

I take a breath. "Harley, I don't want you to hear this from anyone else, but I'm going to hand in my resignation."

"I told you that wouldn't change anything."

"You're not understanding me. I'm not just resigning from the school. I'm going to resign from the hospital as well."

"Why would you do that?"

"Because I can't be anywhere near you and not have you. I'm completely fucked up in the head over you. I couldn't possibly live in the same town as you and not be with you. I need to leave Philadelphia."

She looks shocked. We're both quiet for a few moments as I see it all begin to register with her. I see her getting emotional. "Where will you go? Back to California?"

"I'm going to go there for a bit over the summer for a visit, but no. I've been offered an incredible fellowship in Sweden. They've been calling for years. I've just never considered it until now. They're running several drug and surgical technique clinicals with patients who suffered the same injury as my mother. It's really state-of-the-art stuff."

I run my fingers through my hair. "I need to get out of here. It would be unhealthy for me to stay."

She has tears silently running down her cheeks. She whispers, "I'm so sorry, Brody." I can see her shaking.

"I know you are. It's not your fault."

I give her a forced smile. "I want to wish you all the luck in the world. You don't really need it, you're brilliant, but I still wish it for you. You're going to be an incredible surgeon." I shrug my shoulders. "Perhaps our paths will cross again one day."

The tears are now flowing down her beautiful face. I hand her a tissue, and she takes it. I give her a few moments of silence to compose herself. I know it's also my last few moments getting to see her face, and I want to hold onto it.

I eventually get up to show her to the door. I offer her a hand to help her stand. I go to escort her toward the door, but she tightens her grip on my hand and pulls me to her.

She slowly runs her hands up my stomach, and then my chest. She moves them behind my neck, as she brings my head down toward hers. Her soft lips take mine in a tender kiss. It's a goodbye kiss. I close my eyes to commit her taste and smell to memory. I know this is the last time I'll ever have either. I can feel my own tears dripping down my cheeks, mixing with hers.

I hold her body tight to mine, wishing we could stay like this. She ends the kiss and wipes my tears. She holds my hand over her heart. I can feel it beating a million times per minute. She looks at me in the eyes and whispers one last time, "Bye Brody."

I know that the sadness I see in her eyes will never leave me. No doubt mine mirror hers.

It's the morning of Dad's wedding. I had to spend the past few weeks tying up some loose ends at the hospital.

I only arrived yesterday morning, but I met Melanie, and she's lovely. They're cute together. I'm thrilled for Dad. It's a little weird thinking of him married to someone else, but he certainly deserves happiness.

It's just he and I in the room getting dressed in our tuxedos. He sits down next to me. He places his hand on my shoulder as he looks at me. "What's wrong, Brody?"

I give him a fake smile. "Nothing, Dad. I'm so happy for you. This is a great day."

"I know you are. That's not what I mean. You're not my happy, good-time son right now. What has you down? Talk to me."

I'm not surprised that he can see right through me. He always could. "It's not a big deal. I think I'm nursing a little bit of a broken heart."

If there was ever a picture to capture a shocked face, it would be Dad's right this minute.

"I don't know what to say to that. I've never seen you date anyone seriously, let alone seriously enough to have your heart broken. Of course, it's a big deal. You're very clearly hurting right now. You obviously care about her. Does she feel the same way as you?"

"Yes, she does."

"Tell me about her."

"Today is your day, Dad. We can have this talk another time."

"I'm your father every day, Brody. The job never ends. It certainly doesn't take a day off. Tell me what's happened."

I stand to look out the window. I take a long breath. "I fell for a student of mine." I turn back to him, fearful of a disappointed look on his face.

He brings his lips together. "I see. Is that why you left Philadelphia? They found out and forced you to leave?"

"No. Nothing scandalous like that. It ended before it really ever started. She ended it because of our precarious position. No one knew about us. I just can't be *around* her and not be *with* her."

"I hate to say it, but she's right. She sounds smart."

"She's the smartest woman I've ever met. That's half of the appeal."

He chuckles. "Half, huh?"

I roll my eyes. "It doesn't hurt that she's also the most stunning woman I've ever seen."

"I see. She won't be your student forever."

"That's not how she sees it. She believes that if we were ever to date, her integrity regarding her time as my student would be called into question. Part of me understands it, and part of me doesn't."

He stands and puts his hand on my shoulder. "Brody, have you ever heard the story of how your mother and I met?"

"Only that you were friends for a long time before you got together."

"That's true, but did you know that she was engaged to marry Uncle Max?" Max is Dad's best friend from childhood.

I'm surprised to hear it. "No, I didn't know that."

"Yes, they were engaged. I always had feelings for her, but she was with Max, and that was the end of it. At some point, she knew things weren't right between them and she broke it off. It was messy for a while. They both separately cried on my shoulder."

He walks around the room as if deep in thought. "After a few months, I told her about my feelings. She told me that she returned those feelings, but wouldn't ever do that to Max. Neither of us saw a way to be together without hurting him, so we decided that we wouldn't pursue a relationship."

"We waited another year, but our feelings never waned. I decided to have a man-to-man talk with Uncle Max. He was upset but appreciated that we were forthcoming and spoke with him before acting on our feelings. He had met Aunt Rene by then. Eventually, he came to accept our relationship."

He gives me a sympathetic smile. "Brody, if we approached him earlier, it would have been a mess. But timing sometimes matters. Perspectives change. Priorities change. Circumstances change. Take it from an old man who's been around the block a few times. People change over time. Opinions and feelings change over time. Things that we think we care about change over time. Just give it that time, Brody. If both of your feelings remain strong after this thing in Sweden, you'll go back and fight for what you want. Maybe she'll be ready for you then. Maybe you'll make her see why love is sometimes worth the risk."

I'M ALONE in a café in Stockholm. I've enjoyed the past few months here. Everyone in the clinic is nice. There are several single people, so we all go out together in a big group.

The women here are certainly beautiful, but none as beautiful as Harley Lawrence. I still can't get her out of my mind. It's early though. I probably just need a little more distance.

I'm sipping my coffee when I receive a text notification.

> Harley: Hey Brody. It's been a few months. I hope that Sweden is treating you well and that you're settled in. It's the first day of my third year. It made me think of the first day last year when you walked into the classroom. I nearly had a heart attack. :) Anyway, just thinking of you. Thought I'd say a quick hello.

I'm frozen. I didn't think I'd hear from her ever again. All of the emotions of letting her go come flooding back to me. I type out twelve different responses, but ultimately send none of them. I can't.

ONE YEAR LATER

I'm out at a club with Mikael. He has become my closest friend in Sweden. He's a doctor at the clinic, though he lives here permanently. He's been good for me. He likes to go out several nights a week. Most of the time, he's able to get me to come with him.

We're both dancing with beautiful women. The woman

dancing with me certainly seems interested. She's draped all over me.

I'm a million miles away though. As much as I've tried, I can't get Harley out of my mind. When you find perfection, the woman who was seemingly designed for you, it's nearly impossible to move on. It's nearly impossible to even feign interest in other women. I thought time and distance would make letting her go easier. It hasn't. It's only made me realize that I will never find anyone like her.

Dad's words play over and over in my head. Will there be a time that her reservations fade away? It's almost worse that he mentioned it to me. It's given me a sliver of hope.

I'm slightly ashamed to admit that I try to find her on social media. She doesn't have accounts, but her sisters do. She makes occasional appearances in family photos, but never when they're out at night. I know the day is coming that there will be a picture of her with a man. There's a part of me that fears that day, and a part of me that thinks it may be what I need to move on.

All of a sudden, I feel my arm being pulled. I look and see Mikael dragging me back to our table.

"Brody, get it together." I pinch my eyebrows together in question. "You had a beautiful woman all over you on the dance floor and you were frozen still."

"What do you mean? I was dancing."

He shakes his head. "You *were* dancing. You've been frozen in place for the past five minutes. You didn't move a muscle."

"Oh. I didn't realize it."

"You're thinking of her?" I blow out a breath and give him a resigned smile. "You haven't caved and called her, have you?"

"No. I'm determined on that front. If I ever talk to her again, it'll be in person."

He holds out his hand. "I assume you're still stalking her on social media. Let me see her picture again."

"I'm not stalking her. I just need to see her face sometimes."

"So, you're not checking to see if she's with other men?"

I give him the finger as I pull up one of Reagan's social media accounts and find a picture. I hand him my phone. He studies the photo. "Well, I certainly understand the appeal. She's definitely gorgeous."

"It's not just that. It's everything about her. I don't see how I will ever find anyone that remotely matches up. She's the full package."

While my phone is in his hands, I hear my text tone. He mutters, "åh skit." [*Translation: Oh shit*]

"What?" I grab my phone. The air is knocked out of my lungs. It's Harley.

> Harley: Hey Brody. Today was the first day of my final year. Once again, I was thinking of that day seeing you walk through the door. In all honesty, it's not the only time I've thought of you. I hope it's going well there. I read up on what you're doing. It sounds amazing. I hope you're enjoying yourself.

I reread it five times. My text tone goes off again.

> Harley: Sorry for the text. Mom is moving out of my childhood home this week. Feeling a little emotional. Playing a few "what ifs" in my head.

My head is spinning. I can't believe she's still thinking about me. I haven't heard from her in a year. I assumed she'd have long since forgotten about me. Knowing she hasn't means *everything*. These feelings aren't going away, for either of us. I didn't imagine this connection.

Dad was right. I have some more time here, but I think I know what I need to do when I get home. For the first time in a while, I feel hope.

HARLEY

I walk into my childhood home for the last time. There are so many memories here. Mom needs this though. She needs closure on this part of her life to truly move on. Every part of this house reminds her of him.

We've been telling her for the past year that she needs to move. As much as it hurts to let go, I'm proud of her for finally doing it.

I see her sitting on the ground with Skylar and Reagan. They're all crying. I look at them. "Come on you guys. No crying. We've had enough tears over the past two years to last a lifetime. Let's fill this house with laughter one last time. That's what this house really means to me. Let's remember the happy memories. They drastically outweighed the sad ones." I hold up two bottles of wine and a package of plastic cups.

Mom wipes her tears and smiles. "You're absolutely right Harley. Come sit with us. There's pizza on the counter if you're hungry."

I grab a slice, open the bottles, and sit on the ground. I fill a cup for everyone. We toast to forgetting sadness and remembering happiness.

For some reason, Brody's face crosses my mind. I've been so unhappy since he left. I don't remember the last time I was truly happy. I texted him again today. I don't know why. I just needed to somehow feel closer to him.

I can't look at other men. I really needed to hear from him, but he didn't reply. Maybe he changed his number in Sweden. Or maybe he's over me and doesn't want to talk to me. Whatever it is, it hurts.

I went on a date this past weekend. It was a guy that has asked me out at least ten times. He's a year older, so he's done with medical school now. I figured if it didn't work out, at least I wouldn't have to see him.

He was cute and nice, but I felt nothing. I feel like Brody was a man, and these guys are just boys. He wasn't just any man. He was the perfect man. I miss him. I miss the way I felt around him. I'm afraid I'll never feel the same way about another man.

"Harley, are you participating?" Reagan looks at me like I'm crazy.

"I'm sorry, what?"

"We're sharing funny memories from this house. You suggested we laugh instead of crying. Any of this ringing a bell? It was one minute ago."

I give her a dirty look. "I'm in. In fact, I'll go first."

I give her a little smirk. "Remember Reagan's eighteenth birthday? I came home from school, and we decided to all go into her room to wake her up to bring her breakfast in bed. To our surprise, Dexter had the same idea, and we walked in on Reagan naked, bouncing up and down on top of him. Now *that* was funny."

Reagan jumps on top of me. "I hate you." We're all laughing. She's got me pinned and is tickling me.

"Stop, I'm going to pee in my pants." She finally stops. I grab my phone. "I think I still have the video. Anyone want to see it?" She jumps on top of me again and we're all giggling.

Aunt Cass walks in as we're laughing. "I like that sound. What are you guys laughing about?"

Mom hands her some wine. "We're reminiscing about when we all went to wake Reagan up on her eighteenth, and we caught her and Dexter in bed."

Skylar laughs, "Dad covered my virginal eyes and quickly dragged me out of the room. I vividly remember Dexter screaming in embarrassment, scrambling to grab his clothes, but Reagan barely caring."

Aunt Cass smiles. "I still have the video if you guys want to see it."

Reagan looks mad. "What? Why do you have the video? You weren't even here."

"Your Mom sent it to me that morning. I thought I was seeing a sweet video of your family wishing you a happy birthday, but instead I saw your cute little ass, with Dexter's hands on it, and then the phone drops to the floor and mayhem ensues."

Reagan huffs. "This family is deranged."

Aunt Cass just smiles. "Speaking of deranged, Dick pissed on my bed this morning while I was having sex."

We all look at Aunt Cass in confusion. I ask, "Whose dick pissed in your bed?"

"Dick, my dog, pissed in my bed."

"You have a dog?"

"Yes."

"And his name is Dick?"

"Yes."

"I know I will regret asking this, but why is his name Dick?"

"So that I always have dick in my bed. Duh." We all burst out laughing again.

"When did you get a dog? Why don't we know this?"

"Last year after your mother kicked me out of her bed. I missed having a warm body, so Dick keeps me warm at night when I don't have actual dick."

I shake my head. "I have no words for you, Aunt Cass. You're one of a kind." She takes a bow. "So why did he piss in your bed."

"I'm not sure. Dennis and I were going at it. I don't know if Dick was mad that I wasn't giving him attention, or he was freaked out by my screams, but he jumped on my bed and took a piss. It was disgusting." We all laugh.

"I'm still not over the fact that you have a dog named Dick."

CHAPTER EIGHT

THE PRESENT

HARLEY

We had a nice family Christmas. My grandparents visited. Jackson took us all to a hockey game. Aunt Cass got kicked out of said game for getting handsy with a player. She is legitimately the craziest person that I know.

I've watched Mom fall madly in love over the past four months. For over three years, she was stuck in a depression, mourning the love of her life. Somehow, she pulled herself out and found love again. I guess Jackson really pulled her out, but nonetheless, she's out, she's in love, and she's happy. I wouldn't be surprised if they get married.

Yet here I am, over three years since the night I met Brody, and over two years since I've last seen him, and I haven't moved on. I've been stuck in the same place for all this time.

The fact that I know he still exists out there is messing with my head. I think I must have loved him. That's the only explanation for my inability to move on. I'm so confused.

It's New Year's Eve. I decided to come by myself to the Jersey shore. I need some time alone. Away from the hospital. Away from my family. Away from my friends.

My phone rings. It's Reagan.

"Hey there."

"Hey, sis. Are you coming out with us tonight?"

"No, I came down the shore."

"Is there a party down there? Who are you with?"

"No, I'm by myself. I'm at Megan's family's house. They're not using it."

"You're alone? On New Year's Eve?"

"Yes."

"Harley, what's wrong with you? Talk to me. Please."

"I need to sort through some things in my head. I promise we'll talk soon." I have tears welling in my eyes. "Reagan, I've got to go."

"Harley. You're scaring me. Are you okay?"

"No, but I will be. I'm just about to go for a walk on the beach."

"It's like thirty-five degrees out."

"I'm bundled up. Have a great night."

"Okay. I'll see you at Sunday night dinner, if not before then."

"Yes. Happy New Year."

"You too, sis."

I walk on the beach for over an hour. I'm just thinking about the events of the past few years, and all that I've given up to finally have this title of doctor. Brody's handsome face pops into my mind. What could have been? I'm not sure it was worth it. I'm not happy. I'm not fulfilled.

Dad was right. I haven't lived my life at all. I've lived to become a doctor, and now that I am, I still don't feel happy. I don't do anything besides work. I rarely have fun. I don't date. I'm a mess.

I'm officially determined to make a change. I pushed Brody away. Far away. My New Year's resolution is going to be to allow myself to meet someone. To really put myself out there. To be open to something new. To take a risk on something that might make me happy. I know I've said it before, but I mean it now. I can't go on like this.

My head is down, and I'm not paying attention to the people I pass when I hear a familiar voice. "Harley, is that you?"

I look up and see Brody. It can't be. I must be hallucinating. My heart rate picks up. I blink my eyes several times to make sure I'm really seeing him. "Brody?" He smiles. Oh, that smile. That chin. That dimple. I feel it in my whole body.

I need to keep it together. "I thought you were in Sweden?"

"It was a two-year fellowship. I just moved back." He pauses. "Congrats on your graduation. I know it's been a little while now, but congratulations, Dr. Lawrence."

"Thank you. Are you back at Pennsylvania Hospital or somewhere else?" Please say somewhere else. I can't bear to see him every day.

"I'm back at Pennsylvania Hospital." He sees the disappointed look on my face. "I guess that means I'll be working with you."

"It means I'll be working *for* you." We're silent for a few moments. I'm not sure what to say. My head is spinning.

"Are you down here with anyone?" I shake my head no. "Have dinner with me tonight?"

I shake my head again. "You know I can't risk being seen with you."

"I know an out-of-the-way place. You'd never see anyone you know. Certainly, no one from the hospital would ever be caught dead there."

I shake my head again. "It's not a good idea."

He takes my hand in his. His touch does something to me and he knows it. I see the corners of his mouth rise. I close my eyes and exhale, trying not to give away the sensation currently running through my body. A sensation I haven't felt in a long time.

"Fine. Let's just go now. Before I change my mind." He smiles and continues holding my hand as we walk off the beach.

It most definitely is an out-of-the-way place. An old, dingy, out-of-the-way place. We sit down and order drinks. He looks up at me. "I was surprised to hear that you ended up doing your residency here in Philly. I thought you'd want to get away from Dr. Waters. Not see him every day."

"I do, but Dr. Powers reminded me that Pennsylvania Hospital is the best. I couldn't pass up working with her, and my family is here. When I made the decision, Mom was still in a bad place. I didn't want to leave her. I thought she'd need me around."

"She's still not managing the loss of your father? Wow. It's been a long time."

"I made that decision over six months ago. She's in a much better place now. She met someone right around the time my residency started. She's totally in love now. He's amazing. He's completely obsessed with her. They're very cute together, and definitely very happy. I honestly wouldn't be surprised if she gets remarried."

"That's great. Good for her." He looks at me knowingly. "It's weird to see your parent with another person though, isn't it?"

"It is, but I'm still excited for her. Did your father meet someone?"

"Yes, he got remarried right after I last saw you."

"Wow, that's wonderful. Yes, it's weird, but not bad weird. Just different weird. Jackson brought Mom back to life. I didn't think she'd ever be okay again. He's a miracle as far as I'm concerned. I'm so thankful for him."

"That's incredible. I'm happy for her. You and your sisters must be thrilled." I nod. I see him gulp. "Are you seeing anyone?"

"I see my friends and my family."

"That's not what I meant."

"I know it's not. I don't want to go there, Brody."

I look down and then back up at him. I think we need to address this head-on. "Why are you back here in Philly? Why didn't you go back to California?"

He leans forward and stares right at me, with a fiery look that has me practically gasping for air. He takes my hand and kisses it. "Harley, I won't lie to you. I came back for you. I can't get you out of my mind. I tried. God knows I tried. I want you, Harley. I can tell you still want me too. I won't take no for an answer this time. I'll do whatever it takes to convince you to be with me."

Holy shit. This can't be happening. I close my eyes for a moment to let it sink in.

"Nothing has changed, Brody. If anything, the situation is worse. Not only are you a former professor of mine, but you're also now one of my supervisors. I won't become a cliché, Brody."

He takes my hand in his. "I see it differently. We're no longer a student and a teacher. We're co-workers. Co-workers can date." I shake my head. "Tell me what I can do to change your mind?"

"Nothing. Please. I can't go through this again." I whisper, "I don't think my heart can take it."

I feel tears welling in my eyes and wipe them. "We need to

move on to a different topic or I'm going to leave?"

"Okay." He holds up his hands. "Guess what? I bought a new beach house. I settled on it today. That's why I'm here."

"If you're going to be a true Philadelphian, you can't call it a *beach house*. You have to call it a *shore house*. The *shore* is the area. You now own a *shore house*. You can only say *beach* when you refer to the actual sand and ocean." We both smile. "What made you buy down here?"

He looks at me without a single moment of hesitation. "Because you said you like it here. I bought it for us. When you change your mind about us, and you will change your mind, we'll have somewhere to come and relax when we're not at the hospital."

"I asked you to stop talking like that."

"You asked me why I bought the *shore* house. Would you rather I lie?"

I pause for a moment. "Let's move on. Tell me about Sweden."

We talk for the next few hours. He fills me in on his time in Sweden. The new surgical techniques he's learned. When I do my neuro rotation, I'll get to see him in action. I'm excited to see what he's learned.

He also tells me that for the past few months, since he's been back in the United States, he's been in California working on building a rehabilitation center that's being named for his mother. He's really proud of the work they'll be doing there.

I tell him about my last two years of medical school. I leave out the bad parts, which include desperately missing him, and dodging the near-constant advances of Dr. Waters. At least I haven't seen him much at the hospital, but that'll change now that we're moving to the surgical floor. It also means I'll see Brody almost every day.

Our conversation flows easy as if no time has passed. My feelings for him are as fresh as they were the day he left.

I need to be honest with myself. Despite the silent promise I made only hours ago, I don't see a realistic chance of me ever moving on from Brody Cooper. I know I'll never feel the same way about another man.

At the end of the night, he walks me back to Megan's house. It's almost midnight, so we sit outside on the front deck with blankets. He has his arm around me. It feels right.

The clock is just striking midnight, and we can see fireworks blazing through the sky in all of the various Jersey shore towns, just as they do on the fourth of July.

I turn to him. "Happy New Year, Brody." I give him a hug. I then grab his face to give him a kiss on the cheek, but he quickly turns his head and softly kisses my lips. A bit more than a peck, but nothing crazy.

He slides both of his arms around my body, pulling me close, while my hands remain on his face. We stare into each other's eyes, locked in the embrace.

We slowly move our lips back toward one another. His lips take mine in a kiss. It's not just any kiss. We both pour all of our pent-up emotions and years of longing into that kiss. Our mouths are open, and tongues embracing.

It's genuinely as if no time has passed. He picks me up and pulls me back down so that I'm straddling his thighs. I wrap my arms around his neck.

I feel him in every part of my body. My long-dormant libido is awakened all at once. I don't know if I have the power to continue to deny myself this.

I tighten my legs, pulling him closer. He reaches a hand between us and grabs one of my breasts. My body is reacting in a way that it hasn't since the night with him in the alley behind the club. I'm totally lost in the moment, just as I've always been with him.

All of a sudden, I feel the vibration of my cell phone buzzing in my pocket. It brings me back to earth. I pull off the kiss and gently push his chest away. "Stop. We can't." He sighs in frustration. "I'm sorry Brody. Find someone who can give you what you need."

"That someone is you. You're the *only* woman who can give me what I need. The *only* woman I want. The *only* woman who can possibly quench the insatiable thirst I have for you."

"I'm not the woman for you."

He stands up and places me back on the couch. He takes my hand and kisses it. I look down, but he grabs me roughly by the hair. He jerks my head so that my eyes meet his.

"Look at me." I do. "Hear me. I need you to *really* hear me. The next time we kiss, we won't be interrupted. The next time we touch, we won't stop. This is the year of Harley and Brody. It's going to happen for us. We will never spend another New Year's Eve, or any other holiday, apart. It would be a lot easier, and a lot more fun, if you just accepted that. Make no mistake, you and I are happening. I came back for you. You've never seen this side of me, but I'm a determined man. You're going to be mine, Harley Lawrence." He kisses me hard, releases his grip on my hair, turns, and leaves.

I'm trembling at his words and actions. Part of me wants him and was really turned on by what he just did, and the other part of me is simply scared.

I eventually look down at my phone. It's our family chat, and the interrupting text was Mom wishing us all a happy New Year. She's in Colorado with Jackson, so it's only 10:00 there, but she's wishing us well for our New Year.

I put my face in my hands and start crying. What the hell am I going to do? I cry for another minute, but soon realize that it's extremely cold out here without Brody holding me. I mean that in every sense possible.

I stand up to go inside, but I see both of my sisters standing there on the sidewalk, with their hands on their hips. I'm in total shock that they're here. Reagan moves her arms and crosses them. "Clearly we need to talk."

I'm completely overwhelmed with emotion right now. Emotion that I saw Brody after all this time. Emotion that he came back for me. Emotion at his declaration. And emotion that my sisters canceled their New Year's Eve plans because they knew I needed them.

I walk up to both of them and wrap my arms around them. I put my head down and start sobbing. "Thank you for coming."

They hold me tight and let me cry for a few minutes.

Skylar eventually pulls my arm. "I'm literally farting snowflakes out here. Can we go inside and get warm?" All three of us start laughing. Talk about a tension breaker.

I wipe my tears. "Yes, let's go inside." We go in and sit down on the sofa. They're on either side of me.

Reagan opens her bag and pulls out three bottles of wine. She opens them all, handing them out so we each have our own. It looks like we're going straight from the bottle for this conversation.

Reagan looks at me. "I'm going to tell you what I know. After that, you're going to tell us *everything*. Every. Fucking. Detail. Am I understood?" I nod.

"You've been in a depression for three years. Five weeks ago, you shocked us and told us that *the one* got away. That you pushed him away. We had never remotely heard of him. Tonight, we watched you kiss a man like no kiss I've ever seen. Certainly not one I've ever seen from you. We couldn't hear everything he said to you before he left, but we did hear him say that you two were happening, even if you didn't accept it. As he's leaving, I notice that said man looks awfully familiar to me. He looks a lot like the friend of my ex's brother who we met at a club one night. The same night you and he disappeared at exactly the same time. Care to fill in the Grand Canyon-sized holes in this story?"

Skylar looks at me. "That was the same guy from the club?" I nod.

I take a long breath. "Remember right after Dad died, when I had sex with a random stranger on the roof of Club Liberty?"

Skylar nods and Reagan rolls her eyes. "Obviously we remember that."

"Well, it was Brody."

Skylar looks confused. "Wait, who's Brody?"

Reagan smacks her leg. "The guy that just left here you moron."

I nod in agreement. "Even though we didn't exchange any information that night, he showed up two days later as one of my medical school professors." Skylar gasps. Reagan's hold on my hand tightens.

"We had a year of extreme sexual tension, but I wouldn't let anything happen. It came about as close as it can that night at the club, but it didn't happen."

"I knew it was weird that you both disappeared. Skylar, you told me there was no way she went home with a random guy."

"I didn't know she knew him."

"Anyway, I told him we could never be together, and he took it really hard. He quit his job and accepted a fellowship abroad. I texted him a few times over the years, just to check-in, but I never heard back from him. He told me tonight it was too hard."

"He showed up today and told me that he's moved back here

to fight for me, and that he won't take no for an answer. And to make matters worse, he's going to be one of my bosses at work."

Reagan looks at me. "Let me get this straight. You've been pining after this guy for years. You told us a few weeks ago that he's the one that got away. He's now back for you and desperately wants you. What's the problem?"

"I can't be with him. He was my professor and now he's my boss."

"Who the fuck cares? You're obviously in love with him. People meet at work, Harley."

"I'll be a joke."

"I'd rather be a happy joke than a fucking miserable surgeon." Man did she just hit the nail on the head.

"Maybe after my residency."

"That's in three years!"

I put my head down. "I know."

Skylar is watching us like it's a ping pong match, seemingly deep in thought. "Harley, let me ask you something." She looks at Reagan, and then back to me. "When was the last time you slept with someone?" I look at her with tears sliding down my cheeks, but I say nothing.

Reagan gasps. "No!" She moves her eyes between Skylar and me. "That cannot be true." I think she chugs half of her bottle of wine in one go.

I put my head in my hands. "It's not like I made a decision not to sleep with anyone else. It's not like I didn't try. I am not attracted to any other man. My body physically doesn't react to other men. I can't help it."

Reagan's mouth is wide open. "Holy fuck. I'm speechless. For the first time in my life, I'm speechless. Does anyone else know?"

"Aunt Cass knows. She doesn't know that he's back, since I only found out tonight, but she knows the rest."

Skylar looks confused. "You only found out he's back tonight?"

"Yes."

"How did he know where to find you?"

"We bumped into each other walking on the beach, but he told me he settled on a house down here today that he bought for us. He remembered me saying how much I love the shore, so he bought the house here so that the two of us would have somewhere to go and relax."

Reagan runs her hands through her hair. "Wow. He's in love with you, Harley."

"I don't know. Maybe. We've certainly never said those words to each other. I'm not sure we know each other well enough for that. It's not like we ever dated. We had a few deep talks that first year, but we haven't truly gotten to know one another. There's obviously chemistry, but I don't know if it's love."

Reagan lifts her eyebrows. "I watched that chemistry unfold. There's *definitely* chemistry."

She puts her arms around me. "Harley, we love you. We both vote that you fuck his brains out and live happily ever after. It would be super awesome for my sister to not be so miserable. Let Mr. *Best Sex of My Life* fuck the misery right out of you." We all laugh.

Skylar hugs me too. "Yea, Harley. Who cares what other people think? If you want him and he wants you, go for it."

"Let me see how the next few weeks play out at work." I look at both of them. "Thank you both so much for ditching your plans and coming down. You two are the best sisters. I mean it."

We spend the rest of the night drinking our wine, laughing, and doing what sisters do.

CHAPTER NINE

THE PRESENT

HARLEY

It's Wednesday and I'm back at the hospital after the New Year. This will be our first day on the surgical floor. I'm excited because this is what I've waited for my entire life. I'm nervous because I'll be around Brody. We haven't communicated since he left the porch just after midnight on New Year's.

Michele, John, Marc, and I are all waiting for Dr. McCrevis. I've become very close with Michele and John. I adore them.

Marc hasn't really made an effort to socialize with us. He may have a social anxiety disorder. I don't know that he has an official diagnosis, but I wouldn't be surprised. He keeps entirely to himself.

I've had drinks with John and Michele a few times. John is a character. That's for sure.

We see Dr. McCrevis walking toward us with an entire team. Brody is walking with him. My heart starts to race. He's so handsome. I find myself involuntarily licking my lips. He gives me a subtle wink.

Michele whispers in my ear. "Wow, the tall blonde is hot." He sure is. I quickly nod in agreement.

Dr. McCrevis shakes all of our hands. "Good morning. I know this is the day you all thought you'd be having four months ago. I hope you can now understand why I felt it was important to start in the ER as a bit of a crash course."

Dr. McCrevis was completely right about the ER. We were able to see so many different injuries every single day. We would never have seen so much on the surgical floor. While we didn't really get to work on surgical techniques, the experience was invaluable, and I'm appreciative of him giving us that time to immerse ourselves into things and observe so much.

We all nod in agreement. "Wonderful. Now it's finally time to dive into surgery. Your time will be split. Half in the labs working on techniques, and half with this brilliant group assembled here. I want to introduce you to our team. For roughly the next year, you'll rotate among all of these doctors. First up is cardio. Please let me introduce you to Dr. Elizabeth Powers."

She smiles, steps forward, says a little about her background, and shakes hands in introduction individually with Michele, John, and Marc. When she gets to me, she gives me a big smile and a hug. "Harley, it's so wonderful to see you here. Oh, I mean Dr. Lawrence."

She gives me a warm squeeze with both hands. "I'm thrilled that you chose this hospital. I'll be fighting with all of these guys for your time."

I smile back. "Thank you, Dr. Powers. You're a big part of the reason that I'm here. I look forward to learning from you."

We go through similar introductions with Dr. James Alexander, head of orthopedic surgery, Dr. Sarah Murray, head of obstetric surgery, and Dr. Monica Lipson, head of general surgery.

We finally get to neuro. "Last but certainly not least is neurology. We have two department heads here. We have Dr. Gregory Waters, who you all met briefly in the fall. He specializes mostly in brain surgeries. And Dr. Brody Cooper, who has just today returned to us from a two-year spinal surgery fellowship, his specialty."

Dr. Waters makes his way down the line shaking hands. He gets to me last. His touch makes me sick. "Dr. Lawrence. A pleasure as always. I look forward to working *closely* with you." That was drenched with innuendo. I see Brody clench his jaw and turn bright red in anger.

Brody then makes his way down the line. He smiles appropriately at me. "Dr. Lawrence, it's been a few years. It's thrilling that the brightest mind I've ever taught is now here to work with us. I'm incredibly happy to work with you."

"Thank you, Dr. Cooper. I learned so much in your class. I'm excited to learn even more." He gives me a little extra squeeze and smile. I hope no one saw that.

OVER THE NEXT TWO WEEKS, we do exactly as Dr. McCrevis mentioned. We spend time in the labs where we're taught surgical techniques, and we observe several surgeries from the gallery. We're still another few weeks from being allowed to scrub in, but it's fun to watch these people work. It's fun to see the techniques from the lab brought to life.

It's Saturday night, and we're having a big family meal at a nice restaurant.

"To Darian and Jackson. May they have a happy and long marriage."

We join all of our champagne glasses with that of Aunt Cass, and in unison say, "To Darian and Jackson."

Mom and Jackson got engaged shortly after the New Year. There was a bit of drama after he proposed on New Year's Eve, with Mom freaking out, but she eventually proposed back to him live on the jumbotron at the Eagles game.

It was all over the news. Everyone at the hospital saw it and got a good laugh. My whole new big family is out for a celebratory dinner.

Trevor interrupts my thoughts. "I would also like to toast to the latest and greatest version of the Brady Bunch. To my new sisters, who are going to be so good to me, and hook me up with all their hot friends."

He holds up his glass, but only Reagan hits it with hers. She winks at him. "I've got you, brother. It goes both ways though." They high-five. I swear they're twins separated at birth.

Mom and Jackson are beaming. I'm so happy for them. Seeing Mom bounce back after such heartbreak is giving me hope.

It's getting hard for me to continue to resist Brody. Seeing him every day is basically making it impossible to consider moving on. I couldn't move on when he was on the other side of the world. Now his handsome face is in my face every day. I don't stand a chance at staying away from him for much longer. On some level, I know we're inevitable.

He leaves daily notes in my locker letting me know he's thinking about me, wanting me, and waiting for me to change my mind. Some days he leaves thoughtful gifts.

Yesterday he left me really good sushi. He remembered from the first day of class when I said that good sushi is my favorite food. The other day he left me a key to his shore house, with a note letting me know the house is as much mine as it is his, and that he can't wait until I change my mind so we can spend time down there together. He left me my underwear from that first night we were together, with a note that he doesn't need the memory anymore since he'll soon have the real thing. It's constant, and my defenses aren't going to hold up forever.

If I thought seeing his gorgeous face all the time was breaking me down, watching him perform surgery is next level. It's basically my own personal form of porn. I get turned on every time I watch him perform surgery.

I feel an elbow from Reagan. "Are you awake?"

"Yes, sorry. My head was elsewhere."

"Was it between Brody's legs where it belongs?"

A giggle. "Maybe a little."

"Good. What's going on there?"

"He's relentless. Every single day he does something to pursue me."

"Let him succeed."

"You know my reasons."

"They're stupid. Grow up. Stop being so fucking concerned about what other people think. Do what makes you happy. Look at Mom right now." I look up and she's on Jackson's lap with her arms around him. He's constantly kissing and touching her. She's literally beaming.

"Look how happy she is. Don't you want that? Don't you think you deserve to have that same shit-eating grin that she has right now? I don't want that right now, I'm too young, but I want that one day. Exactly that. You're ready for it, and have it in the palm of your hand, yet you're doing nothing about it. How long do you think this guy is going to keep begging? Men that look like him don't beg forever."

"I'll think about it." She's definitely given me a lot to consider.

Fortunately, she changes topics. "Are we on for Operation Spygate tomorrow night?"

I roll my eyes. "Are we seriously doing this?"

"Absolutely. Skylar is in deep with this guy. We need to find out once and for all if he's cheating on her. I don't mean to be a bitch, but she may need to physically see it to believe it and move on. The three of us are meeting in front of his apartment at 9:00 tomorrow night. Skylar said she thinks he'll be leaving around then. Make sure you're wearing all black."

"Are you kidding me? This is so stupid."

"No, it's not. It needs to be done. You better be there."

———

It's 9:00 the following night, and we meet in front of Jason's apartment. The three of us are dressed in black. We're just sitting there in Reagan's car. Skylar looks like she's going to puke.

I rub her back. "Are you okay? We don't have to do this."

Before she can answer, Reagan smacks my hand. "Yes, we do. She needs to find out the truth so she can move forward one way or the other."

After about thirty minutes, we see Jason come out. He's dressed in ratty clothes and mud-caked boots. I look at Reagan. "He certainly doesn't look like he's going on a date."

Skylar smiles in triumph. "No, he doesn't. He always dresses well when we go out. I've never seen those boots."

Reagan pushes our heads down. "Duck, he's about to pass us."

I push her hand away. "This is genuinely the dumbest thing you've ever done. Somehow, I'm here doing it with you."

He gets in his car, so we follow him. We drive for about forty-five minutes, seemingly to the middle of nowhere.

Reagan is flustered. This isn't what she was expecting. "Maybe he's a serial killer."

Skylar shakes her head. "He's not a serial killer, Reagan. I told you I think he has some job that he doesn't want to share."

He finally pulls into a long driveway. The sign out front reads "Farm Day School".

Reagan looks at us. "What the hell is this place? Google it."

I take out my phone but have no bars. "There's no reception here."

Skylar gives Reagan the evil eye. "I suppose that explains why he never responds to my texts when he's missing."

"Hmmm. Maybe. Reach into the glove compartment."

I point at her. "If it's a gun, I'm leaving."

"It's not a gun. It's one of the devices from my store. It's some sort of extender that grabs onto the closest WiFi."

We power it up, and I'm able to get connected. I google the school. "The Farm Day School is a hands-on school for severely autistic kids. They learn through farming activities, like horseback riding, milking cows, gathering eggs, feeding livestock, tending to gardens and fields, brushing the animals, and generally taking care of the animals."

Reagan pinches her eyebrows. "Maybe he's dating someone that works here." Skylar and I look at her like she's crazy, but she returns our stares. "If it's a day school, why is he here at night?"

I sigh. "Just follow him so we know once and for all."

We follow his car through the farm. He stops in front of what looks like horse stables and goes inside. Skylar looks at Reagan. "What now?"

"Do you think he's into Beastiality?"

"Reagan! Cut it out. You're making Skylar crazy. Come on. Let's just go see."

Like the psychotic trespassers we are, we sneak around the side. We watch Jason shovel horse shit for about five minutes. Skylar sighs and starts walking straight into the barn, in plain sight. Jason lifts his head at the noise. "Skylar? What are you doing here? How did you find me?"

"I'm sorry, Jason. My psycho sister thought you were cheating on me, so we followed you." She looks around, likely feeling a little embarrassed. "So, what is it you're doing here?"

He puts his head down like he's ashamed. "I wouldn't cheat on you. You know I care about you too much for that. I work here. My little sister goes to school here, but my family can't afford the full tuition. I do some of the grunt work a few nights a week to help work off her tuition payments. She loves it here, and I don't want her to have to leave because of finances. This place has helped her a lot."

Skylar turns her head toward us with unshed tears in her eyes. She then looks back toward Jason and walks right up to him. She grabs his face and gives him a searing kiss. He immediately drops his shovel, and wraps his arms around her, returning the kiss.

I grab Reagan's shirt. "Come on. Let's give them privacy." We walk back out to the car.

"I hope you feel like an asshole. We're complete assholes."

"I don't. At least now she knows." Reagan bites her lip. "Maybe a little bit of an asshole."

A few minutes later, Skylar comes out. She goes straight for the trunk and grabs a blanket. I look at her. "What are you doing?"

"I'm going to stay. I'm going to give Jason a *really* good memory of this barn, and then I'll help him with whatever he does here. You guys can leave. I will ride back with him."

I rub her arm. "We're sorry."

She waves her hand. "It's fine. At least I know now. The uncertainty was brutal."

Reagan mouths to me, "I told you."

We hug her and head back.

CHAPTER TEN

THE PRESENT

HARLEY

There was a major pile-up accident on the highway, so they asked us four residents to assist in the ER for a few hours. They need the extra hands, and we're more than happy to help. We're missing a few major surgeries, but this is where we're most needed.

It's been an absolute madhouse. We've seen severed limbs, head injuries, all kinds of broken bones, and several cases of internal damage. It's been a few hours, and it's finally starting to calm down.

I'm with a teenager, Monica, who hit her head hard. She's being monitored for a severe concussion. We don't see any other brain damage. I'm leaning over checking her vitals when she sits up and pukes all over me. Puking is completely normal for concussed patients, but I'm drenched in it. It's on my clothes, my body, and my hair.

One of the ER doctors tells me to go to an on-call room to shower and change. I don't want to leave Monica alone though. She's freaking out, and she's all alone.

I turn to the ER doctor. "Will you please stay with Monica until her parents arrive? She's just a kid and she's afraid to be left alone."

"No problem, Dr. Lawrence. I'll keep her company." She smiles at me.

"Thank you." I head to an on-call room to jump in the shower.

BRODY

I stretch my arms. I'm stiff and sweaty after a long nine-hour surgery. "Melinda, when am I needed again?"

My assistant looks through my calendar. "You have a consult in about ninety minutes. You should go get some rest."

"I intend to. I'm going to rinse off in one of the on-call rooms and grab a quick nap. Call me five minutes before I'm needed for the consult."

She nods. "Will do, Dr.Cooper."

I head to one of the on-call rooms, as they all have both a private shower and a bed. I find one that appears to be empty. I go in and lock the door behind me.

I take off all my clothes and head toward the shower stall. I open the bathroom door.

A plume of steam comes through the door. The moment

it clears, I see a body. It's not just any body. It's the body that I've been dreaming about for over three years. It's Harley, freshly showered, in nothing but a small towel wrapped around that achingly perfect body.

She looks at me with those big, gorgeous green eyes. Everything around me disappears. I'm naked, but I don't care. I can't take my eyes off her. She's fresh-faced, and genuinely the most stunningly beautiful woman in the world.

I see droplets of water drip down from her neck, disappearing into her generous cleavage underneath her towel. More droplets trickle down her long, toned legs. I ache to lick those droplets from her body.

I blink to make sure I'm not dreaming. I'm not. She's standing there, and she's the most magnificent thing I've ever seen in my life.

HARLEY

Brody is in front of me completely naked, frozen in place, just staring at me. I've never seen his body before. The first time we were together, he was entirely clothed.

His body is nothing short of perfection. His abs are muscular with what looks like an eight-pack. His arms are toned with bulging muscles, looking like he hasn't missed a day in the gym for years. He has a broad chest covered in dirty blonde hair, a little darker than the hair on his head. He has the same hair below his belly button heading all the way down.

He has thick, muscular quads. In between them, his arousal is growing tall right before my eyes. I remember thinking he was big when he was inside of me, but seeing it is a whole different ballgame. I can't believe that fit in me.

I'm completely overwhelmed by the chiseled figure before me. I've never seen a man with such a beautiful body. I've never seen anything so perfect. I can physically feel the desire for him pooling between my legs.

We're both standing there in silence doing nothing but breathing heavily and drinking in each other. I don't think I have the power to resist this anymore. We're two magnets, and no matter how much we move around one another, our coming together is inevitable. My body physically needs his.

Without breaking eye contact, I take my hand to the top of my towel, slowly pull it off my body, hold it out, and drop it to the floor.

His eyes widen, as he rakes those big blues up and down my now naked body, taking it all in.

I lick my lips, which seems to snap him out of his momentary trance. He lets out a growl, and charges right at me.

His body crashes into mine as he wraps his arms around me, carrying me back into the shower. He somehow turns the water on. It's still warm considering I only got out a moment ago. He's holding me up, with my warm back against the cold tile wall.

We're nose to nose. Chest to chest. Our lips are so close that we're sharing the same air. His erection lays heavy on my stomach.

I slide my tongue out through my lips, and slowly run it along and around his chin dimple. I've wanted to do that since the day I met him at the club.

He whispers my name. "Harley." He takes a few deep breaths. "I want you so badly. I've dreamt of being back inside your body *every* single night for three and a half years." I close my eyes at the power of his words, knowing that I've felt the same. I no longer *want* him inside of me. I *need* him inside of me.

He moves his lips to mine. His tongue pushes into my open my mouth. I wrap my legs around him and run my fingers through his hair. As the heated kiss rages on, I grind my wetness along his length, begging for relief.

My hands are moving all over his body. I can't touch him enough. I don't know what I want to touch next. I've wanted him for so long, and now that I'm here, I'm like a crazy woman with need. My body feels like a volcano on the cusp of eruption.

He takes one hand and grabs my breast between our bodies, squeezing my nipple. I moan into his mouth and buck my hips, craving more of him. He breaks our kiss. "I need you, Harley. I can't wait another second."

I'm panting with desire. "Neither can I."

He moves his hand down and brings his tip to my entrance. "Are you on the pill?" I nod in the affirmative.

He grabs my ass, moves his hips, and slowly pushes himself all the way in. My head is back, my eyes are closed, and my mouth is open as I let the sensation take over my body. I've never felt anything so incredible in all my life. I've never been so turned on in my entire life. He's completely still inside of me, yet the pleasure is spreading through my body like wildfire.

I bring my head up and open my eyes to look at him. We're nose to nose again. We're both entirely overcome with the sensation of him finally being back inside me after all this time. "Brody," I breathe, "no one has been here since you." I feel him freeze in obvious surprise. He scans my face, realizing the truth and meaning of my statement.

He takes his thumb and rubs it across my bottom lip, just as he did in the club all those years ago. He runs it up my cheek, as he brings his lips to mine again, and starts to move inside of me. The pace of it all increasing over time.

He's pumping into me, over and over. Faster and faster.

Deeper and deeper. I have no awareness of where I am, or the world outside me, only the pleasure that Brody's bringing to me. It's all-consuming. It's three years of pent-up frustration, finally rising to the surface, ready to burst out of me. I feel it everywhere. I feel him everywhere.

He kisses his way down to my neck. I lean my head to the side, giving him greater access. My hands explore everywhere I can reach. His face, his hair, his neck, his back, and his chest. It all feels good. It all feels right. Nothing has ever felt so right for me. Nothing has ever brought me this much pleasure.

He's holding me up with one hand, driving into me, as I scream his name over and over. His other hand is on my breast, squeezing it. He plays with my nipples, driving me wild. "Harley, I've wanted this for so long. Your wet pussy feels so good, baby. I feel your walls gripping me. Sucking me in." My body is an inferno for him.

He pounds into me at a relentless, delicious pace. The sounds coming out of my mouth are like nothing I've ever experienced before. He breathes into my ear, "I don't think I can last much longer. I need you to come with me."

I take his hand from my breast and guide it down to where our bodies join. He puts his thumb on my sensitive bundle of nerves and begins to circle it. I can feel my insides trembling. I'm so close to euphoria. He picks up the pace of both his body in mine, and his thumb on my clit. The sounds of my moans increase. "Oh god, Brody. Yes. Don't stop. Keep going."

Sensing I'm about to scream into my orgasm, he kisses me, muffling out the sounds of my ecstasy. I see stars as I explode into a million pieces, just as he does the same.

He continues to pump into me, helping me ride out my orgasm, as I feel him pulsate through his own.

After a few moments, he stops, and we both remain still with him inside of me, breathing heavy, nose to nose, just as we started.

He continues to kiss me as if we have all the time in the world. He brings his hand to my cheek and deepens the kiss. Neither of us in any rush for this inevitable connection to end.

Eventually, he stops, pulls out, and sets my feet on the ground. He keeps his big body pressed to mine, arms on either side, caging me in. He gives me one final soft kiss as he takes his hand and tilts my chin up so that I'm looking at him in the eyes. "Harley, this is happening. You and I are happening. You're mine."

"I know, Brody. I know."

WE'RE in the shower for another fifteen minutes. He meticulously cleans every single inch of me. He studies me as if he's going to be tested on the intricacies of my body. He dots kisses all over my neck, back, shoulders, and arms. He hasn't stopped touching me, and it feels amazing. It's been so long since I've felt any desire for a man. It's now come flooded back to me, both figuratively and literally.

I look down and see he's ready for more too. He turns off the water and grabs us two fresh towels. He wraps me in mine before he takes care of his own. "I just had a long surgery and need to catch some sleep. Come lay with me."

I look up at the big digital clock in the restroom. Only an on-call bathroom would have a clock. "I should have been back fifteen minutes ago. I can't take a nap."

"Ten more minutes. Please. I want to lay with you. I need to feel your body close to mine. I've waited so long for this. It will soothe me and help me fall asleep." He gives me his best puppy dog eyes.

I can't resist him. "Fine. When you fall asleep, I'm leaving. A max of ten minutes though." He smiles and nods in agreement.

There is only a twin bed in here. We snuggle in close, naked, under the covers. The front of his body pressed to the back of mine. He wraps his big arms around me.

He leisurely moves his hands up and down my body for a minute or two. He then grabs onto my breasts and starts playing with my nipples. I can feel his renewed hardness in my backside. I wiggle and he moans. "Brody, it certainly doesn't feel like you're really trying to fall asleep."

He peppers my back with kisses. "I don't know how I could've possibly thought I'd be able to sleep with your gorgeous naked body pressed against mine."

"I should go then. I don't have time for this." I start to get up, but he squeezes me, not letting me move. He slides his fingers between my legs.

I feel him smile into my back. "Your body betrays your words." It most definitely does. His fingers feel good, as I relax back into him. "You're so wet for me, Harley. I need to be back inside you. I know you want it too. Don't deny yourself." I feel him move his tip to my entrance from behind. He slips all the way in, and I don't make it back out to the floor for another forty minutes.

OUR COMBINED SCHEDULES for the next two weeks cannot possibly be less conducive to spending time together outside of the hospital. We try to squeeze in moments when we can.

I'm walking down the hallway toward the cafeteria after a morning in the lab. All of a sudden, a hand reaches out and pulls me into a supply closet. The door is quickly closed and locked. It's dark. The hand covers my mouth. I smile into it. I can smell Brody's aftershave. His smell, touch, feel, and the danger of what we're doing have me turned on in mere seconds.

He lifts me up on a table, stands between my legs, and takes my mouth in a deep kiss. I run my fingers through his hair, while he pulls the bottom of my scrubs down and off.

He kisses his way down until he's on his knees. He spreads my legs. He growls out something about this being his lunch, and him being a starving man. He parts my lips with his fingers and takes a long lick. He closes his eyes. "I've thought about doing this again for so long. Your pussy tastes so damn sweet. Even better than I remember. Please tell me I'm not dreaming."

I run my fingers through his hair. "You're not dreaming." I look down at him in challenge. "Now get going, you only have a few minutes to get the job done." I push his head back between my legs. He makes me come in less than three minutes.

THE NEXT DAY I'm on the way to observe an appendectomy by Dr. Lipson. Again, I'm grabbed into the closet. Again, his smell and feel overwhelm me. His touch makes me forget where we are. My body reacts to everything about him.

He turns me around, bends me over the table, and pulls down my scrubs. He rubs my ass cheeks as he sticks two fingers inside of me. "You're always so wet, every time I touch you."

"It's you. Only you do it to me." If only he knew how true that is.

"I've thought about this all day long. Seeing you bent over for me like this. Do you know how much I want to fuck you?" He runs his tip through my drenched lips and enters me.

I have no chance at being quiet at this angle. "Oh god, Brody."

He again makes me come quickly, having to cover my mouth with his hand through it all.

THE NEXT DAY I'm determined to get him. I know when his surgery is over. I wait, and when he passes, I grab him. It's not like I can really manhandle his big body, but he goes with it. I lock the door and grab his face, bringing it to mine. I can feel him smiling while I kiss him. "You're full of surprises, baby. How do you want me to fuck you today?"

"This is my kidnapping and I'll do what I want." I pull his scrubs down and drop to my knees. I haven't tasted him yet, and I'm dying to. I pump him a few times, as I lick him from the bottom to the top. I circle the tip with my tongue, and he moans.

I start to take him in my mouth when I see a flash go off. I look up at him. "Did you just take a picture of me sucking your dick?"

"Yes. Please continue now."

I laugh. "Please explain."

"Do you remotely comprehend how much I've fantasized about having you every way possible for the past three and a half years? The fantasy of you on your knees in front of me has imprinted itself in my mind. It's dark in here, I can't see you. I want to see it. I want to remember it. I want the souvenir."

I look up at him. He's struggling to believe this is real. I've damaged him. I've damaged me too.

After I blow his mind, I remind him that we both have the same day off this weekend. I suggest we spend time at his shore house. He can barely contain his excitement.

IT'S LATE FRIDAY NIGHT. We've both just finished at the hospital. We're driving straight to the shore. We get there after midnight.

I walk into his house for the first time. It's incredible. It's three levels, with five bedrooms, a hot tub on the roof, and ocean views from all three decks. "It's beautiful, Brody. Why did you get such a big place?"

He doesn't have to think about it. "Because you have a big family. I know you're close with your mother and sisters. I want them to spend time here too. I'm glad I did. It sounds like your family is getting way bigger."

He really does see this as ours. I don't have the heart to tell him right now that I can't tell my family about us. Aunt Cass and Mom would lose their shit. I suppose I could tell my sisters though.

He comes up from behind me and wraps his arms around me. "You must be exhausted. You just worked a twenty-four-hour shift. Do you want to go to bed?"

I turn and smile at him. I pull his lips to mine. "No. I want to enjoy every second I have with you. I can sleep next week." He grins. "How about we check out the hot tub?"

His eyes light up. "Absolutely. I'll go get it ready. I have a bathing suit already up there. You go get changed."

I walk into the bedroom to get on my bathing suit. The bed is an enormous California King. I see he only has clothes in half of the closet and in half of the drawers. I'm a bit overwhelmed by the fact that he saved me space in both.

I put on a very tiny bikini. I know he's going to flip over it. I wrap myself in a towel and grab one for Brody.

I head up to the top deck. He's already in the hot tub. He has his head back with his eyes closed.

I take a moment to admire the view. The ocean is nice, but I'm talking about Brody, without a shirt, relaxing in the hot tub. I'm already panting for him, and he hasn't touched me yet. I think I must moan because he pops his head up. He smiles at me. "There you are. I missed you. Come get in. It feels amazing in here."

I place his towel on a chair and remove my towel to place it on the chair as well. I turn around, and his chin just about drops to the floor. "Harley, you're the embodiment of every wet dream that I've ever had in my life." I give him a slow smile. Mission accomplished.

I step into the hot tub and sit as far away from him as possible. Of course, I'm joking with him, but he immediately grabs me and pulls me to his lap. I giggle as I straddle his big thighs. He pulls me tight to him. I can feel how ready he is to move this along.

It feels so good to be here with him like this. I want to savor every moment.

I run my fingertips all over the scruff on his face. He's so handsome. I move my head down and pepper him with kisses. I start at his chin dimple and move along his jawline. I nibble on his ear for a bit, until I move my way back towards his mouth.

I place a soft kiss on his lips. He grabs my face with both of his hands and stares into my eyes. He rubs his nose and lips across mine and moans my name.

He stares at me in the eyes with such emotion. "You know I'm in love with you, right?" This moment suddenly feels very heavy. It's so many years of pain and heartache in the making. I'm surprised that I don't freak out. It feels just right.

I place my hands over his on my face and look at the man that I've wanted for so long. "I love you too, Brody." I pause for a moment. "But we've only loved each other from afar. Never like this. We need to learn how to love each other up close."

I move my lips onto his as we kiss. I move my hands across his broad shoulders. I pull back for a brief moment. "I *need* you,

Brody. I've never needed anything or anyone more." I thread my fingers through his hair and kiss him again. Our kisses convey so much emotion. He puts so much into them, and I do my best to return his intensity.

We just sit there and kiss for what feels like forever. We've never been together where we can just take our time with one another. It's always been frantic or rushed. It's nice to go slow, and thoroughly enjoy the moment, and each other's bodies.

He pulls the two small triangles of my bikini top to the side, freeing my breasts. He holds them in his hands and looks at them. "I can't believe I finally get to take my time worshipping these perfect tits. I'm like a kid in a candy store right now." I giggle.

"Better eat your candy, Dr. Cooper." He smiles as he takes one nipple in his mouth. He spends a long time worshipping my breasts, squeezing, licking, and sucking my nipples.

I'm busting with need. I shamelessly rub myself onto him, back and forth. I grab the side of the hot tub for leverage, as I start to grind him even harder. That, along with the nipple treatment, has already got me teetering on the edge.

He sucks one nipple hard, while he pulls the other equally hard. It feels so incredibly good. "Oh god, Brody. I'm going to come." He sucks and squeezes even harder, and I erupt. He doesn't stop until I completely ride out my orgasm. Wow, I don't think I've ever come from just my nipples being manipulated. This is what he does to me.

Before I know it, he's pulled my bathing suit bottoms to the side and has slipped two long fingers inside of me. I ride his fingers and suck on his lips, as I slip his bathing suit down, and pull out his cock. I pump him a few times. "I need this monster cock inside of me, now." He removes his fingers. I place his tip at my entrance, and he grabs my shoulders to pull me all the way down.

I'm still for a moment as I get used to him. I grab his face and kiss him again, until I eventually begin to slowly glide up and down. He feels so deep inside of me. The bliss takes over my whole body.

I completely lose myself, unabashedly riding him without any regard for our surroundings. I feel the sensation from my toes through to my fingertips. I lick and suck my way to his ear. "Brody, you feel amazing."

He starts to kiss my neck and work his way back down to my nipples. "You have the most perfect pussy. I knew it would be like this between us. You're so fucking sexy."

I feel my walls starting to spasm. "I feel you, Harley. I feel what my cock does to you. We're so perfect together. I want you to come with me. All over me. Let me feel you." His words drive me wild. He grabs my ass and slams me up and down a few more times until we both scream into our orgasms together.

We're both breathing heavily, waiting for our heartbeats to return to normal. He kisses around my neck, shoulders, and arms. "Harley, I want this every day for the rest of my life. I want you every day for the rest of my life. Marry me."

CHAPTER ELEVEN

THE PRESENT

BRODY

She starts laughing. "Marry you? Are you crazy? We are *not* ready to get married, Brody."

"Why? I love you. You love me. If I've learned anything in the past few years, it's that I don't want anyone but you. This is it for me. You're it for me. I know it. If you feel the same, there's no reason not to get married."

She grabs my face and kisses me softly. "First, you cannot ask someone to marry you while you're inside of them."

"If I pull out and ask you, will that do the trick?"

She laughs. "No. Stay right where you are. I like you there" She wiggles her hips.

"Brody, we literally just started dating. I told you we've only loved each other from afar. We need to see what it looks like up close. I know we've wanted this for a long time, but this is just the beginning of us. This is where our story begins. We have such an intense physical attraction to one another. We need to make sure it's more than that."

That hurt. I know my face must show it because she immediately regrets her word choice. "I'm sorry. I didn't mean it how it came out. I know it's more than just physical." She sighs. "I meant that I think we need to spend real time together. Something we've never had the opportunity to do. We haven't even told our families that we're dating."

"I told my father everything. He's my only family."

"What? You did? When did you tell him?"

"Two and half years ago when I came back heartbroken, he told me to be patient, and if I still felt so strongly for you after my fellowship, then I should go back and fight for you."

He strokes my face. "You know I went home to California for all those months between Sweden and moving back to Philly. He asked me if my feelings had changed. I told him not in the slightest. He said that I should know what needed to be done. He knew I was moving back to Philly for one reason and one reason only. To get my girl. And that I wasn't taking no for an answer this time." She seems stunned by my words.

"Wow, Brody. I don't know what to say to that." She runs her hands through my hair. "Just know that my feelings never changed either. I've thought of you, and wanted you, every single day since the day we met."

"Does your family know about me?"

"My sisters were there on New Year's. I didn't know they were coming. They were worried about me. They arrived just as you left. They saw you, so I had to tell them. My mother doesn't know anything about you. Her best friend, who's basically a member of the family, knows a little about you, but she doesn't know that you're back in my life."

I'm not sure I understand why her sisters were worried. What am I missing? I tuck her hair behind her ears. "Why were they worried about you, Harley?"

She takes a breath, as tears well in her eyes. She looks like she's in pain, and it breaks my heart. "Because the past few years have been a struggle for me, Brody. You heard what I told you in the on-call room." I nod. How could I possibly forget that she hasn't been with another man since me. No statement has ever shocked me more.

"I spent three and a half years unable to be intimate with another man because I was so hung up on you. It's been hard on me. It's been lonely. I've been incredibly unhappy. My sisters are my best friends. They knew I wasn't okay. They knew I needed them."

I wish I did things differently, but I'm not sure it would have mattered at the time. I look at her trying to convey all the love that I feel. "I'm so sorry. I should have fought harder for us then. You never have to be without me again, Harley. I never want to be without you. I love you. Marry me. Let's never spend another night apart."

"Brody, I'm not saying no. I'm saying not right now. I want us to get to know one another. We need to be a real couple for a while. We're still a secret from most people. We need to figure out how this will go down at work. I don't want issues on my end, and I don't want you to get fired because of me?"

I look at her in surprise. "Why would I get fired?"

"Your predecessor got fired for sleeping with a resident."

"No, he didn't. He got fired for stealing narcotics. He's losing his medical license too."

"Oh. That's not what I heard. What's the policy on attendings and residents dating?"

"They don't like it. They can't forbid it, but they definitely don't like it. It would be more my problem than yours. I'm fine with whatever ramifications there may be."

"The issue with regard to my integrity is still there, Brody. Just because I caved to your good looks doesn't mean that the issue still doesn't exist. I want to think through how we reveal this at work. We need to do it right. I won't make an impulsive decision. It's not how I work."

I hate this. I want to love her openly, but I know she's not ready for that. "Okay. We can wait for a while. It's going to be hard to hide." I run my fingers all over her body. "I have an uncontrollable need to touch you."

She kisses my lips again and smiles at me. "Why don't we go inside, and you can touch me all night?"

That's exactly what we do.

HARLEY

I wake up on Saturday, and half-open my eyes. I see the sunlight filter through the windows, so I know it's morning.

I'm surprisingly aroused right now. I don't know how it's possible given how much sex we had last night. I feel like I'm going to come again. I move my head down and see the reason. Brody's head is between my legs. I run my fingers through his hair. He looks up and smiles. "Good morning."

I give him a lazy smile back. "It certainly is a good morning."

He puts his head back down and gives me a nice long lick before returning to my clit. He adds two thick fingers inside of me, and starts to slide them in and out. "Ahh. Brody. Feels good. Keep going. Don't stop." He curls his fingers. I squeeze my thighs together around his head. He moans into me and that sets me off. I writhe and scream his name through my orgasm.

As soon as I'm done, he flips me over, spreads my legs wide, and immediately slams into me from behind. I yell out.

He slides his hands under my body and grabs onto my breasts as his leverage. He plows his big body into me over and over. I don't think I've been fucked this hard in my entire life. I'm being catapulted to a new level of pleasure that I've never reached before. He's squeezing my nipples. I can't believe I'm already on the cusp of another orgasm.

I tilt my ass up to better the angle, while I grab the sheets to hold myself in place. "Harley, use that pussy and squeeze me hard." I do. "That's it, baby. I'm going to come so hard. Your pussy feels so good. Give me your juices." His dirty words further ignite the fire inside of me. The relentless pace has me spiraling into another orgasm. I shatter uncontrollably into my climax, as he grunts hard into his own.

I've never been with anyone with a dirty mouth like Brody's. I wouldn't have thought I'd like it, but I do. It drives me wild. Maybe it's just those words coming out of *his* mouth that turn me on, but it pushes me to dizzying heights.

I don't remember any dirty talk from our first night together, but I also don't know that I was completely with it and hearing him that night. It's certainly been there every time we've been together since then, and I find myself unexpectedly loving it. Craving it.

We're both completely sweaty and spent, as we lay there for a moment to catch our breath, with his front still draped over my back.

He begins to lift up. He rubs my ass. As he sits up, he runs a finger through the crack in my ass. I freeze. "Harley, has anyone been here before?" I shake my head no. "Good. It's going to be mine. Soon."

WE HAVE a wonderful few weeks together. We sneak away any chance we get at the hospital. Any night that we both have off, we spend together. I'm happier than I've ever been in my entire life. I have the career I've always wanted, and the man that I love.

It's a Wednesday, and I'm standing with Jess reviewing surgical notes when I see Payton roaming the hallways. "Payton?"

"Oh, hey Harley. How are you?"

"I'm good. What are you doing here?"

"Kylie has an ultrasound. I went to the room number she gave me, but she wasn't there. I'm a little lost."

"Well, that's probably because you're on the wrong floor."

"This isn't the fifth floor?"

"No, we're on the fourth."

He smiles. "I guess it makes sense why she wasn't there." I feel a nudge from Jess.

"Payton, this is Jess. Jess this is my brother-to-be, Payton. His *wife* is pregnant, and he's headed to her appointment."

"Oh, nice to meet you. I guess he's not the sweet twin?"

"No, there's a third brother you haven't met."

Payton turns to Jess. "I suppose that means you met Trevor. I apologize for anything he may have said." Jess laughs. He looks back at me. "Harley, are you looking forward to Mexico?"

All of a sudden, I hear Brody's voice behind me. "Dr.

Lawrence, you're going to Mexico?" Oh shit. I haven't told him about that.

I turn around. "Yes, Dr. Cooper. My mother is marrying Payton's father in Mexico in a few weeks."

"I hadn't heard. Congratulations." He doesn't seem pleased. He nonetheless introduces himself to Payton.

Payton says his goodbyes. Brody turns to me. "Dr. Lawrence, I have some good news for you. I just spoke with Dr. McCrevis, and you're going to scrub in on my surgery next week.

I momentarily forget that he's pissed at me. "Really?" He nods. "Thank you. Can I review the file so that I can familiarize myself with everything?"

"Yes, it's in my office. Why don't you come with me, and we'll discuss it *now*." He's definitely mad at me.

"Great." I fake smile at Jess and make my way toward Brody's office.

He closes the door. "Were you ever going to tell me about Mexico, or just call me once you were sitting by the pool with a margarita and guacamole?"

He's really upset. I rub his solid arms. "I'm sorry Brody. I should have told you."

"I want to come with you."

I shake my head. "No."

"Why not?"

"I'm not ready to tell my family about you. And Mexico is *a lot* of my family. They're a different breed. Trust me, you're not ready to handle them. It also won't look great if we're both gone the same week and come back with tans. I'm not there yet. I'm sorry."

He looks hurt. "When will you be ready?"

"Soon. We'll talk about it more after Mexico." I bite my lip.

"Am I really getting the surgery, or was that just an excuse to talk to me about Mexico?"

He gives me an exasperated look. "You're really getting the surgery. Though maybe I should reconsider now." He smiles. I know he wouldn't do that. "I did just speak with Phil about it. We both feel you're ready. If you're a good girl, I'll let you close the patient at the end of the surgery."

I have a huge smile. I wrap my arms around his neck and kiss him. "I promise to be a good girl tonight." I bat my eyelashes at him. "Do you want to discuss the file before you go?"

"No, I'm done for the day. I want to get to the gym. I've been distracted by a hot chick lately and haven't gotten in my workouts."

"I assure you; you've been working out plenty."

He laughs and gives me a kiss. "Read the file on your own and then we'll discuss it. When are you off for the night?"

"I'm done in about three hours. Why don't you head to my place after the gym and order us some food. After we eat, I promise to make it up to you." I kiss his lips. "Or better yet, be naked in my bed and I'll make it up to you before we eat."

He's still pouting but musters a, "Fine."

———————

A LITTLE OVER three hours later, I walk into my apartment. I hear voices. As I walk further inside, I see Brody in boxers and a t-shirt talking to Reagan. This can't be good.

Reagan sees me and smiles. "Hey, sis." She's got that devilish twinkle in her eyes. "Imagine my surprise when I came to see you tonight and there was a hot, naked guy in your bed."

Brody laughs. "It only took a little fondling for me to realize it wasn't you." My chin nearly drops to the floor. He and Reagan both laugh. "You were right. She believed me." The two of them are hysterically laughing now.

I give him the evil eye. "Just what she needs, another partner in crime to torture me."

Brody jumps up and comes over to me. He wraps his arms around me and gives me a deep kiss, as he rubs his hands all over me. "Baby, there's not a chance I would ever confuse someone else's body for your perfect body."

Reagan whistles. "I suppose that's my cue to leave." She starts walking toward the door. "Brody, it was a pleasure to meet you, though I suppose we sort of met before. I want to thank you for the big ass smile that's been on my sister's face for the past few months."

She smiles at me. "Harley, being the thoughtful sister I am, I showed Brody your three black bags. Now he knows where to find all the goodies. You're welcome."

I narrow my eyes at her. "You're seriously the devil, Reagan."

She laughs. "I know. It's so much fun. Bye kids. Make sure you do everything I would do." She leaves.

I turn to him. "Sorry for my embarrassment of a sister."

"I like her. She's funny. I also *really* like the bag of tricks she showed me. We're going to use it all."

CHAPTER TWELVE

THE PRESENT

BRODY

Harley's first surgery is today. She's busting with excitement. She's not actually performing it, she's just scrubbing in, but she's studied for it enough that she probably could perform it. I love how excited she gets about surgeries.

We're in the seventh hour of the surgery. I'm almost done. I've really enjoyed having Harley here watching. Her eyes have been glued to me. I look up at her. "Dr. Lawrence, would you like to close the patient for me?"

I can only see her eyes because of the surgical mask, but I can tell that she's surprised that I'm allowing this. "I would love that, Dr. Cooper. Thank you."

I get a few looks from the nurses. It's a little early to allow this, but I think she's up for it. No one practices harder.

She grabs the proper instruments and begins. I'm slowly talking her through it, but she doesn't need my instructions. She's got it.

I'm mesmerized watching her. Her enthusiasm for doing what she loves is exhilarating. Being a part of her first-time performing surgery is an image I'll never forget.

My dick starts to twitch. I can't believe I'm getting turned on watching her perform surgery. I can't believe I'm getting a semi in the O.R.

She glances my way. She takes a deep breath as she quickly scans down my body, stopping at my pants. She knows exactly what this is doing to me. What she's doing to me. If eyes could smile, hers do. I have to turn around and adjust myself so that everyone doesn't know what Harley does to me.

She finishes the procedure perfectly. We head to the sink to scrub our hands. The need to touch her is overwhelming. "Dr. Lawrence, would you like to assist in my post-surgical notes. It's important to learn how to do them properly."

"Yes, Dr. Cooper. Thank you."

"Let's head up to my office and I'll *teach* you." She gives me a look. There may have been some innuendo in that last comment.

We quickly walk up to my office. As soon as I close the door, she grabs my cock. She stands on her tippy toes and bites my lower lip. She slowly tugs on it, eventually letting it snap back into place. "Dr. Cooper, did you get hard watching me perform surgery? Does surgery turn you on, dirty boy?"

I look down at her with the heat I feel. "*You* turn me on." I bite her lip too. I know she can feel me getting harder. She tightens her grip on me.

I grab her shoulders and quickly turn her, so her back is to my front. I pull her hard against me with one arm, and with the other, I slip my hand down into the bottoms of her scrubs. "It takes one to know one. Does my dirty girl get turned on watching *me* perform surgery?" She's soaking wet. Just as I thought. I slowly run my fingers through her lips.

She moans. "Yes. Always. It's better than porn. I love watching you. It's my personal porn." We're equally demented. I slide two fingers inside of her and rub my thumb on her clit. She nearly collapses as she yells out.

She digs her nails into my arm, already on the cusp. It won't take long to push her over. I pump in and out of her, while maintaining the methodical circles on her clit. It takes her less than thirty seconds to scream out my name into my other hand as she comes.

When she eventually recovers from her orgasm, she turns around and shoves me toward my desk chair. "I need your dick in my mouth. Now." She pushes me down onto my chair and drops to her knees in front of me. She quickly frees my now straining cock, grabs it, and pumps it a few times while circling her tongue around my tip, swallowing down what's already oozing.

She sucks me into her mouth while maintaining her tight grip on the base. I feel it everywhere. This woman electrifies my body in a way I've never experienced. I don't know that I'll last much longer than she did.

She grabs my balls with her other hand and squeezes me. I watch my cock slowly disappear into her luscious mouth, all the way in and all the way out. Her head is bobbing up and down. It's the most perfect image. "Harley, I could watch you on your knees in front of me, sucking my cock, all day long."

I'm gripping the arms of my chair so hard I might break it. I can feel her throat squeezing me. I look down as her eyes find mine, and she sucks just a little harder.

Her tongue is working its magic on me. "Harley. That's it, baby. I'm coming." If possible, she takes me even deeper and sucks me even harder. I feel the sensation through my whole body as I come hard and long down her throat. She doesn't flinch as she licks at all up.

Just then, I hear my door handle. I quickly scoot Harley and my bottom half under my desk. Phil pops his head in. "Brody, do you have a minute?" I guess I forgot to lock the door when she was gripping my cock.

"Umm..well..."

"Just a quick moment."

I don't think I can get out of this. "Of course. Please come in." I look down at Harley underneath my desk. She's got terror in her eyes. I need to move this along quickly.

He sits. "What can I help you with? We need to make it quick. I'm trying to get my surgical notes recorded while it's all still fresh in my mind."

"This won't take long. It's about your surgery. It's been reported to me by several people in the O.R. that you allowed Harley Lawrence to close in your surgery today."

I nod. "Yes, I did."

"It's highly irregular to let a resident do so this early. It's the first time she's scrubbed in."

"Yes, it is, but you've seen her. No one logs in more hours in the lab or watching in the gallery. I knew she was ready.

Remember, she was a student of mine. I know her abilities. They run *very deep*." I look down at her and smirk. She pinches my leg and I flinch.

He looks at me skeptically but nonetheless carries on. "Frankly, I think it was a bit careless. It's very unlike you to take such a risk."

"Phil, I was with her every step of the way. I could have intervened at any point if I was needed. She was flawless. Did anyone say differently?"

"No, they agreed that she executed it to perfection. No one is saying otherwise in that regard."

"Well then, we have one resident well ahead of schedule. Isn't their progress our goal here?"

He nods in contemplation. "Maybe you're right. I suppose they have to jump into the deep end at some point. She's going to make a fantastic surgeon. I know Liz thinks extremely highly of her abilities as well. Dr. Lawrence *is* pretty extraordinary." I see Harley smiling.

"That she is, Phil. That she is."

He gets up. "Well, I guess just be careful. I certainly don't want any issues with our surgeries. And you know the other residents will now all be begging for the same treatment."

"When they're ready, they'll have the same opportunity. The others aren't ready yet."

"I agree with that. Thanks for your time, Brody." He sticks out his hand for me to shake it. I almost stand up until I remember that my dick is hanging out. I shake his hand from my seated position. It's awkward, but I imagine the alternative would be a lot more awkward.

He goes to leave. "Can you close my door, Phil? I'm

trying to finish these surgical notes. I don't want to be interrupted before I finish them."

"You should have Dr. Lawrence come help with those. It's another learning opportunity for her."

"Great idea, Phil. Thanks."

He leaves and closes the door. Harley pops up as I tuck my dick back in my pants. She's freaking out. "Oh my god. That could have been bad." She runs her fingers through her hair. "We can't keep doing this here."

"Or we could just tell them that we're together."

She puts her hands on her hips. "Would that make me sucking your dick under your desk okay?"

"Maybe not okay, but less surprising." I laugh, but she looks like she's going to strangle me.

"This isn't funny. We need to cool it at the hospital."

"I'm pretty sure that I'm irresistible to you. You'll never last." She narrows her eyes at me, but I just smile as I take her into my arms.

CHAPTER THIRTEEN

THE PRESENT

HARLEY

We arrived in Mexico tonight for Mom and Jackson's wedding. We have a week of festivities before their wedding ceremony on our last night here.

I miss Brody already. I may have made a mistake not bringing him here with me. Perhaps it's time to come clean with Mom. I just don't want to interfere with her wedding week. This should be a drama-free week for her.

It's going to be a struggle for me to admit the whole truth. The thought of disappointing her sickens me.

Jackson rented us an enormous villa. We each have our own rooms.

It's around midnight here, and I'm in my bed wishing Brody was next to me. Holding me. Touching me.

My cell phone rings. I see it's Brody and I smile. "Hey, handsome."

"Hey, beautiful. I miss you already. My bed is lonely without you."

"I miss you too." I pause for a moment. "I'm sorry I didn't bring you, Brody. It was a mistake. This is the last trip I'll go on without you."

"You know I can get on a plane tomorrow and be there by dinner."

I wish he could. "No. Now isn't the time. I don't want to make myself the center of attention. This is Mom and Jackson's week. If you come here, that's all anyone will focus on."

"You're a good daughter."

I smile to myself. "She's a really good Mom."

I sigh. "Ugh. I can't believe I have to survive a week without your hands on my body. I'm sort of addicted to you."

"Me too, baby." I hear him let out a breath. "Are you in bed?"

"Yes."

"Do you have a private room?

"Yes."

"Is your door closed?"

"It is." I hope he's headed where I think he's headed.

"Go to the side pocket of your suitcase. To the left of the handle. I left something in there for you." I reach for the side pocket. I didn't know the pocket existed. I open it and pull out a vibrator.

It's not exactly what I expected. "Have you been going through my black bags, Dr. Cooper?"

"I told you we'd use it all. It's going to start tonight. Turn on your video chat." I do. I see his face. I get a lump in my throat. It's only been a few hours and I truly miss him already. I've gotten used to seeing him all the time.

He looks me up and down. "Take off your shorts and panties and position the camera in front so you don't need your hands to hold it. I need to be able to watch you. To see all of you."

I do as I'm told. "I want to watch you too, Brody." He pulls out his hard dick and gives it a few pumps. He's the perfect male specimen. My body immediately reacts to the sight of his. I lick my lips as my breathing picks up.

"I see you licking your lips. That drives me crazy, Harley." He strokes himself harder. "Now touch your pussy, baby. Put your fingers in. Make sure you're nice and wet for me."

"Brody, the second your big dick made it onto my screen I was wet."

He laughs. "Show me." I do. He smiles.

"Take the vibrator and run it up and down. Cover it in your sweet juices." I do what he says. "Very good. Now slide it into my heaven. Slowly. That's it. All the way in. Pretend it's me. That's my cock inside of you." I love the way he commands me and takes control. "Lift up your shirt so I can see those perfect tits." Again, I do as I'm instructed.

I squirm. "It doesn't feel as good as you do, Brody."

"Turn it on." I flick the switch, and it starts to vibrate. That feels good. I close my eyes. "In and out, baby. It's me moving in and out of your perfect wet pussy. I own that pussy. It's mine." I moan. Damn, I love when he talks dirty to me.

I arch my back. "Brody, you feel so good."

I can hear his breathing pick up. "I can feel your tight walls squeezing me."

"Oh god, Brody."

"Faster. I want to see your tits bouncing. Good girl. Now

deeper. You know how I like it. You know how deep I get inside of you."

"Brody."

"That's it, baby. Take your other hand and touch your clit. That's it. Fast circles. Faster."

"Ahh."

"Now move your hand up and grab your nipple. Squeeze it hard, just how you like it. That's it. Harder."

"Brody, I'm going to come. Come with me."

"I am."

I look up in time to see white streaks shoot out all over his muscular stomach. That image is enough to send me over the edge, and I yell out his name over and over as I convulse through my own climax.

We're both breathing heavily as our heart rates come down. I've never done anything like that before. It was insanely hot.

I turn off the vibrator and grab the phone. "Thank you, Dr. Cooper. Can we make an appointment for the same time tomorrow?"

He laughs. "You got it, sexy. Get some sleep. Good night. I love you."

"I love you too." I end the call and slip my sleep shorts back on.

My throat is dry after that. I need some water. Maybe I'll head out to the beach for a short walk. I need to figure out how to tell my family, and how to deal with this at work. I don't want to hide anymore. I want to love him openly.

I walk into the kitchen and grab a bottle of water. I'm about to head outside when I hear a voice. "I wouldn't go out there if I were you."

I startle, not realizing anyone else is awake. I turn and see Aunt

Cass sitting on the couch with a glass of wine. "You scared me. What are you doing here in the dark?"

"I had the same thought as you to go outside, but your mother and Jackson have been going at it in the hot tub for at least half an hour. It doesn't look like it's ending anytime soon."

Like a car crash on the side of the highway, I can't help but turn and take a peek. Sure enough, Mom is on top of him moving up and down. At least I only see her bare back, and things are mostly shaded by the water and the night, though his head and hands are clearly on her boobs. I quickly turn my head away. "Ugh. Gross."

"Do you really mean that?"

"No, I don't. I'm happy for her. I don't think I need to see it, but I'm happy for her."

She smiles. "Did you ever think she'd get here?"

I shake my head. "Never. I still find it hard to believe at times. Thanks for being there for her, and for pushing her. It wouldn't have happened if you didn't force her to get out of the house."

"She's my best friend, Harley. I would do anything in the world for her."

"I know you would. You're the sister she never had. She's lucky to have you. We all are."

She nods to one of the chairs. "Come sit with me. Let's talk."

I sit down across from her and wrap myself in one of the blankets. "Tell me about the person you've been sleeping with for the past three months."

I shake my head as I smile. "Why do you know this? I honestly don't understand how you always know these things."

She laughs. "It's my gift in life. I sense when people are getting laid. At least when it's good sex. And you, my girl, have been getting it very good for the past three months."

I can't help but smile. "I certainly have." I look around as I think of what to say. I don't want to lie to her. I owe her the truth. My face turns serious. "It's him."

"Him who?" I look at her for a moment and wait for it to register. I see the moment it does. "Oh. I thought he was gone for good."

"He was. He came back for me."

"I see." I can't read her face right now.

"Aunt Cass, I love him."

She brings her lips into a tight line. "I thought you might. Does he love you?"

"Yes. Are you upset with me?"

"Are you happy?"

"Yes."

"Then, no. I'm not upset with you. I've never seen you happier than you've been the past three months. How could I be upset with that?"

"That's it?"

"That's it."

"What about me not becoming a two-dollar whore?"

"The circumstances were different then, Harley. He was your professor. That was a long time ago though."

"He's one of my supervisors at the hospital now."

She blows out a breath and closes her eyes. "That's not ideal. I suppose employer/employee isn't quite as problematic as teacher/student, but it's not great. You know that."

"He's not really my employer. More of a supervisor. A mentor." She nods. "No one knows yet."

"Ride that out a little longer if you can. Make sure it's really worth the shit storm it's going to cause."

"I'm trying. He wants us to tell everyone."

"You have more to lose in the reputation department than he does. It's your call."

"I know. He's respecting my wishes." I pause for a moment. "He asked me to marry him."

She looks surprised. "Wow, Harley. Things have *really* progressed. Is that what you want?"

"Yes, but not now. Not while we're still a dirty secret. In the future. He's definitely my future though. I'm sure of that, but I told him no for now."

"You need to talk to your mother. She knows nothing and she doesn't deserve that."

"I know. I will. I didn't want to take anything away from her wedding. She's been on cloud nine the past few months. I do wish he was here with me, but this wasn't the week for it. Another time."

"You're delaying the inevitable, Harley. It needs to be soon."

I nod. "Yes, soon."

IT'S BEEN A FUN WEEK. We drank our way through Mexico. I don't think I've ever had this much to drink over the course of a week in my entire life.

My new brothers are party animals. Well, Trevor is. He and Reagan together are a recipe for disaster. I think we've all had to pray to the porcelain Gods at least three or four nights this week. Yet, it hasn't slowed us down at all.

Today was our last full day, and the wedding day. Mom was a stunning bride. She was genuinely glowing the entire day. Jackson had a smile from ear to ear that didn't waiver for one minute. The rest of us leave tomorrow, but Mom and Jackson are staying for another week.

It's nighttime and I'm sitting outside with my sisters, Trevor,

Hayden, and Payton. They really have become brothers to us. We all get along so well.

The six of us were the bridal party, with Trevor being the self-appointed flower girl. He made everyone laugh as he danced down the aisle, spreading flower petals everywhere.

We all have drinks and have been chatting and laughing for over an hour. Mom and Jackson disappeared hours ago. I don't want to know what's going on in that room tonight.

Reagan loves using these opportunities to get information out of people. "Okay, so hottest place you've ever had sex. Payton, you go first."

He smiles as he looks over his shoulder. He's likely looking for Kylie. She's about six months pregnant and went to bed early. "Well, we had sex on top of the Eiffel Tower during our Honeymoon."

Trevor high fives him. "Bro, I didn't think you had it in you."

"There's a lot you don't know about me, little brother." He throws a smirk Trevor's way. "It was pretty hot. We almost got caught but didn't. You can see all of Paris from there. It's amazing."

Reagan looks at me. "Harley?"

There's zero chance of me saying anything about all the various rooms at the hospital. I don't think there are many places left we haven't had sex at the hospital. Reagan knows what I'm thinking and smiles in challenge. "I guess I'd have to say the roof of Club Liberty."

The boys all laugh. Trevor fist pumps me. "That's actually kind of hot."

I smirk at him and raise my eyebrows. "It was *very* hot. I can assure you of that. I highly recommend it."

Reagan nods toward Hayden. "You're up."

"Ummm..."

"Hayden's a virgin." Trevor laughs.

Hayden throws a beer can at Trevor. "I am not, you asshole." Hayden gives me a sheepish grin. I have no idea why. "It was... well..it was in a supply closet at the hospital."

Trevor and I at the same time yell, "What?"

"Yep."

I'm shocked. "With whom?"

He smiles. "I'm a gentleman, Harley. I would never tell you that."

I smile back at him. He's adorable. But I'm going to find out who.

Reagan nods toward Skylar. "You wouldn't think it unless you've done it, but the barn a few weeks ago was crazy hot. It may have just been the circumstances of following him and how great the sex was, but getting down and dirty in the hay was hot." We all laugh.

Reagan wiggles her eyebrows. "Ride 'em cowgirl?"

Skylar smirks. "Yes, I did."

Reagan looks deep in thought. "Hmm. I've definitely had sex in some unusual places, but I think the hottest was in college when David and I snuck into the dean's office and had sex on his desk. The possibility of getting caught by the head of our school made it all the hotter."

Skylar scrunches up her nose. "Ugh. I was in that office last week. I hope I didn't touch the desk."

Reagan looks at her deadpan. "Trust me, Skylar, there are tons of surfaces you've touched that I've had sex on." She gives a devious smile, and then turns to Trevor. "Okay Trevor. I'm equally excited and afraid to find out your answer."

He thinks for a moment. "Well, I did have sex on a ride at Disney World, but I don't think it was the hottest. It was kind of uncomfortable. I think the hottest was in the lifeguard tower on the beach at the main hotel."

Reagan looks at him in surprise. "As in here? As in this week?" Trevor gives a smile and nod in the affirmative. "With whom?"

"Like Hayden, I'm a gentleman and would never kiss and tell."

Hayden throws him an elbow. "You're no gentleman. Does the girl whose eye you came in think you're a gentleman?"

"I took her to the hospital, didn't I?

We all laugh.

CHAPTER FOURTEEN

THE PRESENT

HARLEY

I've returned from Mexico convinced more than ever that Brody is the one for me, and we need to come up with a plan to let everyone know. I suppose that starts with my family, especially Mom.

I feel terrible keeping this secret from her. While I never wanted to burden her when she was in a bad place herself, she's in a great place now and I need to confide in her. She's going to be hurt that she's just learning of us now, but I need to peel off the band-aid. The longer this drags on, the worse it is.

She's gone for another week in Mexico, and then we have Skylar's college graduation just after that. Maybe once the celebration dies down, it'll be the right time.

I pass Dr. McCrevis in the hallway. He stops to talk to me.

"Dr. Lawrence, we have a group of first year medical school students coming through today. Considering the fact that they attend to your alma mater, I volunteered you to talk to them for a bit. Maybe you can show them around. Do you mind?"

"Of course not. I'd be happy to. My brother is in that class. I was hoping I'd get to show him around."

"Wonderful. They'll be up here in about twenty minutes or so. Thank you for doing this."

I smile at him. "My pleasure."

About a half an hour later, the group makes their way up to the surgical floor. I immediately find Hayden and hug him. "Hey baby bro. How's it going?"

He looks embarrassed. "Hey Harley. I thought I might see you."

"Yes, they asked me to show you guys around." I gather the group. "Hi everyone. I'm Dr. Lawrence. I went to the same school as you. I graduated last year. I'm a first-year surgical resident here now, and the very fortunate older sister of this handsome devil here." Hayden puts his head down in embarrassment.

"I'm going to give you guys a tour of the surgical floor. Feel free to ask any questions. Follow me." I motion for them to follow.

We start walking down the hallway. I hear a few students ask Hayden about being related to me. He's all of a sudden become a very popular student. It makes me smile.

We get to the administrative area, and I introduce the group to everyone. I make sure to introduce Hayden to Jess, since I know she was anxious to meet him. As soon as I do, Jess looks at me with terror in her eyes. "I know Hayden. I didn't realize that he's your brother. He's the one you previously mentioned?" I nod.

She turns back to him. "Good to see you, Hayden."

Hayden turns fifty shades of red. "Good to see you too,

Jessica." As we turn to leave, I catch them briefly touching hands out of the corner of my eye.

I show the group several operating rooms and tell them about some of the special surgeries we perform up here. At some point, when the opportunity arises, I link my arm with Hayden's. "Anything you want to tell me about you and Jess?"

"Umm...nope."

I'm smirking now. "Have you by chance spent any time with Jess in a hospital supply closet?"

He turns red again as he looks at me. "Harley, I told you that a gentleman doesn't kiss and tell."

"But you could have said no. I think I have my answer." He rolls his eyes and I giggle. "If it matters, I think you two are so cute together. I love her. She's fantastic. And obviously I love my baby brother. It's a perfect match."

"Please don't tell Trevor. I may introduce her to the family in a few weeks, but for now, I don't need him in my business."

"Don't worry. Your secret is safe with me."

He nods in appreciation. "She said that you previously mentioned me. What did you say?"

"Well, she met Trevor when he was in here for his friend's special eye treatment." We both laugh at that memory. "I told her that Trevor's twin brother is much sweeter and equally as good looking. That you're a great catch. Looks like she already caught you though." I giggle again. He smiles in triumph.

"Thank you for saying that."

"I meant it, Hayden. You're kind, smart, and extremely attractive. Anyone would be lucky to have you." I don't know why he has such little self-confidence. It's such a contrast to Trevor.

"Thanks Harley."

After I finish the tour and say my goodbyes, I head to the break room to grab a quick cup of coffee before heading to the lab.

As I'm leaving, Dr. Waters walks in. He grabs my arm unnecessarily hard. "Hey Harley."

I pull my arm away. "I'm just headed to the lab. I'll see you later."

"Harley, I'm very sad that I haven't gotten any time alone with you. That's going to change at some point. How would you like to scrub into my surgery tomorrow? We can meet tonight and review the file along with a few surgical procedures."

"Sorry, I can't. I'm with Dr. Powers tomorrow."

"Does she have a surgery? I didn't see anything on the board."

"No, she's going to teach me a few of the techniques she learned at her conference last week."

"Wouldn't you rather scrub into a surgery?"

"I know that I want to go into cardiothoracic surgery, so I think my time is best spent with her. That, and I know she already booked time for me in her schedule. Thanks anyway."

"I have another surgery the day after. How about that?"

"I'm scrubbing into one of Dr. Cooper's surgeries that day."

"Yes, I've noticed that you scrub in for an awful lot of his surgeries."

"I appreciate the opportunities he gives me."

"Earned, no doubt."

"I work my ass off. That's how you earn opportunities." I give him my best fake smile. "Have a good day."

I turn to leave, but he grabs my arm again. "Our time will come, Harley. Don't you worry your pretty little head."

I pull away and leave. I can't stand that guy. I have tears welling in my eyes as I round the corner, straight into Brody. He takes one look at me and knows that I'm upset. He pulls me into a closet. He rubs his hand down my cheek. "What's wrong?"

I look down. "Nothing. Just the normal dose of weekly harassment from Dr. Waters."

He sighs. "Please let me report him. It's out of control."

"No, it's not worth it. He's been doing this to me for years. He's mostly harmless. I think he just likes to get under my skin and ruffle my feathers. I won't give him the satisfaction of knowing that he's succeeded. It's my word against his anyway. I just want to keep my head down an learn everything I can. In the next few months, I'll pick my specialty and work solely with Dr. Powers. I need to stick it out until then."

"How about he and I have a chat?" I shake my head. "I can only take so much of this, Harley. One day I'm going to punch him, and it will give me great pleasure to watch him go down."

"Please don't. Then he'll know something is going on between us. I'm pretty sure he already suspects it."

"How about I tell the administration of lewd comments he's made about you? I can't imagine they'd be too happy about that."

I didn't know that. "Like what?"

"He's made a few comments to me through the years about your body and your tight ass."

I take his hands and place them on my ass. "This tight ass is yours and only yours." I pull his face to mine and kiss him.

He nibbles at my lips. "I wasn't aware that your ass is available to me. Good to know. I plan to take advantage of that very soon." He gives me a squeeze and another kiss.

I look up at his gorgeous blue eyes and run my fingers over his stubble. "I *really* missed you last week."

"I missed you too." We kiss again, but as it gets more intense, he breaks away and grunts. "I have to stop. I'm headed into surgery. Now I have to do it with a boner."

I smile up at him. "It wouldn't be the first time, Dr. Cooper."

"No, it wouldn't. It's a hazard of working with the sexiest woman in the world." He kisses me one last time before we exit that closet. Of course, when we do, Dr. Waters is walking by.

He gives us a fake smile. "What a surprise. The two of you coming out of a closet together."

"We don't have time for your nonsense, Greg. We are allowed to need supplies. Dr. Lawrence, after you." He motions for me to walk ahead of him, and I do.

THE PAST FEW weeks have flown by. I've worked hard and played with Brody equally as hard. We're so happy in our private love bubble. I don't want it to burst, but it seems inevitable. I feel like it's the calm before the storm.

I wake up one morning enveloped in warmth. Brody's naked body is holding mine close to his. I love the way he feels and smells. It gives me such a sense of contentment. I've never had this before. I know that it's exactly where I belong, and I'm finally willing to fight for it.

He's fast asleep on his back, and my front is on top of his. His arms are around me. I look up at his face. He's so damn handsome. I've honestly never seen a more beautiful man than Brody Cooper.

My attraction to him can best be described as feverish. My desire for him is unquenchable. I always want more.

I reach up and softly run my fingers through his chin dimple. I can't help myself.

He wakes me up at least one morning a week with his head between my legs. I want to return the favor. I kiss my way down his God-like body until I slide under the covers and get to my target.

Despite him being fast asleep, it's somehow already rock hard and ready to go. I take him in my hand and give him a nice, long, slow lick. He stirs a bit but is still sleeping.

I take him in my mouth and suck hard. His eyes pop open as he looks down. He runs his long fingers through my hair and smiles. I stop for a moment and look up at him. He playfully pushes my head back down. "Don't stop, keep going. It feels great." I get back to work and take care of business.

When I'm done, I try to get up to shower, but he grabs me and pins me on my back. "It's your turn."

"It's a very tempting offer, but I need to go."

"I thought you were off today."

He's about to freak out. "I am, but I have Skylar's graduation."

"What? Why didn't you tell me? I would've taken off."

"Brody, I need to tell my mother about us before you start coming around."

"You still haven't told her?"

I sigh. "No. I'm sorry. I just haven't found the right time." He's pouting.

"Brody, it's going to be a big a deal. I couldn't bring you to the wedding because that was Mom's time in the sun. I can't bring you today because it's Skylar's. I was thinking about it. Jackson and Mom are having a Memorial Day barbecue. That's probably a good time for them to meet you. It's just a few weeks away. Does that work?"

Now he's smiling. "Yes. I think I have a surgery that day, but I should be done by mid-afternoon."

"Perfect. I'll make sure to talk about it with her before then and tell her that you're coming. Now I need you to let me go so I can shower."

He pulls me back down onto my back. "No. I crave your sweet taste. I can make you come in under two minutes." And he does.

WE WATCH Skylar walk at her graduation. Mom is crying. I'm just relieved that they're happy tears.

After the ceremony. Mom moves up through the crowds to take pictures of Skylar and her friends. Reagan and I run into one of Dad's old high-school friends. He kisses Reagan and then me on the cheek. Reagan gets distracted talking to someone else, so I'm stuck with him on my own. "Hey there, Harley. I guess it's Dr. Lawrence now?"

"It is. Hi Nelson, how are you?"

"I'm okay."

"Did Julian graduate today?"

"He did. He's taking pictures with his mom right now. We have to rotate our photo opportunities. God forbid we should do it together."

That's a shame. Now it's kind of awkward. "Well, congratulations to Julian. Please tell him that we said hello."

"I will. Is your mother here?"

"Yes, she and Jackson moved up to get a few pictures of Skylar with her friends. We're hanging back waiting for them to finish."

"Oh, she's still with Jackson."

"Umm...yes. They got married a few weeks ago." I'd assume he'd know this.

He looks like his head is going to explode. What's that about? "Oh right. I think I saw them get engaged on the news."

I laugh. "Yep, that was them."

"Have fun celebrating Skylar. Tell your mother that I said hello."

"Will do."

Reagan turns and looks at me. "That was strange, right?"

"Totally."

Just then Aunt Cass comes up to us. "Was that Nelson?"

"Yes, and he was acting weird."

"He is weird. I can't stand him. I never understood why your mother used to hang out with him."

"Now that you say it, she's completely stopped seeing all of those guys. She used to watch football with them every Monday night. Do you know why? Is it because of Jackson?"

"No, it's because Nelson professed his undying love to her, so it got a little awkward."

Reagan and I look at one another in surprise. "Really? When did that happen? We had no clue."

"It was shortly after she started seeing Jackson. Nelson went all caveman on her when she told him about Jackson. He told her he was in love with her, and some nonsense about her belonging with him. She was pretty upset about it, but I think Jackson helped her through it."

"Jackson is a God send. She never said anything to us about it."

"She's a mom. Her job is to protect you from the bad. And yes, Jackson is a Godsend."

She looks around. "By the way, your mother asked me if you're seeing someone. Harley, you're clearly a changed person over the past several months. It's obvious even to people without a sixth sense."

"You mean a sixth sense?"

"No, I mean a sexth sense. I have a keen and intuitive sense for sex. It's my sexth sense."

"You're ridiculous."

"Whatever. Anyway, she knows something's up. I'm really not comfortable lying to her. I need you to tell her."

"I was planning to talk to her later today. I'm inviting Brody to meet everyone on Memorial Day at their party."

"Finally. I can't handle this anymore. I don't keep secrets from your mother, Harley. She's the healthiest relationship I have in my life, and I can no longer manage keeping this from her."

"I'm telling her. I promise."

We're having lunch to celebrate Skylar. I'm next to Mom and she's partially distracted by Skylar. This is the perfect time to slip it in. "Hey Mom?"

She turns to me. "Yes, doll."

"I'm sort of seeing someone. Can he come on Memorial Day to your pool party so that I can introduce him to you?"

She has a big smile. "Of course. How did you meet him?"

"He's a doctor at the hospital too."

"That's fantastic. I'm happy for you. I was wondering if you were seeing someone. I thought you might be."

"Yep, I am. You'll meet him then."

"Great."

I get very ugly looks from Aunt Cass and Reagan. Yes, I know. I'm a chicken.

CHAPTER FIFTEEN

THE PRESENT

TREVOR

My friends James and Anthony come with me to Dad and Darian's house for a Memorial Dad barbecue and pool party. We walk in and don't see anyone else, but as we get deeper into the house, we can hear loud music by the pool.

We walk outside to the pool deck area. Laying on lounge chairs in bikinis are Harley, Reagan, Skylar, Darian, and Cassandra.

James and Anthony stare with their mouths wide open. James looks at me. "Dude, are we at the Playboy Mansion?" I laugh. "Who are these goddesses?"

I point to them. "Those three are my stepsisters, that's my step mom, and that's her best friend."

Anthony slaps my back. "Trevor, you are the luckiest man on the planet."

I shake my head. "No, I'm not. I'm now related to those four. That makes me the unluckiest man on the planet."

James laughs. "I guess you're right. More for us."

Just then, Dad comes out and smacks me on the back of my head. "Stop gawking. All three of you look pathetic." He says this as he's staring at Darian with drool practically coming out of his mouth.

I roll my eyes. "Yeah, Dad, we're the pathetic ones."

He goes over to Darian and hands her some clear drink with a lot of limes. He bends down to peck her on the lips, but she grabs his head and pulls him into an open-mouthed kiss. He stands up looking a little dazed. He discreetly adjusts himself. Ugh. Gross. He catches me staring and gives me the stink eye.

He looks back down at her. "I think you need some more lotion, sugar."

"I just put some on, Jackson."

"I'm pretty sure you need more." He smiles at her as he wiggles his way in behind her and straddles her chair. He shamelessly rubs her entire body with lotion, reaching places that clearly don't need any. He turns to me and winks. Asshole.

James and Anthony don't miss it. Anthony looks at me. "Your stepmom is a MILF."

"I'm more than aware of that."

"Her body is ridiculous. Those tits."

"I'm also aware of those."

"It clearly runs in the family. Introduce us to your stepsisters."

"Okay, but to be clear, you have zero chance with them.

They get hit on about a hundred times a day. I've witnessed it. I promise you that they're immune to your nonexistent charms."

I raise the volume of my voice. "Hey sexy ladies." I say that staring directly at Cassandra. She smiles at me without even needing to look my way.

They all pull down their sunglasses. Skylar sits up. "Hey Trevor. We didn't hear you come in. How are you?"

"I'm good. These are my friends James and Anthony." Everyone makes the appropriate introductions.

We sit down in our own chairs and have a few drinks. Payton and Kylie come at some point, followed shortly thereafter by Hayden.

He walks out to the pool area hand in hand with a really cute girl. She's a petite brunette, with big chocolate brown eyes. I just about fall out of my chair at the sight. I don't think I've ever really seen him with a girl. Maybe some high-school puppy love, but that's it.

"Hey guys. Sorry I'm late. I want you to meet Jessica. She can only stay for a little bit because she has a shift at the hospital, but I wanted to bring her by to meet everyone. Jess, this is my dad, Jackson, my stepmom, Darian, her friend, Cassandra, my brother, Payton and his wife Kylie, my other brother, Trevor, his friends James and Anthony, and my stepsisters Skylar and Reagan. Of course, you know Harley."

"Hi everyone, nice to meet you. Good to see you again, Trevor and Payton. Good to see you too, Dr. Lawrence."

"Jess, call me Harley when we're not in the hospital."

"Will do. Thanks."

We sit around drinking, eating, chatting, and swimming all afternoon. Everyone is getting along. James and Anthony take their swings with the girls but are immediately shot down. Jessica takes off after a little while, as do James and Anthony.

At some point I see Cassandra go inside. I quickly follow her in. She's got her back to me at the sink. She looks so damn hot in that bikini. She has an amazing body, particularly her butt.

I sneak up behind her and reach my hands out to give her ass a nice, long squeeze. She startles for a moment but doesn't turn. "Trevor, not here." She wiggles her ass onto my dick anyway.

"How'd you know it was me?"

"The options of men here that would grab my ass are exactly one. That and I certainly know the feel of your big hands at this point."

I give her another squeeze. "You look edible in this bikini. I want to bend you over right here." I bite her neck and she giggles.

She peeks over her shoulder to the pool area, and when she doesn't see anyone looking this way, she turns around, grabs my face, and gives me a red-hot kiss. She gives my cock a little grab and rub too. "There, that will have to satisfy you for a while. You can come over again later tonight if you want to finish this."

I point down to my now rock-solid dick. "Does this look like I'm currently satisfied?" She laughs.

HARLEY

I get a text from Brody that he's finished with his surgery and is on his way over. I'm nervous for him to meet my family, especially Mom.

I walk inside toward the front door when I know he's about to arrive. I open the door as soon as I see his car.

He's walking toward me looking sexy as hell in a low hung bathing suit, and a tight t-shirt stretched across his muscles. I'm practically drooling. He stops in front of me and looks me up and down. "Jesus Christ, how about some warning if you're going to greet a guy looking like that. I'm going to meet your family with a huge boner."

I laugh and reach up to kiss him hello. When I pull away, he points down. "That did not help matters."

"If you behave, I promise to take care of that later."

"Still not helping." We both laugh as we walk through the house toward the pool area. "Wow, your mother has a really nice house.

"Thanks. My stepdad designed it. It's beautiful. I love it here."

I give him a look. "One last warning. My family has no filter and no boundaries whatsoever. My sister Reagan, stepbrother Trevor, and Aunt Cass being the worst. Please be prepared."

"I can handle it. I've already met Reagan. How bad can it be?" He has no clue.

"Oh, and my sisters and Aunt Cass are the only ones who know our whole history. No one else knows everything."

"You didn't tell your mother everything?" I shake my head and he sighs in frustration. "I thought you were telling her everything. We're not doing anything wrong. I don't know why you feel this is necessary."

"Please just respect my wishes. I have my reasons." He reluctantly nods. We head out back hand in hand.

I haven't introduced a boyfriend to my family in over five years, and certainly not since our family doubled in size with the Knight crew. "Everyone, this is Brody Cooper. Brody, this is everyone."

I go through all of the introductions. When I introduce Reagan and Skylar, Brody says something about it being nice to see them again. I see Mom turn her head, not realizing they had met.

I save Mom for last. "This is my mom, Darian Lawrence Knight."

He gives her a warm hug. "It's so nice to finally meet you, Mrs. Knight." After he pulls back, he smiles. "Wow, you and Harley really do resemble each other. It's remarkable."

She smiles at him. "Thank you, Brody. I certainly take that as a compliment. And please, call me Darian."

I notice Reagan checking him out in that bathing suit and the tight shirt. "Damn sis. You snagged yourself a full-fledged hottie. Well done." Brody laughs. I give him the *I told you so* look.

Trevor crosses his arms. "Not as hot as me though, right?"

Reagan shoos him away, but Aunt Cass strokes his ego by reassuring him of his hotness. The two of them have a strange relationship that I'd rather know nothing about.

I think maybe the safest place for us is in the pool. "Brody, it's hot out here. Why don't we jump into the pool?"

"Okay." He puts his bag down and takes off his shirt. Even though I've seen it nearly every day for the past four months, I never get used to how hot his body is.

Aunt Cass comes by and wipes my chin. "You have some drool."

"Do you blame me?"

"Nope."

I grab us two drinks, and we get in the pool. He wraps his arms around me as we sit in the corner. We talk as he aimlessly moves his fingers all over my body and kisses my shoulders and neck.

I try to pull away, but he tightens his grip. I turn to him. "Stop it. Not in front of my family."

He won't let me move. "No. I'm really fucking sick of always having to hide my feelings for you. Everyone here knows we're together. I will touch you when I want to, where I want to." He turns my head so that our eyes meet. "And I *always* want to touch you, Harley." He takes my lips in a kiss.

Trevor yells out, "Get a room." We break the kiss and smile.

Mom and Jackson are cuddled up on a chair, fondling each other, but Aunt Cass slips into the pool, and swims over to us. Brody has his arms wrapped around me. I go to move away, but he squeezes me close. I look at her. "Hey Aunt Cass."

"Hey." She wastes no time as she looks at Brody. "So, Brody, how do you see the playing out?" She's never been one for mindless chit chat. I suppose this conversation was unavoidable.

"How do you mean, Cassandra?"

"I mean the shitstorm that will head Harley's way when news of your relationship breaks at the hospital."

"My preference is to head it off. I'd rather go to HR and the administrative team to inform them that we're in a serious relationship. I personally think it would be worse if it came out any differently. It'll look like we're trying to hide things. But Harley is calling the shots right now, and she wants us to remain a secret."

"She has more to lose than you."

"I'm not sure that I agree with that, but regardless, I would never want this to negatively impact her."

She stares at him. "It's unavoidable."

I can tell that Brody's getting angry. "What is it you'd like to hear from me, Cassandra? I love her. I want to spend my life with her. Are you suggesting I walk away from her? I won't do that. I'll do everything in my power to protect her, but I won't walk away from her. We did that before, and we were both miserable. If there's something else you'd like me to say or do right now, why don't you just spit it out."

Aunt Cass turns to me. "I like his backbone."

She sighs. "Look you two, there's a storm brewing and it's headed your way. We'll see what you're made of when it's time to weather it. Both as individuals and as a couple."

She gives Brody a long, intimidating stare. "Brody, Harley is like a daughter to me. She and her sisters are the closest thing I will ever have to my own children. If you fuck her over, or hurt her in any way, I'll hunt you down and kill you." She gives him a big smile. "Enjoy your day." She swims away.

He looks down at me. "You family is kind of intense, and kind of crazy."

I laugh. "I told you so."

We have a little fun after that. Trevor gets a volleyball game going and we have a blast.

Brody is a great athlete, but Mom's competitiveness wins out in the end. He potentially let her team win to keep her happy.

Jackson has been cooking on the grill for the past hour. We sit down at the outdoor table to start eating.

Mom turns to Brody. "So, Brody, I understand you work at Pennsylvania Hospital as well. Is that where you two met?"

Brody clearly doesn't know how to respond, not wanting to lie, so I respond for him. "Yeah, Mom. I thought I told you this already. We kind of met once or twice before, given my time working at the hospital during medical school, but we didn't start dating until the past few months." Aunt Cass gives me a death stare.

"Oh, I don't recall you telling me that. Does the hospital have a policy against attendings and residents dating? I assume Brody is an attending." Mom doesn't miss a thing.

"He is. It's not a precise policy, Mom. More like discouraged. We're not remotely flaunting it at the hospital for the time being. We're keeping it private." She nods her head and gives me a *we'll discuss this later* look.

"Darian, please know that any unfavorable reaction will be directed my way, not Harley's. Harley's doing nothing wrong. I'm the attending. Any and all consequences of our actions will be mine. I would never let anything jeopardize her career." I squeeze his hand in thanks, but Mom still doesn't look satisfied.

Trevor breaks the tension. "So, do you get it on in the on-call rooms?" Brody starts coughing. Trevor and Reagan laugh while high fiving. "I told you, Hayden. It's exactly like Grey's Anatomy."

Jackson, always the voice of reason, puts an end to Trevor's antics. "Trevor, that's enough. Excuse my six-year-old son, Brody. Why don't you tell us a little about where you grew up. I understand it was out west. I grew up out west as well, in Colorado."

Brody smiles at Jackson. "I love Colorado. We used to vacation there. I grew up in Southern California. The Huntington Beach area. My Dad still lives there. He got remarried a few years ago. He and his wife live right on the beach."

Mom asks, "Is your mother still out there?"

"She actually passed when I was a teenager."

"I'm sorry to hear that."

"Thank you."

Trevor asks, "Do you surf?"

"I do. I own a place now at the bea..." He smiles at me. "...

shore so that I can keep up with surfing now and then. Though the waves here aren't quite the same as Huntington Beach."

Mom looks at me. "Harley, have you been to his shore house?"

"I have. It's beautiful. You know I love it down there."

She looks at Brody. "How long have you had the place?" She's fishing for information. She knows my story doesn't quite make sense.

"I settled at the end of December when I moved back to the area. I told Harley this when I bought it, but you're all more than welcome down there. I bought it with family in mind. It has plenty of space." Mom gives me a look. She knows something is off. Why does she have to be so damn smart?

Trevor smiles. "Sweet. I may take you up on that. I love it down there too. What else do you do for fun?"

"I'm fairly athletic, so anything along those lines when I can find the time. Frankly, my job keeps me busy, but I love to go dancing with Harley." He winks at me. Reagan and Skylar smile.

Trevor laughs. "I didn't realize that Harley ever goes out. What's your favorite spot?"

"I guess we like Club Liberty, right Harley?" He winks again. This time Reagan, Skylar, Payton, Trevor, and Hayden all burst out laughing, now knowing exactly who was there with me for my hot roof sex.

Jackson looks at them like they're crazy. "What's so funny about that?"

Trevor grins. "Nothing, Dad. We've heard the roof there is an especially nice spot."

Brody nearly spits out his food. Aunt Cass has now caught on and she's trying to contain her smile. Jackson looks at Mom. "Darian, I feel like we're the only two missing something here."

Mom responds to him but is looking right at me. "It sure does,

Jackson. We're most definitely missing a few things here. We'll figure them out soon though. Don't worry." I gulp.

The rest of the meal is uneventful. It's the normal Knight-Lawrence banter.

Brody and I are about to leave, but before we do, Mom pulls me aside. "Which day this week should I come and meet you for lunch? I think we have some things to discuss."

I give Aunt Cass a look, and Mom picks up on it. She turns to Aunt Cass. "Cassandra, do you know what's going on with my daughter and her bullshit story?"

"She's an adult, Dare. This is her life and her story to tell. Not mine."

Mom turns back to me. "Harley. Which day shall Aunt Cass and I meet you for lunch? I know she'll make herself available." Aunt Cass nods.

I put my head down. "Friday." I'm trying to buy as much time as possible. I know this conversation is going to be a nightmare. I should've told her everything before it came to this.

CHAPTER SIXTEEN

THE PRESENT

HARLEY

Friday comes around quickly. I'm scrubbing in early this morning on a coronary artery bypass graft with Dr. Powers. You take a blood vessel from another part of the body and attach it to the coronary artery when there's a blockage. It allows for a new open passage to the heart.

It's a common procedure for her, and I've watched her perform it from the gallery above about five or six times, but it's my first time being in the room for one.

I'm extremely excited about it. I've probably "performed" the procedure a thousand times in the lab, but this is the first time I'll see it up close and on a real person. Brody said he'd watch from the gallery when his surgery is over.

We're about three hours into the surgery, and I see Dr. Powers stretching her hand and then making a fist, back and forth. I look up at her. She shakes her head. "Just some cramping. I need a minute."

She manipulates her hand in all directions, but after a few minutes, she doesn't seem to be any better. "Can someone please page Dr. Callahan." He's another cardiothoracic surgeon at the hospital.

A nurse responds. "He's not in the hospital today, but I'm sure he can get here in about thirty minutes or so." Just then, the patient's heart rate becomes erratic.

Dr. Powers yells for the nurse to immediately page Dr. McCrevis. She turns to me. "Harley, you're going to have to complete this. At least until we can get Dr. McCrevis in here. I'll talk you through it."

I nod. My own heartbeat is off the charts. I know what to do, but having her talk me through it helps. Before I know it, an hour has passed, and I've completed the entire procedure on my own. The patient is closed, and all of his vital signs are normal.

Dr. Powers looks at me proudly. "You did it, Harley. Congratulations." I give her a huge smile. I don't think I've ever been this happy in my entire life.

Just then, Dr. McCrevis walks in. "Sorry Liz, I was in surgery. Tell me what you need."

"I don't need anything now, Phil. Dr. Lawrence performed the procedure. Flawlessly at that." I'm now grinning from ear to ear, though otherwise trying to play it cool.

He looks at me and holds out his hands. "Congratulations, Dr. Lawrence. That's quite impressive."

"Thank you. I'm just thrilled to have been able to help." I leave to scrub out of the surgery.

There's only one person I want to see right now. I can't wait to tell him and share my happiness with him. I didn't see him in the gallery, but I was so focused, I'm not sure that I noticed anything outside of what I was doing.

I quickly scrub my hands and run out of the O.R. I see Brody turning the corner. He has a huge smile. "Congratulations, Dr. Lawrence. I heard the good news."

I don't know what comes over me. Maybe it's the adrenaline rush or the pure euphoria of the moment. Perhaps it's the fact that I'm in love with him and want to share this moment with him. Without thinking of anything else in the world, I run to him and leap into his arms.

I wrap my legs and arms around him and kiss his lips. It's not a peck either. It's a real, sensual kiss. He tightens his arms and I grab onto his hair, as I let the utter bliss wash over me.

As I pull away, I still have a big smile, but that smile quickly fades when I see his face. He whispers, "Harley, we have company." He motions behind me.

I turn my head and see Dr. McCrevis and Dr. Powers standing there. Both look completely shocked at the display in front of them.

I turn back to Brody and close my eyes. This cannot be happening.

I unwrap my legs. He places my feet back on the ground. He looks at me with both love and compassion, knowing this is the moment I've feared.

Dr. McCrevis clears his throat. "Dr. Cooper, Dr. Lawrence, a word in my office please." We both nod and follow him in silence to his office.

Just before we enter, Brody whispers into my ear. "I love you. We're in this together."

We enter the office and Dr. McCrevis closes the door. We sit down in the chairs in front of his desk.

He moves to his side of the desk and sits. He briefly closes his eyes and takes a breath. He then waves his finger between the two of us. "How long has this been going on?"

Brody answers, "About five months."

"So, the entire time that you've been back?" Brody nods. Dr. McCrevis twists his lips. "Interesting. Did anything go on while she was in medical school?"

Brody looks at me. I put my head down and sigh. This is the moment I've been fearing for nearly four years. This is the moment that I'm going to lose everything I've worked my entire life to achieve.

I lift my head back up and answer for him. "Yes, it did."

Dr. McCrevis holds his lips in a straight line. He looks at me. "Dr. Lawrence, you are an excellent doctor, and have shown signs of becoming an exceptional surgeon in the making. Unfortunately, I have a duty to report this to the Medical Board. I know that Dr. Cooper was a professor of yours, and he controlled some of your grades. They'll need to investigate the propriety of those grades. Do you understand what I'm saying?"

I nod. "I do."

I can see Brody getting angry. "Phil, this is complete bullshit. She's obviously highly intelligent. Do you honestly think she wasn't deserving of top grades?"

He shakes his head. "I have no doubt that she was deserving of her grades, but it's not my call to make. I risk the hospital's accreditation and my own medical license if I don't report this. Truth be told, Dr. Waters has expressed concern over the nature of your relationship, but I told him that I saw nothing inappropriate. Clearly, he was right."

Brody pounds his fist on the desk. "Greg Waters is a piece of shit who has wanted and harassed Harley for years. He can't manage the rejection. He's out to get her."

"Brody, don't lash out. It won't help her. Frankly, Greg Waters doesn't have anything to do with this."

"He has *everything* to do with this, Phil. Everyone turns a blind eye to his overt harassment of women, yet the integrity of an intelligent woman like Harley is being brought into question, and her entire career is in jeopardy, all for her involvement in a *consensual* relationship."

Brody's furious. He points his finger at Dr. McCrevis. "I'm telling you, Phil, if she so much has one mark on her record, I am resigning. Good luck maintaining a reputable neurosurgery department with me gone, Greg at the helm, and the stink of the Mancini debacle still fresh."

I grab his arm. "Brody, stop. We knew in the back of our minds that this day was always coming. As soon as our relationship started, we knew. It was always only a matter of time. It was never an if, it was a when. Don't get angry with him. He's just doing his job. It's not his fault. It's ours. Ultimately, it's mine. It's time for me to face the music and let the chips fall where they may."

Brody takes my hand and kisses it, not caring at all that Dr. McCrevis is right in front of us. "I'm so sorry, Harley. You don't deserve this." He rubs my cheek and I lean into it, letting him comfort me.

Dr. McCrevis clears his throat, breaking our moment. "Dr. Lawrence, you're suspended pending the outcome of a hearing of the Medical Board. Dr. Cooper, I'll have to talk to the hospital administration, but you'll likely receive some sort of letter of reprimand in you file for having an intimate relationship with someone in your charge, and failing to report it to HR."

"That's it? I get a stupid, meaningless letter, and her entire career hangs in the balance. What a bunch of sexist bullshit." He stands and grabs my hand. "Let's get the fuck out of here, Harley."

He turns his head to Dr. McCrevis one last time. "I'll be back when Harley is welcome back. Not a minute before then."

We start toward the door when Dr. McCrevis interrupts. "I'm sorry, Harley. I certainly take no pleasure in this. You're one of the brightest minds we have here. The good news is that the Board will want to deal with it quickly. It's Friday, so it won't happen this week, but likely next week. You should think through your testimony over the weekend. Brody, you'll be asked to testify as well."

We walk out in stoic silence, but as soon as we get to the car, the dam breaks. I sob, while he holds me, whispering reassurances and apologies in my ear.

After about twenty minutes of crying, I wipe away my tears. "I have lunch with Mom. I need to fill her in on *everything*. She going to go all lawyer apeshit on this, but I think I need her help."

He nods. "I'll come with you."

I shake my head. "No. Absolutely not. She doesn't know the whole story. She's going to blame you when she hears it. I have to finally tell her everything. I've kept so much from her the past few years. It's going to be rough. I don't want you there. I need this time alone with her."

I WALK INTO LUNCH. I had texted ahead that I'd be a few minutes late, so they're waiting for me at the table when I walk in.

As soon as I see them, the dam breaks again. Aunt Cass mutters, "Shit," under her breath.

She looks at me. "The storm arrive?" I nod.

Mom is clearly struggling with whether to be pissed for being in the dark, or compassionate that her daughter is in tears. In the end, she moves over next to me and wraps her arms around me. She lets me cry for just a few minutes before she wipes my tears and tells me it's time to talk. I know she's right.

I tell her the whole story, from the rooftop to the year of medical school, to the end of our relationship, to the rekindling of it, through to the events of this morning. I leave nothing out.

Her head is in her hands. "Jesus, Harley. I can't believe you of all people slept with your professor."

I'm on the verge of tears again. "What's that supposed to mean?"

"It means you're too damn smart to make mistakes like this. You've always been so level-headed. You've never had an irresponsible moment in your entire life. I don't know how you got so out of control?"

The tears start to stream down my cheeks. Her blatant disappointment in me is my biggest fear coming to life. "I didn't know he was my professor when I slept with him. I was a mess at the time. Dad had just died, and you wouldn't even get out of bed."

I wipe my tears and straighten my back. "For once in my life, I did something out of character, and a little reckless. I'm not perfect, Mom. But I won't say it was a mistake. It wasn't a mistake."

She shakes her head in anger. "You're wrong. It was a huge mistake. Maybe the biggest of your life. It could cost you everything."

I'm getting mad. I take a minute to collect myself before responding to her. I refuse to look at Brody as a mistake. "Mom, I met the love of my life that night. I acknowledge that the circumstances are horrific, but I won't say it was a mistake, no matter the outcome. I never once slept with him during the time I knew he was my professor. And let me assure you, it was the hardest thing I've ever had to do."

"Why wouldn't you have just immediately transferred out of his class? That's the part I don't get."

"I had some issues with the other professor. There's no need to get into it."

"Did you sleep with him too?" I gasp.

Aunt Cass grabs Mom's arm. "Dare, that's enough. That wasn't fair. This is Harley we're talking about here. You owe her an apology."

Mom looks back at me and drops her head. "I'm sorry. She's right. I'm just in shock. This is so unlike you. Why didn't you talk to me? Why am I just hearing about this now? Maybe I could have helped you."

I go to speak but Aunt Cass interrupts. "Dare, you weren't in a good place for a very long time. You know you weren't. I don't blame her for not talking to you then. She talked to me about it. We discussed her ending all communications with him, and she did. She was completely broken-hearted over it, but she did it. Cut her some slack here."

Mom thinks for a moment. "He was the adult in this situation. He was the professor. He should have known better."

"Mom, I'm an adult too. He respected my wishes every time I asked for space. He moved to the other side of the world to give me the space I asked for."

"But he just had to come back, didn't he?"

"Because he was miserable, and so was I. I know you had your own shit going on, but didn't you notice how unhappy I was all those years?" She slowly nods her head.

"Haven't you noticed how happy I've been for the past five months?" She nods again.

"It's him. It's all him. I love him. You, of all people, should understand that love sometimes comes at unexpected times, from unexpected places."

"Christ, Harley." She looks down and massages her temples. Eventually she looks up at me again. "Tell us about the Board hearing. We need to figure out a plan. I won't let this ruin everything you've worked for."

I tell them what I know. That it'll be a three-member panel, with a simple majority vote. They'll decide if my relationship with Brody impacted my grade in his class, therefore nullifying my Medical Board Certification. As far as I know, only Brody and I will testify. They tell me that they want to meet with Brody too so they can discuss our testimony.

CHAPTER SEVENTEEN

THE PRESENT

HARLEY

It's Wednesday morning, the day of my hearing. It's been a long five days since our big reveal.

I've been with Mom and Aunt Cass strategizing a vast majority of the time. Brody tried to be helpful, but Mom was extremely cold to him, and mostly shut him out. They spent a brief amount of time with him discussing his testimony, Aunt Cass more so than Mom.

I walk with Aunt Cass and Mom into the room for my hearing. There are three panel members already sitting at a long table. It's comprised of two women and a man.

I see Dr. McCrevis. He stands as he notices Mom and Aunt Cass on either side of me. "Dr. Lawrence, this is a closed proceeding."

"They're my attorneys."

"This isn't a legal proceeding. You don't need counsel. We're simply here to investigate the propriety of your grades, and its bearing on your Medical Board Certification."

"They're my mother and my aunt. They're here for moral support."

Aunt Cass can't help herself. "We're not leaving. Call security if you have to."

Dr. McCrevis looks around, clearly not wanting a scene. "Very well. They can stay. They must be quiet though."

I look at him. "That won't be a problem." Yes, it will.

I sit down. Brody and Dr. Powers are in attendance too. They're already sitting together on the other side of the room. I didn't know that Dr. Powers would be here. I'm not sure what it means.

Brody smiles and winks at me. It helps to ease my nerves. I subtly smile back at him.

Eventually the panel starts the proceeding. They introduce themselves. I learn that the two female Board members are Dr. Griffith and Dr. Goldwater. The male Board member is Dr. Branch.

None of them have any affiliation with the school, or with this hospital. I suppose that's how it's supposed to be.

Dr. Branch speaks first. "Dr. Lawrence, we're here today regarding your medical certification. It has come to our attention that you engaged in an intimate relationship with Dr. Cooper, both currently, and at the time he was a professor of yours, just over three years ago. It is only your relationship at the time you were a student that has any real bearing on this procedure, but the current status of your relationship will be pertinent to discern the previous nature of it. Do you understand?"

I nod. "I do."

He turns his attention to Brody. "Dr. Cooper, we ask that you approach for questioning."

Brody walks up to the small desk with a microphone just in front of the panel. He sits down. "Dr. Cooper, while we're not a court of law, and there is no official swearing in, do you understand that your standing as a Board certified physician hinges on you telling the truth here today? There will be severe ramifications if any of your testimony is proven false."

"I understand. Of course, I'll be truthful."

"Dr. Cooper, what is the current status of your relationship with Dr. Lawrence?"

"We're dating."

"Is it casual?"

Aunt Cass and Mom both jump up and yell, "Objection." Aunt Cass continues speaking. "That's a vague term and it needs to be better clarified."

Dr. Branch looks annoyed. "Excuse me, but this is not a legal proceeding. We can ask any questions we want."

Aunt Cass takes a step forward. "Well, that's bullshit. She should have some rights here."

Brody turns and looks at her. "Cassandra, it's fine. I'm okay to answer this question. Thank you though."

He looks back at the panel. "No, it's not casual. I'm in love with her. She'll one day be my wife." Mom squeezes my hand.

The panel looks surprised. "Dr. Cooper, are you and Dr. Lawrence engaged to be married?"

"Not yet, but only because she was afraid of this very thing happening."

"And what is that, Dr. Cooper?"

He looks angry. "A witch hunt."

"Please tell us the nature of your relationship during the year you taught her in medical school."

"I was her professor. She was my student. That's it. That was the extent of our relationship."

"Did you date during that time?"

"No, we did not."

"Did you see her outside of classes?"

"I saw her in the lab, in the hallways, and at other school related activities?"

"I mean did you see her outside of school?"

"I briefly ran into her once and only once. It was accidental. It wasn't planned."

"Are you saying that you did not have a sexual relationship with Dr. Lawrence when she was your student?" Aunt Cass goes to stand up, but I look at her and shake my head.

"I did not." They all look confused.

"At any point from the day classes began that year, until the final day of class, did you have a sexual relationship with Dr. Lawrence?

"No, I did not."

"Were you attracted to her in that same timeframe?"

"She's an objectively beautiful woman. I doubt anyone, including yourselves, could possibly say you have no attraction to her."

"So, is that a yes?"

"Yes, I was, am, and always will be, attracted to Dr. Lawrence."

"We understand that you moved away for a period of just over two years. Did you have any contact with Dr. Lawrence during that time."

"I didn't contact her at all."

"Did she contact you?"

"She texted me twice. Once to see how I settled in, and once approximately a year later to let me know she had researched the clinical and was quite impressed by it."

"You didn't respond?"

"No, I did not."

"What were your thoughts on Dr. Lawrence as a student?"

"That she was brilliant. She was easily the most intelligent person in her class. I wasn't the only professor to hold that opinion of her." He looks back toward Dr. Powers and she smiles in the affirmative.

"When did you first begin a sexual relationship with Dr. Lawrence?"

He hesitates for a moment. He looks back at me and I nod. "In September. Nearly four years ago." The panel members look at one another in confusion.

"Dr. Cooper, you said that you didn't have a sexual relationship with her while she was your student."

"I didn't."

"So, when exactly did the sexual relationship begin?"

"It was two days before classes began that year." There's discussion among the panel again.

"To be clear, you claim that you had a sexual encounter two days before classes began, but not during the entirety of the school year?"

"That's correct. Once we realized the teacher student nature of our relationship, Dr. Lawrence wouldn't agree to any contact beyond the classroom."

"Is that what you wanted?"

"No, it was not. But her studies came first to her, and it was her decision that she and I not continue to pursue a social relationship. The integrity of her schooling meant something to her. I respected her wishes."

"Why didn't Dr. Lawrence request a different professor?"

"I think you'd have to ask her that. I can't speak for her."

"We intend to. Thank you for your time, Dr. Cooper."

"Can I say one more thing?"

"Of course."

"Dr. Lawrence was an exemplary student and is an exemplary surgeon. Her dating me has no bearing on any of this. Why don't you spend five minutes with her. You'll quickly realize that this proceeding is a complete waste of time, and an insult to the intelligence of a fine physician, and a fine person, like Dr. Lawrence."

"Thank you, Dr. Cooper. You're dismissed."

They turn to me. "Dr. Lawrence, please have a seat in front of the microphone."

I stand up and sit at the small desk. My throat is suddenly very dry. I take a few sips of my water.

Dr. Griffith speaks. "Dr. Lawrence, I'll be questioning you." I nod. "Dr. Lawrence, was Dr. Cooper's testimony here today entirely truthful?"

"Obviously I can't attest to his attraction to me, but I can otherwise tell you that he was entirely truthful with regard to the facts in his testimony, and the recollection of events."

"It's entirely accurate that you did not have a sexual relationship with Dr. Cooper while you were his student?"

"That's correct?"

"After your time as a student, when did you again begin a sexual relationship with Dr. Cooper?"

"A few weeks after he moved back to this area this past January. I can't tell you the exact date. I don't know it."

"Can you please tell us where this relationship began?" I see Aunt Cass and Mom getting antsy, but I give them a look to just let it be.

I sigh. "In the hospital."

"Your first sexual encounter in January was physically on the grounds of the hospital?"

"Yes, that's correct."

"Where did this encounter take place?" I look back again and try to communicate to Mom and Aunt Cass that they need to calm down. I just want to answer the questions truthfully.

"It was in one of the on-call rooms."

Aunt Cass yells out objection again. "This has no relevancy to her time as a student. It's unnecessary to humiliate her for the sake of hospital gossip."

Dr. Branch interjects. "Miss, if we hear from you one more time, you'll be asked to leave." I turn around and *again* indicate that she should just sit. I shouldn't have brought them with me today.

Dr. Griffith turns her attention back to me. "Dr. Lawrence, let's cut to the chase. Have you ever been offered better grades, or other beneficial academic or career opportunities in return for sexual favors?"

"Yes, I have." Everyone in the room has a shocked look on their face except Brody. I see the corner of his mouth rise in amusement.

"It's your testimony here today that Dr. Cooper offered you better grades or other opportunities in return for sexual favors?"

"I never mentioned that it was Dr. Cooper. Dr. Cooper would never do anything like that. He's an honorable man."

"Who is it that made you these offers?"

"It was Dr. Gregory Waters."

The panel members look at each other and shrug their shoulders. "Can you please tell us exactly what happened?"

"On multiple occasions during my schooling, Dr. Waters would trap me in his office and offer me better grades, or help securing a residency, in return for sexual favors. I turned him down on every occasion."

"Did you ever report this behavior?"

"No, I did not."

"Why?"

"Because I know what happens to women who report on men like Dr. Waters. I never wanted to draw attention to myself or be known for anything other than being a hard-working student. Creating a circus was never my goal. Becoming the best surgeon possible was always my focus."

"Are there any other witnesses to this alleged harassment?"

"Dr. Cooper once saw me run out of Dr. Waters' office crying. That is as close as it ever came to being witnessed."

She turns to Brody. "Dr. Cooper, is this true?"

He stands. "It's true. She was quite upset about it. She immediately told me what happened. I offered to report his actions, but she declined for the same reasons she stated here today. Further, on more than one occasion, Dr. Waters has made lewd comments to me with regard to Dr. Lawrence, her physical appearance, and her sexual prowess. He even once went so far as to suggest that I offer her extra credit for sexual favors. I told him that I don't make it commonplace to sexually harass my students."

"Thank you, Dr. Cooper."

I turn back toward the microphone. "It's also worth noting that the harassment I've suffered at the hands of Dr. Waters has continued into my time at this hospital."

"We'll certainly pass that information along to the hospital administration to investigate. Thank you, Dr. Lawrence." I get up to return to my seat.

"We have one more witness here today. Dr. Elizabeth Powers." Dr. Powers sits down at the desk.

Dr. Goldwater appears to be the one to question Dr. Powers. "Dr. Powers, you contacted this panel and asked to testify here today, is that correct?"

"It is. I taught Dr. Lawrence in medical school, and work

directly with her here in the hospital. I also know Dr. Cooper fairly well, having worked with him at the school and at two different hospitals. I thought I might be able to provide valuable, impartial insight into both parties."

"How do you know Dr. Cooper?"

"I originally met him when we both worked at the same hospital California."

"Do you consider him a friend?"

"I would say that we;re friendly as co-workers, but not friends, as we do not socialize outside of the hospital. I may have at one time hoped for a more friendly relationship, but he wasn't interested." I didn't know that. That can't help. Now I'm worried as to what she's going to say.

"What is your opinion of him?"

"He's a wonderful doctor and person."

"What's your opinion of Dr. Lawrence?"

"Dr. Lawrence was the brightest student I've ever taught. I have now also worked with her at this hospital the past year. She's a gifted surgeon and deserves the opportunity to succeed. She's going to save lives as a cardiothoracic surgeon. It would be a tragedy to deprive the world of her skill."

"Thank you for your time, Dr. Powers."

"I'm not done. I agree with Dr. Cooper. Dr. Lawrence is an objectively beautiful woman. I imagine that if she didn't look the way she does, this ridiculous proceeding wouldn't even be happening."

"While you may not feel compassion for her, I've watched for years as her looks have actually worked against her. I've witnessed firsthand as other students, professors and co-workers degrade her because of her looks. They don't believe she could possibly be that attractive *and* that smart. They assume she uses those looks to help secure good grades or other opportunities. I've observed her for nearly five years now. I can tell you firsthand, without a shadow of a doubt, that she's earned every grade and every opportunity with hard work and merit."

She reaches into her bag and pulls out a stack of papers. "I have fifteen sworn affidavits from other professors of Dr. Lawrence attesting to the fact that she was the most gifted student they've ever taught, and that they never witnessed one moment of impropriety from her."

"We're not here today to discuss her sex life, which I am personally appalled she was put through, but to simply decide whether she received an unearned grade from Dr. Cooper, nullifying her Board certification. I think it's entirely clear that her grade was earned. It matches every other grade she received throughout the entirety of her time in medical school."

"Thank you, Dr. Powers."

She stands and looks at Dr. Griffith and Dr. Goldwater. "I was recently reacquainted with the famous Madeline Albright quote. *There's a special place in hell for women who don't help other women.* You would be remiss not to remember that. We have a highly intelligent, motivated woman right before us. Let's make sure she's given the opportunities she's more than earned." She delivers the affidavits to the panel members.

"Oh, and I've witnessed crude comments and unsavory behavior from Dr. Waters. There's not a doubt in my mind as to the veracity of Dr. Lawrence's statements in that regard."

She turns to walk out of the room, but before she does, she looks at me. "Dr. Lawrence, I assume I'll see you in my O.R. tomorrow morning." She leaves and winks at me on the way out. I do my best to stifle my smile.

Dr. Branch stands. "The panel will convene and get back to you with our findings. You should hear from us by tomorrow." They stand up and leave the room.

Mom has tears in her eyes. "I didn't know things were so hard for you, Harley. I'm sorry that I wasn't there for you. I was so caught up my own grief, that I forgot my most important job. Being a mother to my girls. I'm ashamed of myself."

I hug her. "It's not your fault, Mom. I never told you anything. I didn't really tell anyone. I chose to deal with it all on my own."

Aunt Cass hugs me too. "That's because your daughter is a certified bad ass, Dare. Toughest chick I know. Always has been." She gives me a squeeze of support. We're all a bit of a teary-eyed mess.

BRODY

She's being embraced by her mother and Cassandra. I need to go to her and comfort her. I can't help myself. I walk over, take her hand and kiss it. She stands and wraps her arms around my body. I hold her as she sobs into my chest.

"It's going to be okay." I kiss the top of her head, as I rub my hands up and down her back. Darian is staring at me. I can't read her expression at all.

I grab Harley's face with my hands and wipe away her tears with my thumbs. "Baby, you're going to be okay. If they revoke your medical license, we'll move to Africa and work there. We'll be together practicing medicine somewhere, even if it's not here." She nods her head.

Just then, the panel reemerges. Dr Branch speaks. "Dr. Lawrence, the panel has already reached a decision. My co-panel members feel very strongly one way, and have indicated that there's no way they will change their minds. So ultimately, my vote doesn't matter." He looks pissed.

"It's the majority vote of this panel that there was no impropriety with regard to your medical school grades, and therefore you will maintain your medical license. While we do not have any jurisdiction over the hospital, it is recommended that you be reinstated immediately. Let the record also reflect that Dr. Phillip McCrevis submitted a letter on Dr. Lawrence's behalf, stating that she is an exemplary resident, and he has no doubt as to the merit of her grades."

"It's the recommendation of this Board that the actions of Dr. Gregory Waters be investigated. That brings this hearing to a close. Thank you."

Harley looks up at me in shock. "Did that just happen? This is over?"

I smile at her and nod my head. "It's over." I bend down and take her lips in mine. It's tender at first but gets a bit deeper as our mouths open.

Cassandra nudges us. "Get a room you two." We break our kiss as we laugh.

Darian and Cassandra hug Harley. The girls all cry again.

Darian and Cassandra offer to take her out to celebrate, but she says she just wants a quiet evening at home with me. I couldn't agree more. Maybe not so quiet, but we need to get home and celebrate.

WE BURST through her front door with her legs wrapped around me, and our tongues dancing in each other's mouths.

She pulls her lips away. She's looking at me in a way I've never seen from her before. "Brody, I want you to do everything to me tonight." She nibbles at my lips. "Anything you want."

I growl as I rip her blouse open. Buttons scatter all over the floor. I pull her lace bra down and take her nipples in my mouth. She bucks around me. "Oh god, Brody. I want you. Please. I need you."

We stumble our way into her bedroom. I set her down on her feet. "Get naked, now!" She quickly does as she's told, while I grab what I need.

She's now standing in front of me completely exposed. Her eyes shaded with lust. I've never been hungrier for anything in my entire life. I tear off my jacket and tie. I walk around her, like I'm stalking my prey. Her body could start wars.

I run my fingers around her as I walk, and revel in her shiver. "Harley, undress me. Slowly."

She takes her time unbuttoning my shirt, kissing her way down my chest and stomach. Once my shirt is removed, she unbuckles my belt. She looks at me in the eyes as she unbuttons my pants and pulls down my zipper. She pulls my pants and boxer briefs down and off at once.

She slowly rakes her eyes over my body, as I'm now standing naked before her. I see her cheeks flush, and her nipples harden.

We do nothing but stand there and stare at each other, as our deep breaths become one. It reminds me of that night in the on-call room where we took the time to properly appreciate the person before us.

I take what's in my hand and rub it across her neck and down her chest. I circle her nipples. She moans. I run it down her stomach, and through her drenched lips. I pull it out and back up. I slide it into her mouth. "Suck on it." She does as she's told.

I rub my hand down the side of her body as I pull her to me. "Turn around and bend over, Harley." Again, she does as she's told. I rub my hand all over her perfect ass, as I slowly slide it into her back entrance, until it's all the way in. She tenses at first, but then gives in with a small whimper and a moan.

"Stand up and face me." She turns and looks up at me. I run my thumb across her plush bottom lip. I move to take it in my mouth, but before I do, I whisper, "I'm going to make you come so fucking hard tonight." I suck her lip, and her legs nearly give out.

She runs her hands up my stomach and chest and breathes, "Yes."

I kiss my way to her ear. "Harley, I'm going to own every hole in your body."

She closes her eyes and whispers, "Yes."

I run my fingers through her hair. "Get on your knees. Now."

She smiles and drops down right away. I grab her hair in my fist and feed my aching cock into her mouth. "Take it all the way in." I slide it straight to the back of her throat. She doesn't flinch. She wraps her lips tight around me. I move in and out. She grabs my balls with one hand and squeezes them. "Yes, baby. Like that."

"Touch yourself with your other hand. I want you to feel what I do to you." I see her other hand disappear between her folds. "It's so wet, isn't it?" She nods.

I pull her hair a little harder and move in and out of her mouth at an increased pace, yet she does nothing but moan in ecstasy. Her tongue teases me as I slide in and out of her. She's so good at this.

I watch her own fingers slip all the way inside of her. I desperately want to be there. I need to be there. I can't take it anymore.

"Time for me to taste that sweet pussy of yours." I lift her off of me and toss her onto the bed. I lay down on top of her, between her legs. They immediately open wide in invitation.

I crash my mouth to hers. Kissing her is everything. I love her lips and her taste.

I eventually work my way down to her nipples. Nipple play drives her absolutely wild. Her nipples are so sensitive, which will make what I have in mind tonight all the better for her. I suck each one into my warm mouth while I hold her perfect, heavy tits.

I reach down for the nipple clamps I left nearby. Her eyes open wide as I bring them into view. I secure them to each of her nipples. She squeezes her eyes shut in anticipation of pain, but I see the moment she realizes that it's only pleasure.

She arches her back. "Oh my god. This feels so good." Her mouth is wide open. She bucks her hips. "Brody, I need you to touch me. Please."

I kiss my way down her body. I reach up and stick two long fingers in her mouth. "Suck." She sucks my fingers hard. I pull them out, move them down her body, and slide them into her entrance.

I pump my fingers in and out of her soft walls as I take my first long lick. She again bucks her hips. "You taste so damn sweet. I could eat you for every meal." I reach my other hand up and tug on her nipple clamps.

"Ah. Brody. I'm so sensitive." Immediately I latch onto her clit, while I make sure to apply some pressure to her back entrance. She twists and turns, while squeezing my head with her thighs. Even though she fights me, I push them back open. She's on sensory overload, already so close to her first orgasm.

I continue to revel in her juices. She's barely hanging on. She screams my name over and over, as her body spasms, without inhibition, into a long, hard orgasm. I pump, suck and lick her all the way through it.

When I know she's finished, I pull my fingers out and I move my way up her body. She grabs fistfuls of my hair and brings my mouth to hers. She tastes herself as she kisses me with everything she has.

I slide my cock through her sensitive, dripping lips. She reaches down and moves my tip to her entrance. "Brody, I need you."

I slowly slide all the way in until I completely disappear inside of her. I don't move. "Oh god, Brody. It's so good." She's extra tight with the plug in the back. We can both feel it.

I take her hands in mine as I move them above her head. I spread my legs, to make sure to give her everything she needs. I start to move. Long, hard, deep thrusts.

I'm pretty sure I see her eyes rolls to the back of her head. Her body is moving in ways it's never moved before. She's in another universe right now.

Seeing the pleasure on her face is pushing me to the edge, but I'm holding back.

"You feel me deep inside of you, baby?" She nods, unable to speak. I pound and pound until I feel her shudder around me, as she screams and orbits into another powerful orgasm.

I slow down as her shaking subsides. I kiss her jaw. "You ready for the finale, baby? You're going to feel me everywhere." She nods, barely able to move any other part of her body. I pull out and pull off her nipple clamps. I suck each nipple into my mouth to sooth her.

After I take care of her, I flip her over, and lift her ass, while her head remains on the bed. I gently pull the plug out. She cries out in mourning at the loss of sensation. I bend down and whisper in her ear. "Don't worry, it's about to get a lot better."

I grab for the lube and squeeze some onto my hand. I rub it on myself and all over her back entrance. I easily slide two fingers in. She's ready.

I place my tip at her back entrance, and slowly push in. Inch by inch she sucks me inside her. She whimpers at first, but it quickly turns into pants of pleasure.

Once I'm all the way in, I remain still for a moment to give her the chance to acclimate to me. I move my hand around and start to play with her clit. I lean over and pepper her back and neck with kisses.

"Loosen up for me. Open up, baby." I feel her body start to relax.

She pulls her head up. "Brody, I'm good. You can go."

I start to move in and out, slowly at first, but eventually picking up the pace. I slide two fingers into her sex. I can feel my cock through her walls. "Harley, your ass feels so tight around my cock. You feel so good. Tell me how it feels for you. Use your words."

She can barely get out the word, "Amazing," as she tries to endure the dual sensation. I move my thumb to her clit and begin to circle. She reaches back and grabs my hips, pulling me even closer to her, if possible.

She's practically howling as she screams my name over and over. I feel her walls squeeze both my fingers and my cock.

She screams out, "Brody, oh my god, I feel like I'm going to explode." She starts to convulse. Her entire body spasms as a monster truck of an orgasm plows through her. She screams louder than I've ever heard her. It's such a turn on.

As soon as I feel her final squeeze, I pull my fingers out, grab her hips, and pick up my pace. I'm driving into her hard.

My balls tighten, and my spine tingles, as I finally give into my release, and come over and over. I don't think I've ever come that hard. I don't think anything has ever felt so good.

We both collapse onto the bed. I slowly pull out of her and lay on my back. I pull her front to mine and kiss her.

I peel away her hair from her sweat covered face. I look into her deeply satisfied face. "I love you, Harley."

She gives me a sleepy, lazy smile. "I loved *that*." I laugh. "There wasn't an inch of my body that you didn't pleasure. I felt you everywhere, Brody. It was the most incredible thing I've ever experienced. Thank you."

I kiss her again. "For me too." We lay for a few more minutes in content silence, listening to each other breathe.

At some point, I squeeze her arm. "Let's rinse off and go to bed." She nods. I practically have to hold her up in the shower given how spent she is, but I don't mind keeping her body close to mine. After we rinse off, we fall into bed into a deep, sated sleep.

CHAPTER EIGHTEEN

THE PRESENT

HARLEY

I'm awakened early the next morning by the voice of my sister Reagan as she's walking through my apartment and into my bedroom.

"Harley, I heard the good news. Congr...." She sees Brody and I and looks around the bedroom. "Damn. Looks like you've finally used all the toys. Aunt Cass will be so proud. Should I call her? Maybe take some photos? She'll want to see this."

Brody and I are naked and only partially under the covers, yet she doesn't seem to care. I pull my head up and look at her. "Reagan, you have some serious sisterly boundary issues. We're going to need to talk about that."

She laughs and waves her hands at me as if I'm speaking nonsense. "There's no such thing as boundaries with sisters."

She climbs into bed with us. I stare at her. "You do realize some of the shit that went on in this bed last night?"

She shrugs. "Whatever. I'm so happy for you. You deserved it." She hugs my now sheet covered body and gives Brody a fist bump across me.

Brody looks at us. "This whole sister thing is peculiar. Can I expect this to be a regular occurrence? Is a full bed something I need to get used to?"

We both say, "Yes", at the same time and giggle. I look at him. "It's not always like this." I smirk. "Sometimes Skylar is here too." Reagan and I giggle again.

Brody shakes his head. "I actually need to go get in the shower and head to the hospital."

He's looks at Reagan, clearing inferring that she leaves so he can get out of bed, but she just smiles. "Go ahead. I don't mind."

I push her out of my bed. "Go turn on the coffee machine. I'll be out in a minute."

"Ugh. Fine. I'll go. Why do you need to deprive me of a little eye candy?" I roll my eyes and shake my head.

She leaves my bedroom and closes the door behind her. Brody rolls on top of me and kisses my neck. "I love waking up with you." He kisses me a few more times. "Let's move in together to make sure we have this every single morning."

I stretch my arms above my head. "Okay."

I think I've shocked him. "Okay? No resistance? No excuses? Just like that?"

I cup his cheek and smile at him. "Just like that."

His eyes light up. "Great. I'm going to call a realtor to start searching for places near the hospital."

"Okay."

"You're awfully agreeable this morning, Dr. Lawrence. It's kind of bizarre."

I laugh. "I feel like the weight of the world has been lifted off of our shoulders. I have everything I want. For the first time in as long as I can remember, I simply feel content."

"Good. Let's keep you that way. I like content Harley."

I run my fingers through his hair. "Brody, yesterday ended nearly four years of battling obstacles to be together. There are no more walls to climb. No more hurdles to jump. We're through them all. We came out on the other side, and we're still together. We made it."

He dots kisses all over my face and neck. "I love you, Harley. Our open, happy life begins today."

He's right. What an amazing feeling. I smile as I hold him close. "Yes, it does. I love you too."

He gives me one last long kiss and gets out of bed. "Are you coming into the hospital with me?"

"No, I'm not due in for a few more hours." Dr. McCrevis called me immediately after the hearing to invite me back to the hospital.

"I'm going to sit with Reagan for a while and then maybe get some more sleep. Between the events of the past week, and my animalistic boyfriend, I'm exhausted."

"Rest up. Your animalistic boyfriend will be ready for another round tonight."

I lick my lips. "Yum. That sounds good to me."

He reluctantly leaves to take a shower while I throw on clothes, and head into the kitchen.

Reagan is sitting there with two coffee mugs. She hands me mine. "Thank you."

"You look awfully happy and relaxed, sis. I honestly don't think I've ever seen you this way."

"I have no reason not to be. It's a really nice feeling."

Brody comes out looking showered, fresh, and gorgeous. He

says goodbye to Reagan, kisses me goodbye, and walks out the door.

Reagan watches him leave. "He really is very good-looking."

I give her a dreamy smile. "I know. *All* of him is good-looking."

She laughs. "So, what's next for you guys?"

"He actually asked me to move in together this morning."

"What did you say?"

"I said yes, of course."

"Wow. Is this it for you?"

"This is it for me, Reagan. He's the one." I sigh in content. "We're finally not a dirty secret. There's absolutely nothing standing in our way now."

"I'm so happy for you." She leans over and hugs me. "I love you."

I hug her back. "I love you too."

She stands up. "I've got to get to work. Let's try to go out over the weekend and celebrate."

"That sounds good."

"Content, agreeable Harley is freaky."

I laugh. "Brody just said the same thing. I'll see you later."

When she leaves, I go to my bathroom. I pull out the brown bag I've been avoiding for a few weeks and take care of business.

A FEW HOURS LATER, I pull into my spot in the hospital garage. My shift begins in about thirty minutes. I smile as I get out of my car. For the first time ever, Brody and I have nothing standing in the way of our happily ever after. It's almost hard to believe. I can't wait to talk to him, and truly begin our life together. Just then, I smell something strange, and my world goes black.

BRODY

"Jess, is Dr. Lawrence here yet?"

"No, and it's kind of odd. Her shift starts right now. Not only is she never late, but she's always at least thirty minutes early."

I call her cell, but it rings and then goes to her voicemail.

I text Reagan to see if she's still with her, but she replies that she left Harley at her apartment hours ago.

"Jess, can you please pull up Dr. Lawrence's contact form."

"Sure thing, Dr. Cooper."

She presses a few buttons on the keyboard. The information pops up on the screen. I scan it until I see what I'm looking for. I dial the number on my phone. I hear a female voice. "Hello."

"Hey Darian, it's Brody Cooper."

"Oh. Hello, Brody. What can I help you with?"

"Have you spoken with Harley this morning?"

"No, I haven't. Why do you ask?"

"I don't want to worry you, but she's late for work, and it's kind of unlike her. She's not answering her cell."

"Brody, you *are* worrying me."

"I'm sure it's nothing. She probably hit some traffic. I'm heading to the garage to check if her car is here. I'll call you back and let you know what I find."

"No, I'll stay on the line with you." Her voice is getting shaky.

"Okay. Just give me a minute to get there." I hear her yell for Jackson. She fills him in on things.

As I approach the garage, I see her car. Phew. She must be here somewhere. Maybe she went to see her friend Megan before her shift.

I speak into the phone. "Darian, I see her car. She must be somewhere else in the hospital."

"Oh, thank God."

I'm about to turn back towards the hospital when I see something on the ground near the driver's side of her car door. I walk over and start to panic. I see her purse, keys and cell phone scattered on the ground. "Darian, don't freak out, but her purse, keys and phone are on the ground right next to her car."

I hear Darian starting to freak out. "Darian, put Jackson on the phone."

I hear his voice. "Brody, what's happening? Darian is flipping out."

"Jackson, I think someone has taken Harley. I have a pretty good idea who would do this. Can you conduct a quick property ownership search for me?"

"Of course. Let me open up my laptop." I hear Darian in the background yelling about calling the police.

"Okay, I have the program up and running. What am I searching for?"

"Look up Greg or Gregory Waters. He's about forty years old. I'm pretty sure his main residence is in or near Olde City. I want to know if he owns any other properties." I hear Jackson quickly typing.

"I see a million-dollar condo in Olde City. I also see a small walk-up unit in West Philly, that looks like a rental property. I can't tell if it's currently occupied."

"What's the address in West Philly?" He gives it to me. "Jackson, I need you to call the police and give them that address. Tell them about what I found at her car, and that Greg Waters has an axe to grind with Harley. I'm headed there now on foot, it's only a few blocks from here."

"Okay, we're on our way. We're about thirty minutes out. Trevor and Hayden are near you. I'll call them to meet you." He pauses for a moment. "Brody, please don't let anything happen to her."

I'm already hurrying out of the garage. "I won't. Please just call the police. Keep Darian calm."

I hear Darian screaming. "Don't you let anything happen to my baby." She's completely hysterical. I don't blame her.

I don't think about anything, I just take off running. I'm playing through worst case scenario in my head, and I am starting to shake. I need to keep it together though.

I arrive about eight minutes later. I hang back a house or two away as I think about what I should do now that I'm here. Should I sneak in, or just break down the front door?

Just then, I see Trevor and Hayden pull up. They look around and find me right away. Trevor has a bat in his hands, and Hayden has a golf club. They walk over to me. "You guys don't need to be here. This could be dangerous."

Trevor looks at me like I'm crazy. "She's our fucking sister. Of course, we're going to be here. What's the plan?"

"I haven't even gotten that far. I just ran here as quickly as I could. I'm going to go over there and try to peek in. I'll be right back."

I duck down as I approach a side window. I carefully lift my head to take a quick look. I see Greg, but I don't see Harley. At least I know he's here. I jog back to Trevor and Hayden. "He's in there. I didn't see Harley though."

"Are you sure he has her?"

"No, but he's the only person I can think of that would want to harm her. He's always had an unhealthy thing for her, but she's rejected him for years. He has a huge ego and isn't used to rejection. At her hearing yesterday, her testimony included some bad shit about him that could get him into some real trouble. This is our only lead. We need to see if he has her."

Hayden looks around. "Maybe we should wait for the police?"

"You two can. I wouldn't blame you. This guy could be dangerous. I'm not wasting another minute though. If he has her, I need to get to her."

Hayden nods. "Whatever you need. We're in."

I think for a moment. "He knows me, and he may recognize Hayden from around the hospital. Trevor, I'm thinking that you ring the bell with some kind of delivery story. Hayden, you go around back. I'll be right next to the door, out of sight of the window. We can come at him from all angles once he opens the door. Hopefully we can surprise him. I'll go in first in case he has a weapon. He's not a big guy. We should be able to easily overtake him." They both nod.

HARLEY

I try to crack open my eyes. I can barely see. I have a pounding headache. My mouth feels like I've been sucking on cotton. I go to rub my eyes, but I can't move my arms. They seem to be stuck.

I feel a draft. I slowly peel my eyes all the way open, and notice that I'm in my bra and underwear. My arms and ankles are tied to a chair. I can't move at all. What the hell is going on?

I suddenly hear a voice. "There she is." I look up. As my eyes adjust to the light, I see Greg Waters.

"Dr. Waters? What's happening? What are you doing?" He's in sweatpants and a sweatshirt and is holding a big knife.

"Thanks to you, I received a call last night that I'm on leave from the hospital. My medical license has been revoked, pending the outcome of a criminal investigation."

My brain is foggy. "I'm sorry, I don't understand what you're saying."

"When word got out about your little hearing yesterday, several women went to the police, and the hospital administration, to file complaints about me. You've ruined my life."

I shake my head. "It's not my fault. You did this to yourself."

He bangs his fist against the table. He's getting angry. He shouts at me. "No, *you* did this."

I look around and notice that I'm in the kitchen of a small, run-down house. I have no clue where I am or how long I was unconscious. No one else probably knows where I am.

I'm scared. He looks unhinged. "What is it that you want from me? I can't help you now. I have nothing to offer you."

He smiles as he walks toward me. He softly runs the knife across the tops of my breasts. I whimper. "I want what I've always wanted from you, Harley. I'm leaving the country tonight, but I'm going to have you as a parting gift. You owe me that."

Realization hits me. Tears are streaming down my cheeks. I manage to croak out, "Please don't do this. I'm begging you. Please." I've never had more to lose than I do right at this moment.

He slowly looks me up and down while giving an overexaggerated lick of his lips. It sends a shiver of fear down my spine. I feel like I'm going to be sick.

"Harley, your body is as hot as I always imagined it to be. You always tried to hide it, but I knew what was underneath. I can't wait to make it mine. You'll never be the same after I'm done with you."

He gets down on his knees and starts to move his hands up my thighs. He pulls them apart. I try to fight him, but he's too strong. With my arms and ankles tied, I can't offer much resistance.

I squeeze my eyes shut, as the tears are free falling. I can't watch this. I silently pray that someone helps me stop this.

Just then, the doorbell rings. I try to scream for help, but he covers my mouth right away. He places duct tape over my lips before I have a chance to do anything. I try to scream again, but it's muffled by the tape.

The doorbell rings again. I hear someone shouting, "Pizza delivery." It sounds kind of like Trevor, but I doubt that's possible.

Greg shouts through the door. "I didn't order any pizza. Go away."

Another shout comes back. "Are you G. Waters? That's what it says on my ticket."

I can only partially see into the area by the door. I can't see all of the front door, just the front half of it, but I do see Greg move toward the front window and peel back the curtain to look out.

I hear a very faint window tap behind me. I turn and see Hayden outside through the window of the back door. He motions for me to be quiet. Tears are streaming down my cheeks as I silently plead with him to come save me.

Greg again yells for the delivery person to go away. The delivery person yells back. "I need you to at least sign my ticket that you're rejecting the pizza. I can't leave unless you do. I'll get fired. I'll sit here all day if I have to." That's definitely Trevor's voice.

Greg places the chain over the door, and then opens it just a few inches. "Give me the damn ticket and then get the fuck out of here."

The door suddenly crashes open, the chain breaking easily. Brody comes barreling through looking like a man possessed. He has a tremendous size, strength, and height advantage over Greg.

He grabs Greg by the neck and lifts him off the ground. His legs are dangling. Greg tries to stab Brody, but Brody easily knocks his hand away. It causes Greg to drop the knife to the floor.

"Where is she? I know you have her." Greg is now swinging all of his limbs in the air.

Hayden crashes through the back door. He quickly removes the duct tape from my lips. I yell for Brody. Brody is distracted enough by my voice that Greg gets in a punch to his face, and Brody drops him.

Greg crawls for the knife, but Trevor gets there first, and gives Greg a hard kick to the face, and another to the ribs. Greg is writhing in pain. It looks like he has a broken nose. Probably a broken rib too.

I hear police sirens as Brody comes to me. He has blood trickling from his lip, which looks split open. I'm crying.

Hayden is untying my hands, as Brody falls to his knees in front of me and unties my ankles. When he's done, he grabs my face and wipes my tears. He has tears in his own eyes. "Are you okay?" I nod. "Are you hurt?" I shake my head. "Did he..." Brody can't bring himself to finish that sentence, as more tears stream down his cheeks.

"No, you got here just in time." I'm fully sobbing now. "You saved me. You all saved me. Thank you." My hands are free now. I wrap them around Brody and squeeze hard. We're both crying.

I see Trevor with his knee in Greg's back, pinning him down. Hayden walks over to help him. The police sound like they're right out front now. Brody takes off his shirt. He places it over my head, pulling it down to cover my body.

He picks me up and cradles me into his arms. He walks out the front door as the police come in. He motions inside with his head. "I've got her. She's okay. He's on the floor inside. He's been subdued."

Brody walks toward the sidewalk, still holding me in his arms. I wrap my arms around his neck, still sobbing at what could have happened.

I see Mom and Jackson pull up. I think Mom gets out of the car while it's still moving. She screams my name and runs to me. Brody sets me on my feet. Mom grabs me and hugs me hard. "Thank God you're okay. Thank you, Brody. Thank you for saving her."

Just then I hear Trevor. "What about me? I'm the real hero here." I stop crying long enough to laugh. Leave it to Trevor to make me laugh under these circumstances.

I look at my brothers, Trevor and Hayden. "All three of them saved me, Mom." She too has tears streaming down her cheeks.

A moment later, Skylar and Reagan arrive. They run up and hug me, along with Mom, who can't seem to let go of me.

An EMT worker approaches me. "Ma'am, we need to check you out."

I wave him off. "I'm fine." I motion towards Brody. "Please check his lip. He was hit and may require a stitch or two." He waves them off too.

Mom unwraps her arms, looks up at Brody, and notices his swollen lip. "Brody, you're injured. Let them look at you."

He shakes his head. "Not until they examine Harley. They need to make sure she's okay. She may be in shock."

She goes up to him and hugs him. "Thank you for what you did. Thank you for saving my baby. I will *never* forget this." He looks at me and hugs her back. This is the first time Mom has shown him any warmth or affection.

"Of course. I couldn't have done it without Trevor and Hayden. They were very brave." She moves to hug them too.

Jackson leaves Trevor and Hayden to come embrace me. "You gave us quite a scare."

I squeeze him back. "I was pretty scared myself."

The EMT hasn't left. "Ma'am, we really have to examine you. We can't let you leave unless we do."

I roll my eyes. "Fine. Let's get it over with." He leads me to the back of the ambulance, and I climb in. Of course, my mother and sisters climb in with me, leaving no room for Brody.

He smiles at me. "I'll be right out here waiting." The EMT closes the door.

He asks me the routine questions. I let him know that no real physical harm came to me, much to the relief of my mother and sisters.

He indicates that he'd like to get me on a series of antibiotics just in case anything happened to me when I was passed out. "Any condition I should know about before I administer the drugs?"

I look around at Mom and my sisters, and take a deep breath. "I'm pregnant."

CHAPTER NINETEEN

THE PRESENT

HARLEY

My mom and sisters are in shock. Mom has tears in her eyes and takes my hand. "Does Brody know?"

I shake my head. "No. I just found out this morning. I took a home test. I wanted to give myself an ultrasound at the hospital today, to be sure, before I told him."

She rubs my arm. "How did this happen?"

Skylar smiles at her. "Mom, do you need a lesson on the birds on the bees? I'm happy to take you in another room and explain it to you."

She gives Skylar a dirty look. "You know what I meant."

"The only thing I can come up with is that I drank too much and threw up a few times in Mexico. It probably screwed up my birth control pills. I didn't think of it when I came back."

I see Mom do the math in her head. "So that would mean you could be nearly two months along?"

"I suppose. I don't think I've had a period since before Mexico, but I won't know anything for sure until I do the ultrasound."

The EMT interrupts. "I can do one in here if you'd like. I have a machine."

I nod my head. "Okay. Let's take a look."

Her performs the ultrasound. I am in fact pregnant. I think this is the first time that the reality of the situation hits me. Tears well in my eyes, and Mom squeezes my hand.

It shows that I'm eight weeks along, as we suspected. We're already able to hear the heartbeat. It's so incredible. I wish Brody knew and was with me for this.

Mom looks at me. "How do you think he'll take it?"

I smile. "I think he'll be over the moon. We know we're going to be together. Maybe we're doing this in the wrong order, but we're going to be together. He asked me to marry him four months ago."

She looks shocked. "He what?"

"He wants to get married. I said I wouldn't consider it until all the secrets were out in the open. They're out now. We can finally have a real talk about our future. I've been avoiding it for so long."

"Didn't you discuss your future last night, after the hearing?"

Reagan interrupts. "I saw the state of her bedroom this morning. There was definitely no talking going on last night." Skylar laughs.

I narrow my eyes at her. "Boundaries, Reagan. You lack boundaries."

I turn back to Mom. "Mom, she broke into my apartment and got into bed with Brody and me this morning. We were naked and she didn't even care."

She looks at my sister. "Reagan, you need to respect your sister's private life. You guys aren't teenagers anymore. She's a grown woman."

Reagan gives me a dirty look. "You're about to become a mother and are still a tattletale."

Mom rubs my leg. "When are you going to tell him?"

"Soon. I want to think of a really special way to deliver the news."

"Okay." She turns toward Reagan and Skylar. "You two keep your big mouths closed. This is her news to share." They both roll their eyes and nod in agreement.

We exit the ambulance. Brody is standing there waiting for me. He immediately moves toward me to wrap me in his arms. Reagan looks at him. "Brody, put on a shirt. It's kind of distracting."

I mouth to her, "Boundaries."

Mom puts her hand on my shoulder. "I want you to come home with us tonight. I need you under my roof."

I look at her. "Mom, I'm going to be with Brody tonight."

She looks up at Brody and smiles. "Of course. I meant both of you. I want you both under my roof tonight."

I widen my eyes at him in question and he nods. "Okay, Mom. We'll come."

Skylar and Reagan look at each other. "We're coming too."

Trevor walks over. "Rumor has it we're having a family slumber party. I hear skimpy nighties are mandatory attire. Pillow fights begin at 9:00."

WE ALL, and I mean *all* of us, stay over at Mom and Jackson's. We eat junk food, watch movies, and laugh. It's like soup for the soul, and I really needed it.

Brody is treated like a member of the family. Both the good and the bad. Though surprisingly, he gives as good as he gets. He doesn't let Trevor or Reagan get away with anything.

At some point he whispers to me, "Is something going on with Trevor and Cassandra?"

"I don't know. I've often wondered the same thing but have ultimately concluded that I don't want to know. They're both flirtatious people by nature, but I agree, there's something odd about their interactions."

I scrunch my nose. "She's more than twice his age, though I know he likes older women. He's told us that before."

"It's strange. Whatever. Not my business." He squeezes me tight. "You, however, are my business." His arms wrap around me, as he interlaces his fingers with mine and kisses my cheek.

He hasn't stopped holding me the entire night. I think the events of today scared him as much as they scared me.

Mom, Reagan, and Skylar also don't seem to stray too far from me. Jackson is working overtime to soothe Mom. I think she's emotional over today. I'm so grateful that she has him to keep her calm.

Mom is being incredibly warm to Brody. I think her past issues with him are now long forgotten. At some point she even throws her arm around him and smiles at him. "Brody, I hear that you're a fairly decent quarterback. You know, I'm a very good quarterback myself."

He smiles back at her. "I was an all-state quarterback, actually. I'm happy to toss the ball around with you anytime."

Skylar interrupts. "Don't get her started, Brody. And don't challenge her. She's a crazy woman on the field. She'll tackle you without a second thought."

Brody laughs, but Mom just gives him a guilty grin. "Brody

and I will settle this at Thanksgiving this year, won't we Brody?" She winks at him.

That's months away. I guess it's a good sign that she's talking to him about Thanksgiving.

We all say good night. Brody and I head to our appointed room.

We get into bed, and he pulls me in close. He gently kisses me. He can't do much more with his mouth because of his split lip.

I trace his two stitches with my fingers. "That's probably going to scar. You should have a plastic surgeon look at it in the morning."

"Aren't women supposed to find scars sexy?"

I smile at him. "Everything about you is sexy, Dr. Cooper."

He nuzzles into my neck. "I'm taking you home tomorrow. We're getting into bed and not surfacing for a few days."

Sounds perfect.

CHAPTER TWENTY

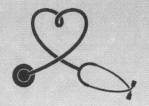

THE PRESENT

BRODY

"Harley, let's go dancing tonight."

"Really? You and me at clubs tends to be an explosive combination." She smirks suggestively at me.

I wrap my arms around her. "That's what I'm hoping for."

She looks up at me. "I'm in."

"Club Liberty?"

She smiles. "Perfect. Back to the scene of the crime." She kisses me. I wince in pain. My lip is still a bit tender and swollen.

It's been a little over a week since the Waters debacle.

The hospital encouraged us to take some time off to rest and recuperate. We took them up on it.

We've been holed up in my bedroom enjoying each other's bodies all week. I hate for the week to come to an end, but tonight's going to be special.

Greg Waters was arrested that day. I don't think he'll see the light of day for years to come.

Harley seems to be handling the circumstances well, all things considered. I'm thankful we got there in time. I suggested that she talk to someone when we get back to the hospital. She said she would. I plan to see to it.

WE ARRIVE AT THE CLUB, and I offer to go to the bar to grab us a few drinks. She says that she's on antibiotics and can't drink, so I don't drink either.

"Let's just go dance. I need to feel your body on mine." She grabs my hand as we head straight for the dance floor. We're immediately all over each other.

Not that we ever let it stop us at a club, but it's nice to not care about who sees us like this. I get to enjoy her wherever and whenever I want to.

I hold her from behind, swaying our hips to the beat, while running my hands all over her body. I take in her scent and run my lips up and down her neck. I whisper in her ear. "Come home with me tonight."

She smiles. "Sorry. I'm not that kind of girl."

I turn her around and pull her to me. I latch on to her bottom lip and suck it. She moans. I motion my head toward the stairwell. Her eyes light up as she nods.

We climb the two flights toward the roof. Just as we're

walking through the door, she turns her body around to me so that she's walking backwards, holding onto my shirt.

She pulls me through the door with her. "Dr. Cooper, did you just bring me to this club to fuck me on the roof aga..." I cover her mouth and turn her around. Her mom, Jackson, her sisters, her brothers, and of course Cassandra are standing on the roof. They're all shaking in silent laughter at her words.

She turns back around to me with her eyes wide open, but I'm down on one knee. She gasps.

"Harley, our love story began on this roof. It was love at first sight for me. You left your mark on my soul that night, and it just wouldn't go away. I know it will stay there forever. I love your beauty, both on the outside and the inside. Your mind and heart are just as beautiful as your stunningly perfect exterior. I love you with every part of myself. I know without a doubt that you're my soulmate. Spend your life with me. Marry me?" I pull out a big, gorgeous diamond ring that my future mother-in-law helped me choose when I snuck out for a little while this week.

Harley has tears in her eyes. She grabs my face and gently kisses my lips. "Yes, I'll marry you, but I have one condition."

I smile. "Oh really, what's that?"

"It needs to be *very* soon."

"That's fine with me, but why?"

"Because, Brody Cooper, this is a shotgun wedding." She smirks at me.

It takes me a moment for it to register. When it does, my face must show it because she laughs.

I look up at her. "You're pregnant?" She nods. The

biggest grin of my life crosses my face, shortly thereafter followed by hers.

I wrap my arms around her and kiss her. I pick her up as I stand back on my feet. She wraps her legs around me. I ignore the pain, as I kiss her long and hard. Trevor and Cassandra both shout, "Get a room." Everyone laughs before they run over and congratulate us.

EPILOGUE

THE PRESENT

BRODY

"Dr. Cooper?"

We both say, "Yes," at the same time. We laugh. Everyone is still getting used to there being two Dr. Coopers at the hospital now.

We got married a week after I proposed. It happened at the shore. I finally started calling it the shore instead of the beach.

It was just her huge family, along with my father and Melanie. The actual ceremony was on the beach at sunset, and it was perfect. She's perfect.

A few weeks ago, she chose her surgical specialty. Much to my chagrin, she went with cardiothoracic. I supposed I understand why, but I miss having her in surgery with me.

I still watch her from the gallery, and immediately corner her somewhere shortly thereafter.

Liz Powers has been a tremendously positive influence on my wife. She teaches her, and supports her in every way, just as she's done since the very beginning. They have a special relationship. I'm so grateful to Liz for everything that she does for Harley.

Jess looks up at us. "You're being paged to the O.R."

I laugh again. "Which one of us?"

"You, Brody."

"Okay, thanks Jess."

I turn to Harley. "Take it easy. Your due date is tomorrow. I don't know why you're not home resting."

"Because I don't need rest, and I'd be bored out of my mind." She wraps her arms around my neck and kisses me.

It's nice to finally be able to express our love out in the open at the hospital. Though we still find time for our secretive rendezvous in on-call rooms and supply closets. "I'll see you after your surgery." I start to walk away when she whispers in my ear. "Brody, I'll be watching." She smirks as she blows me a kiss.

Three hours later, my surgery is over. I walk down the hallway, when a hand reaches out and pulls me into a supply closet. It's dark, but I smell strawberries and vanilla. That's my favorite smell in the world. I smile.

She pulls herself up on the table and wraps her legs around me. "That was so hot. I could watch you cut into people all day." She pulls my face toward hers and kisses me.

"There's something slightly disturbing about your word choice."

She ignores me. "Brody, I need you inside me. Hurry."

I pull off her shirt and look at her. She's even more

beautiful now that she's carrying my baby. "I think your tits got bigger."

She laughs. "I swear I'm carrying this baby in them, not my stomach."

She's not wrong. They're bigger than her little stomach. I pull her bra down and take each nipple in my mouth. She moans. If possible, her nipples may be more sensitive in pregnancy than they were before. I love it.

After a few minutes, she hops down from the table and turns around. At this point in the pregnancy, I have to take her from behind.

I pull down her pants and run my fingers through her lips. She's soaked, as always, especially after one of my surgeries. I take my tip and slowly run it through her lips. "Brody, now."

"So impatient." As soon as my tip is at her entrance, she grabs my hips from behind and pushes back until I'm all the way in.

"Oh god, Brody. That feels good. Please fuck me." It's my turn to grab her hips as I start pumping into her. "Yes, that's it."

I reach up and grab her tits as leverage. I squeeze her nipples, and her moans get louder. She feels so good. I think she's gotten even tighter toward the end of her pregnancy. She's gripping me so hard. I can barely hold on.

She's screaming, completely lost in the moment right now. I grab her shirt from the table and shove it in her mouth. She bites down on it.

I move my finger around to her clit and circle it. She's moaning around the shirt. I feel her walls start to tremble around me. I know she's close. "Give it to me, Harley. Show me what I do to you."

I pick up the pace as she shatters explosively into her orgasm, her screams mostly muffled by the shirt. When I know she's done, I give into my own orgasm.

We clean up and go to leave the closet. As soon as we exit, her water breaks.

HARLEY

My water broke three minutes after we were done having sex. What are the chances?

Brody runs and grabs a wheelchair, quickly wheeling me to the maternity floor. Considering the fact that I was working right up until my due date, I actually have a packed bag already at the hospital.

I text my family to let them know what's happening. By the time I'm in my room, Mom, Aunt Cass, Reagan, and Skylar are already there. "How the hell did you guys get here so quickly?"

Mom laughs. "We were at Reagan's packing. Jackson and the boys will be here in a little bit."

Aunt Cass and Reagan both scan my body. They look at each other and nod in some sort of silent agreement. Reagan asks, "Did you just have sex?"

How do they always know? I turn to Mom and Skylar. "I'm telling you guys, both of them are witches."

Aunt Cass turns to Reagan. "That sounds like a yes to me."

Reagan nods. "Sure does."

Eleven hours later, our baby boy is born. He's perfect and healthy in every way. Brody goes to tell my family, but I tell him not to reveal the name. I want to do that.

My whole Brady Bunch family, along with Aunt Cass, come

into the room. Brody's Dad and his wife are flying in over the weekend.

Mom has tears in her eyes as she sees my baby boy for the first time. I hand him to her. "Mom, meet Scott Lawrence Cooper." She begins to sob, as do my sisters. Even Aunt Cass and Jackson have tears gathering in their eyes.

Mom squeezes me. "Oh Harley, he's so beautiful. He's perfection."

Trevor takes a peek. "If anyone cares, I think he looks like me." Hayden smacks his head.

Trevor picks up the blanket to look between Scott's legs. "*Definitely* looks like me." He winks at Aunt Cass.

Brody grabs the baby into his arms. "Sorry Trevor, those generous family jewels are all me." Trevor smiles.

I roll my eyes. "Can we please stop talking about my son's penis? He's twenty minutes old."

Everyone laughs. The room eventually thins out, and it's just me and Mom. Brody is taking a quick shower in the hospital.

Mom pulls out an envelope and hands it to me. I read the front. *To Harley on The Day You Become a Mom.* I supposed on some level I knew this was coming. I just hadn't thought about it today. I look up at her. "Mom, will you read it to me?" She nods as she opens the envelope. We both already have tears dripping down our cheeks. She begins:

Harley,

Baby doll, it's crazy that this day is here. You're a mom. I can't believe my first baby girl is actually a mom. I still see you as a little girl in my arms. There's not a doubt in my mind that you will be an incredible mother. Look at the example you had. If you can be half the mom that yours is, you'll have one very lucky and very happy baby.

I hope that this means that you have everything you want in life and that you're enjoying yourself. Living life to the fullest. I hope it means that you've stopped to smell the roses. Maybe even the ocean too. I hope you've met someone special that makes you as happy as your mom made me. Someone truly deserving of the sensational woman that you are. Make sure he treats you like a princess. You deserve nothing less.

Guess what? You have it all now. You have a wonderful career and a family. As a father, I couldn't possibly ask for more. I'm so proud of you, baby doll. Do what you need to do to stay happy. Don't ever forget that your happiness means everything.

If it's a boy, I'd like to suggest that Scott is an excellent name. It served me well. Give my grandchild a big kiss from me. I promise that I'll watch out for him or her from above.

Love you always,
Dad

PS: Tell your mom that she's officially a GILF. She'll know what that means.

THE END

If you'd like to continue reading about the Knight and Lawrence gangs, **Cass** is the next book in the series. The prologue can be found at the end of this book.

ABOUT THE AUTHOR

AK Landow lives in the USA with her husband, three daughters, one dog, and one cat (who was chosen because his name is Trevor). She enjoys reading, now writing, drinking copious amounts of vodka, and laughing. She's thrilled to have this new avenue to channel her perverted sense of humor. She is also of the belief that Beth Dutton is the greatest fictional character ever created.

AKLandowAuthor.com

ALSO BY AK LANDOW

Signed Books: AKLandowAuthor.com/Books

PROLOGUE - CASS: CITY OF SISTERLY LOVE BOOK 3

MEXICO - DARIAN AND JACKSON'S WEDDING WEEK

TREVOR

"Trevor, harder." I'm gripping the side of the lifeguard stand for leverage. "Harder."

"You're crazy. I'm going as hard as I can." She's standing, facing the water, with her hands also grabbing the ledge. I'm behind her. We're both completely naked, covered in sweat. We've been going at it all night. We're in a lifeguard stand on the beach in Mexico, overlooking the turquoise blue ocean. It's late at night, and no one is around, but we can see the ocean sparkle from the bright moonlight. It smells like a mix of ocean and sex.

"I'm close. Keep pounding me. Harder. Harder."

"Loca, if I hammer into you any harder, I'll put another

hole in you." That being said, I take it up one final notch to push her over the edge.

"Yes, Trevor. Yes." She screams out my name, as she finds her release. A few more seconds, and I find mine, but as I do, the lifeguard stand tips over, barreling us towards the sand.

As soon as I realize what's happening, I grab her body to shield her from taking the brunt of the fall. We're fortunately thrown a few feet from the now tumbled lifeguard stand, so it doesn't fall on top of us. I land first, with her mostly on top of me.

She rolls off of me, both of us completely out of breath. We lay there naked and sweaty, now thoroughly covered in sand. It's sticking to our bodies. We both look at each other in shock, until we begin laughing hysterically. I hold up my hands. "Was that hard enough for you?"

She gives me her signature devilish smile. "There's no such thing."

I sit up, pull off the condom, and toss it aimlessly.

She looks at me with disgust. "You're not leaving that here. Some poor kid will walk out here in the morning and find it. Throw it away on our way out."

"How about we stop using condoms? Then I won't need to worry about that."

She looks at me like I'm crazy. "Are you insane? Condom free sex is for monogamous couples. We are neither monogamous nor a couple."

"But, what if..."

Before I can finish, she gets up and sprints towards the ocean. She smiles back at me and shouts, "last one in has to talk politics with Payton and Kylie."

I get up to run after her, while screaming, "it's not going to be me." We both dive head first into the ocean at the same time. The water is cool, but not cold. It feels amazing on my severely overheated body.

We break back through the surface, still smiling and laughing. We scrub our bodies free of the sand.

I grab her into my arms. She wraps her arms and legs around me, and crashes her lips to mine. Our tongues dance with one another. I feel myself getting aroused again. She pulls back and smiles. "God, I love being with a younger man. A two-minute turnaround time can't be beat."

I squeeze her. "Loca, *you* do this to me."

She rolls her eyes. "I really don't care for my new nickname. We've been in Mexico for all of three days, and you think you're fluent in Spanish. Somehow, I now have a Spanish nickname. An ugly one."

I smile at her. "What would you like me to call you?"

"How about my actual name?"

"Can I call you Aunt Cass, like my new sisters?"

She gives me a dirty look. "Absolutely not. They are the only three people in the world allowed to call me that. Cassandra is fine."

"What about Cassie? I like that. It's cute."

"No. There's only one person who I ever permitted to call me that, and it's not you."

"Whatever, gorgeous. Maybe I'll just stick with that." I move her shoulder length, dark hair out of her face, so I can see those ice blue eyes of hers. They're particularly bright tonight. "Can we get back to the condom talk? I want us to be a real couple. I'm ready to tell Dad and Darian about us."

She pulls away. "Are you out of your mind? Absolutely not. We can never be a real couple, Trevor. You're a kid, and I'm an adult."

She's pissing me off. "I am not a kid. I'm a twenty-four-year-old man."

"Whose daddy still pays for all of his expenses. I'm twice your age, Trevor. I'm a senior partner at the top Philly law firm, who has been 100% on her own for longer than you've been alive. We will never be a couple. If you can't handle that, we need to stop what we've been doing for the past few months."

I'm pouting now, which I suppose only bolsters her argument. "But I don't want to be with anyone else, and I'm sick of always hiding my feelings for you around my family. I hate that we never go out. I want to take you on real dates. I hate being a secret."

She shakes her head. "I'm sorry, Trevor. Either we sneak around, or we're done. It's up to you."

"Are you afraid of Darian?"

She sighs. "Trevor, I'm not afraid of anyone, certainly not Darian. I don't do commitment. It's not who I am."

"Will you tell me why?"

"It doesn't matter why. I don't do it. And I definitely don't do it with men half my age."

She wraps herself around me again. She presses a soft kiss to my still pouting lips. "I *really* like fucking you, Trevor. I'd *really* like to keep doing it. If you're okay with no commitment, you can grab another condom, and we can make use of that youthful virility of yours. If not, let's just head back to the villa and part ways for good."

I kiss her back, while pulling her ass to me, grinding myself against her. She moans. I love her moan. I pull away and look down at her. "Fine, have it your way." She smiles at me. I carry her up to the beach, while still kissing her.

I'm not done trying, but she doesn't need to know that right now. I grab another condom out of my discarded pants, and we don't make our way back to the villa for another two hours.